"Are we done arguing?" he asked as he watched her eyes change to a deep, rich blue, a color he had seen each time he had kissed her.

"Aye, I believe we are. I think I would like to do something else right now."

"What?"

"I would like ye to kiss me."

He had her in his arms so quickly she gasped. For one brief moment she wondered if she was about to make a very big mistake. Then he kissed her and she no longer cared. She wanted this, needed it. For once in her life she was going to be bold and daring, was going to reach out and take what she wanted without a thought to the consequences . . .

Books by Hannah Howell

THE MURRAYS

Highland Destiny
Highland Honor
Highland Promise
Highland Vow
Highland Knight
Highland Bride
Highland Angel
Highland Groom
Highland Warrior
Highland Conqueror
Highland Champion
Highland Lover
Highland Barbarian
Highland Savage
Highland Wolf
Highland Sinner
Highland Protector
Highland Avenger
Highland Master

THE WHERLOCKES

If He's Wicked
If He's Sinful
If He's Wild
If He's Dangerous
If He's Tempted

VAMPIRE ROMANCE

Highland Vampire
The Eternal Highlander
My Immortal Highlander
Highland Thirst
Nature of the Beast
Yours for Eternity
Highland Hunger
Born to Bite

STAND-ALONE NOVELS

Only for You
My Valiant Knight
Unconquered
Wild Roses
A Taste of Fire
A Stockingful of Joy
Highland Hearts
Reckless
Conqueror's Kiss
Beauty and the Beast
Highland Wedding

Silver Flame
Highland Fire
Highland Captive
My Lady Captor
Wild Conquest
Kentucky Bride
Compromised Hearts
Stolen Ecstasy
Highland Hero
His Bonnie Bride

Published by Kensington Publishing Corporation

HIGHLAND MASTER

HANNAH HOWELL

ZEBRA BOOKS
KENSINGTON PUBLISHING CORP.
http://www.kensingtonbooks.com

ZEBRA BOOKS are published by

Kensington Publishing Corp.
119 West 40th Street
New York, NY 10018

All Kensington titles, imprints, and distributed lines are
available at special quantity discounts for bulk purchases
for sales promotion, premiums, fund-raising, educational,
or institutional use.

Special book excerpts or customized printings can also be cre-
ated to fit specific needs. For details, write or phone the office
of the Kensington Special Sales Manager: Attn.: Special Sales
Department. Kensington Publishing Corp., 119 West 40th
Street, New York, NY 10018. Phone: 1-800-221-2647.

Zebra and the Z logo Reg. U.S. Pat. & TM Off.

ISBN-13: 978-1-4201-1881-0
ISBN-10: 1-4201-1881-1
First Printing: December 2013

eISBN-13: 978-1-4201-3269-4
eISBN-10: 1-4201-3269-5
First Electronic Edition: December 2013

10 9 8 7 6 5 4 3 2 1

Printed in the United States of America

Chapter One

"Six riders at the gate, m'lady."

Triona looked up from the shirt she was mending and stared at young Angus, her heart pounding with a fear she struggled to control. It had been quiet for weeks, a long span of peace they had all enjoyed. Now she feared it was at an end. Even telling herself that six warriors were no real threat even to her poor garrison did not immediately put to rest the unease that now gripped her. Banuilt was weak. She knew it, and any seasoned warrior who looked around would quickly know it, too.

"The Grants?" she asked as she hastily set aside her sewing, almost hoping it was the neighboring laird and his men, for those men would at least not try to kill them all.

"Nay. One of the riders is a woman. She claims she is your cousin." Angus scratched at the few thin red hairs on his pointed chin, which he proudly declared his manly beard. "Lady Arianna."

"Arianna?" Triona frowned as she struggled to

recall her cousin by marriage—and a few times removed, if she remembered correctly. "She is in France."

"Nay, m'lady. She be at the gate."

Triona fought the urge to rub her temples where the pinch of a headache began to bloom. "Lead me to them then, Angus."

He shrugged his bony shoulders. "I be willing, though I am surprised ye dinnae ken where the gates are by now." He strode toward the door leading out of the great hall, waving at her to follow him.

The headache grew a little larger as she followed him, resisting the strong temptation to kick him in his scrawny backside. If she had not known him since he was little more than a child, she would think the violent fever he had survived two years ago had burned away half his wits. Triona then silently scolded herself for those unkind thoughts. Angus was not sharp-witted, never had been, but he was good-hearted and an astonishingly fierce and able fighter. There were too few of those left at Banuilt, all the best having fled to France to fight for coin. Despite how difficult it could be to have a conversation with Angus, she often wished for a few more of his ilk. All the trouble they had been having lately had not cost them any lives yet, but she feared that could all too easily change.

Her attention was swiftly caught by the riders just beyond the gates, all irritation with Angus forgotten. Triona recognized Arianna immediately despite the many years it had been since she had last seen the woman, for there was no forgetting those golden eyes of hers, but her interest was caught firmly by the five men who rode with her. They were all big, strong men and well armed. No matter why her cousin had come to Banuilt, Triona prayed the woman intended to stay for a while and keep her guard with her. If nothing else, she might be able to get Arianna's men to spend a little time training hers.

"Triona!" cried Arianna. "Tell your men to stand down, please. I desperately need to dismount."

"All is weel, men," Triona said. "Let them in and help them with their horses."

It was hard, but Triona pretended that she did not notice the envy her men displayed over the fine horses and weaponry as they moved to help her guests. All of Banuilt's best weapons and horses had gone to Francc with the garrison when it had left, and she did not have the means to replace them. The women who moved out into the bailey, now that it was obvious there was no threat, were overtly interested in the five strong warriors riding with Arianna. Triona was silently preparing a speech to give the women of Banuilt concerning the need to remain chaste if only because they needed no more fatherless bairns to care for, when her cousin reached her side. The moment Arianna hugged her, Triona's concern about the morals, or lack thereof, of the women of Banuilt fled her mind. Arianna was with child. She prayed that was not why her cousin had suddenly decided to visit, for she did not need some angry man arriving at the gates, demanding his child.

"Cousin?" Triona stepped back a little, grasped

Arianna's hands, and looked at the unmistakable rounding of her cousin's belly. "Ye are with child."

"Aye, but I will tell ye all about it later, if I may," Arianna said. "Right now I truly need to use your garderobe." She laughed. "Or a bucket in a corner. E'en a bush to squat behind. Anything. Now!"

The only woman near them was Angus's sister Mary, and Triona sighed. "Mary, love, would you please take Lady Lucette . . ."

"'Tis MacFingal now," Arianna said, "but we can talk about that later, too."

"Oh, aye, that we will."

"My companions will need beds. Most of them are my kin."

"Mary, take her ladyship to a bedchamber so that she might refresh herself."

"Which bedchamber?" asked Mary.

"Whichever one is empty and clean. And we shall need water heated so that all our guests may wash away the dust of a long journey."

"And they are going to be needing bedchambers, too?"

"Aye, just as her ladyship said, but someone else will see to that. Ye will see to her ladyship and call for heated water, please."

"How do I do both?"

Noticing that her cousin was beginning to look pained, Triona said, "Just tell one of the other lassies as ye take her ladyship to her chambers. Now!"

The way Mary's eyes widened told Triona that her growing annoyance had been clear to hear in that one sharp word. To her relief, Arianna took Mary by the arm and pressed the girl to get her to a bedchamber, chattering away so continuously that Mary had no chance to ask any more questions, and led the woman away. It was wrong to be cross with Mary, and Triona knew it, but some days she just grew weary of no longer having well-trained servants around, if only because it meant so much more work for her. After taking a deep breath and letting it out slowly, Triona turned her attention to the chore of seeing that Arianna's escort had their needs tended to.

One look at the five men standing in the midst of her own men told Triona, more clearly than anything else ever had, that Banuilt was sadly prepared to fight the troubles besetting it. Her men were either aging or very young. There were good fighters amongst them, but it was not a strong force, for they had had little training and she could see the recognition of that sad fact in the expressions of the newly arrived men. It was a good thing that they were allies, she decided as she began to snap out orders. She just wished her cousin had taken the time to introduce her to the men. Knowing a name made it a great deal easier to order someone around.

A tall, black-haired man stepped up to her, his green eyes shining with amusement, and bowed. "Sir Brett Murray, m'lady. Necessity robbed our Arianna of her usual precise courtesy."

Triona curtsied. "I am Lady Triona McKee. Welcome to Banuilt."

"Thank ye for that welcome. Now, my companions

here are my brother Sir Harcourt Murray, Sir Tamhas Cameron, Sir Uven MacMillan, and Sir Callum MacMillan," he said as he pointed to each man named and each one gave her a quick bow.

Five knights, Triona thought, praying that she did not look as dazed as she felt. Five big, strong, trained, and honored knights. And all far too handsome for any woman's peace of mind, she decided as she forced herself to calm down and glanced from one man to another. Two black-haired Murrays and three red-haired men, and four of them with differing shades of green eyes. The only man who did not have green eyes was Sir Harcourt, and his amber eyes reminded her all too much of a wolf's. She hastily prayed that his nature did not match those feral eyes. What truly alarmed her, though, was that her gaze did not linger on any of the four men with Sir Brett despite their fine, manly looks, but quickly returned to rest upon him. Just the sight of his tall, lean form made her pulse quicken, and she wanted none of that.

Despite the vast difference in their ages, her husband, Boyd, had made her pulse quicken and she had often wondered if it had just been a foretelling of trouble to come. Now, as a widow of five and twenty and a mother, she told herself she was far too old and sensible for such nonsense. Responsibility also weighed too heavily on her now. Quickening pulses were better left to women who did not have so many people depending on them for their next meal, for everything they needed to survive.

"Allow me to show ye to your bedchambers," she

said even as she turned and headed up the steps into the keep. "I fear ye may find them poor accommodations, less than what ye are accustomed to, but they will be clean."

"I am certain they will be all that we need," said Sir Brett.

The man's voice was deep, with just a hint of roughness. Triona had to bite back a shiver of pleasure as it washed over her. The one time that had happened to her before, she had ended up married to a good man, but one who had little true passion or love for her. She had seen kindness and interest where there had been only a lack of emotion and a need for her dower. Holding firm to that sad reminder, she stiffened her backbone and did her best to get the men settled in their chambers as quickly as possible.

"Did it seem to you that the Lady McKee just scampered out of the room like a rabbit hearing the bay of a hound?" asked Harcourt as he began to shed his travel-stained clothing.

Brett stopped staring at the door Lady Triona had just fled through and walked to the chair near the fireplace. The bedchamber was clean but sparsely decorated, the furniture simple and plain. The hearth was a sign that there had been money once, or money newly gained and used to improve the large fortified manor attached to an old peel tower. He did not doubt that the high, thick walls surrounding the place had emptied the coffers as well.

"She may be unused to guests," he said as he sat down and took off his mud-splattered boots.

"True." Dressed in only his braies, Harcourt walked to the window and looked out. "But there is something nay quite right here."

"Do ye refer to the fact that the men are all young or old? That there is a veritable small army of children running about? Or, mayhap, that the village we rode through is half-empty?"

"All of those things and the fact that nay many of them acted as if they had been weel trained or even trained a little, but simply handed a sword and told to guard the place."

"Nay, they didnae, did they. Most of them acted much like youths who have but begun their training. One or two actually dropped their swords when they tried to unsheathe them. Arianna did say her cousin was a widow. Mayhap the highly trained men, the knights, sought out a new place when they were left with naught but a woman holding rule over them."

"Could be. There are men who cannae abide that. Any objection to my finding out all I can about her ladyship, Banuilt, and its people?"

"None at all. Arianna is here and she needs to be protected. Brian is going to be half-mad when he discovers she left. I have nay wish to see him completely insane because we didnae care for her safety with all diligence."

A hard rap at the door drew Harcourt away from

the window. When he opened the door, half a dozen boys on the verge of manhood hurried inside with a large wooden tub and buckets of water. A girl who was barely a woman, blushing furiously at the sight of Harcourt partially undressed, ran in, dumped some linen on the bed, and ran out again.

Brett watched her flee and shook his head. Even the servants appeared to be new to the work. Something was definitely amiss at Banuilt.

He thought about simply confronting Lady Triona and asking her what was troubling the place, but hesitated. Not only did he not know her well enough to be certain if she would answer truly, but he was not sure he wanted to be in her presence very often. She made feelings stir to life in him that he thought he had killed a long time ago. She made his blood run hot.

And that surprised him. There was nothing particularly alluring about Lady Triona, nothing that would make a man who had known far more women than he should have, intimately, find her attractive. She was neither tall nor short, nor plump and well-rounded, nor too thin, and her hair was neither brown nor red, though it was certainly long, thick, and healthy. Even her eyes defied description, as they were neither blue nor gray but an odd shade somewhere in between. She did have a lovely face, but he had seen many that were far lovelier. Yet something about her caught his interest and refused to release it.

He inwardly cursed. For the past five years he had had little to do with women, despite what his family believed, and despite his best efforts to change that, especially during a time of drunken abandon for two years before that. It was difficult to give in to lust when doing so roused the ghost of a woman he had loved and lost. Nothing could kill a man's desire faster than that, he suspected. That and the guilt over her death, which still ate at him even after seven long years. He did not wish to lust after any woman now but had the uneasy feeling that he could easily begin to lust after Lady Triona McKee.

It was not hard to bring the image of his Brenda to mind, for she was always there; and far too often, that memory was all too real. Lady Triona was nothing like Brenda, so he could not blame that for his sudden, strong attraction to the woman. Brenda had been beautiful, with her golden hair and sky-blue eyes, her body soft and with the sort of curves that made any man ache to hold her. She had also been sweet, graceful, gentle, and loving. Unfortunately, her family had had plans for her that had not included marrying a knight with few riches and no land. He supposed he should not be surprised it had all ended so tragically.

Shaking away that sad memory, he washed up and put on some clean clothes. It would have been better if Triona were actually Arianna's blood cousin, for he could have placed that familial connection firm in his mind and seen her only as another member of his large family. It was something he could still try to do, however, even if he doubted it would be successful. He had never been very good at lying to himself, no matter how much he sometimes wanted to.

Just as he moved to stand beside Harcourt, who was

staring out of the window again, Callum, Uven, and Tamhas entered the room. "Ready to find out a bit more about who and where we have delivered Arianna?" he asked them.

"Aye," replied Callum as he sat on the end of the bed. "Something isnae quite right here."

"That is what Harcourt says."

"Though it fair chokes me to say so, he is right." Callum grinned when Harcourt just laughed. "The first odd thing I noticed was the many children running about, many actually working without an adult about to direct them. Also a great many women with a welcoming eye."

"That should not seem strange to you," Harcourt said. "Ye get that look a lot."

Callum just shrugged. "This welcome appears to come because we are some of the very few adult men here. There are older men, some nay too hale. And a lot of verra young lads, some of whom could be considered men, but much too young for the lasses looking at us as if we were a rich slab of roasted venison and they were starving."

"I, too, wondered at the lack of armed, and trained, men to greet us," said Tamhas, leaning against the bedpost and crossing his arms over his chest. "We may have been a small party approaching, giving no sign of a threat, but there still should have been men of equal strength to greet us and ask our business with the lady. I dinnae think the sight of Arianna was all that made the difference in how we were met at the gates. No one builds such strong walls and then leaves the gates so weakly defended."

"Verra true," agreed Brett. "We need to look around, gather what information we can. I dinnae like Arianna staying in a place where the defenses are so weak. Harcourt has already decided to look round and discover what he can, but I think it would be best if we all do. We will gather what truths we need so we will ken a lot faster that way."

"Agreed," said Callum, and the rest nodded.

"Then let us go down to the great hall and see what food has been set out for us. We can start our watching and listening right there. Do we need to collect Arianna?"

"Nay," replied Uven. "I went to ask, and she said she would have that maid take her down to the hall."

Brett nodded and led the men out of his bedchamber. Banuilt appeared to be a fine fortified manor home, its people friendly enough, but he remained uneasy. His instincts told him there were some secrets to be uncovered, and he was determined to unveil every one.

"Such fine men, m'lady," said Nessa, one of the few older women who had survived the time of the fever. "All the lassies are sighing o'er them."

"I am nay surprised," Triona muttered as she carefully checked that the meal for her guests was all it should be, and reminded herself that she needed to have that stern talk with the women about not needing any more fatherless children at Banuilt. "It has been too long since we have had any true warriors here. Knights, too. Big, strong, weel-armed, and, I believe, skilled knights."

"Are ye thinking they could help us fight that bastard Grant?"

"They could, but should we ask them to? I did wonder if I could get them to train our men but hesitate to ask that, either. It doesnae seem, weel, courteous to have someone come to visit and then usurp their guard for your own purposes."

"Weel, mayhap nay, but something needs to be done about that mon. He is killing us all slowly, is what he is doing. That is all one can think when he tries to end our ability to feed everyone. 'Tis only because his own men dinnae have their hearts in the business that we have survived for so long."

"Sadly true, and we cannae be sure that reluctance will last much longer. If naught else, Sir John Grant has to be becoming suspicious of how little damage all his plans have done to us. Once he sees that his own men are nay helping him much, that they are at fault for his lack of success, he will make certain that they do things right the next time. 'Tis said he has a fierce temper."

"Aye, and then the burying will begin again, only it will be our own allies who set us in the ground." Nessa sighed and shook her head, a sadness clouding her brown eyes, for she had lost her husband and a daughter to the fever.

"Nay, I shall nay let that happen. If it begins to cost us lives, I will bow to what he wants. I just dinnae do it now because I dinnae think he has any right to force me to it, but also because I dinnae believe any of ye would find life beneath his boot all that comfortable."

"Nay, we wouldnae, but we wouldnae ask that sacrifice of ye, either."

"No need to ask. I willnae hold firm if the blood starts to flow, as nothing is worth the lives of the people of Banuilt. We have lost too many already to an enemy we couldnae fight. Now, let us finish this, as I am certain our guests will come down soon. So, no more talk about Sir John Grant. I wish to just enjoy a time with some guests for now, and listen to whatever news my cousin may have brought with her, news that will undoubtedly entertain me, if I recall Arianna as well as I think I do. She was always verra skilled in the telling of a tale."

"Aye, ye deserve that. Ye work verra hard for all of us."

"'Tis for me and Ella, too, Nessa. But tonight I wish to nay think about what work needs to be done, and I certainly dinnae want to think about Sir John."

"Ye do that, lass. Just wish it was as easy to be completely rid of that bastard," Nessa muttered and hurried back toward the kitchens.

So do I, thought Triona, and sighed. Sir John would not be shrugged off so easily, however. He had been a dark cloud in her sky from the moment she had buried her husband, one of the first victims of the fever that had taken so many of Banuilt's people. Sir John did not wish to heed her refusal. Why the man would think she would want another husband, she did not know, but he had even been uncivilized enough to ask her for her hand when her first husband was barely cold in his grave. Something was going to have to be done, something more than just fixing the problems he caused. But, she thought, for tonight, Sir John Grant would be forgotten and she would take pleasure in new faces and whatever news they had of the world outside the walls of Banuilt.

When a little voice in her mind whispered that she would also take some pleasure in looking at Sir Brett Murray for a while, she cursed. That was a danger she had not expected. The biggest danger was not just that he was a true pleasure for the eyes, which he most certainly was, but she had seen handsome men before. There had even been ones at Banuilt before the fever killed some and the rest went to France to try to gain enough coin to help restore Banuilt to the comfortable, pleasant place it had once been. Not one of those men had caused her heart to flutter or her pulse to race.

Then she took one look into a pair of dark green eyes and she went all soft and silly, she thought crossly. It could be just that she saw in him a chance to taste a true passion, something she had never gained in her marriage but had heard other women speak of. She had been willing to find it with Boyd, but, as she had discovered, he had been a rather passionless man. Bedding down with him had been quick and obviously only for the promise of producing a child. He had been kind enough when, after two years of such effort, she had given him a daughter and not the son he craved, and then he had returned to the duty of trying to breed with her. She still felt guilty about the many times when she had dreaded climbing into her marriage bed.

She smiled as she thought of her little Ella with her too-curly red hair and her big blue eyes. Everything else about her marriage may have been a sad disappointment, but never her Ella. For her child she could only be grateful she had spent her youth in a marriage that had brought her no real happiness. She had even endured Boyd's attempts to breed with her again after Ella's birth, for the simple reason that she, too, had wanted another child.

And Ella was one of the reasons she would have nothing to do with Sir John Grant. The man had seen her child only a few times and his disregard for the little girl had ended all thought of him as any more than a nuisance. She had even sensed that he would not welcome her child if she had been fool enough to think marrying him would solve her problems. That chilled her to the bone. Not only would Ella get no love or guidance from the man, but she could not shake the feeling that Sir John could even be a threat to Ella, who could claim a right to Banuilt. Banuilt was, after all, no more than Boyd's first wife's dower property, one deeded over to him on the day of their marriage, when he took the McKee name to please her aging father. And it could go to his child if Ella was suddenly orphaned; or, if Ella herself was gone, it would leave the lands free to go to whatever other child Triona might bear.

Realizing that she was standing by the table, scowling at the floor and drumming her fingers on the top of the table, Triona straightened up and fought to clear her mind of such thoughts. The past was the past and nothing could change it. Thinking on it so much was akin to brooding, and she did not want to fall into that mood. She had guests coming down the stairs even now, could hear the sound of the men's boots on the stairs, and would soon share a meal with them.

She looked over the table set for her guests and smiled. Banuilt may have faltered, so much of what Boyd had planned to do left unfinished, but she could still present guests with a fine feast. She refused to think of the large hole it had to have left in the larder. It had been years since any guests had come to Banuilt, far too long since she had heard any news of what was happening outside the borders of her lands, except that brought by the occasional trader or drover. They could make up this loss and, if Arianna and her men planned to stay for any length of time, she would face the problem of an empty larder when it arose. If nothing else, the men could do some hunting to help feed themselves.

Turning toward the door of the great hall, she smiled a welcome when the men walked in. She could hear Arianna talking to the maid as she, too, came to join them. Tonight was to find out Arianna's reason for visiting, and to enjoy a fine meal. Nothing else, she told herself firmly, pushing aside every concern that never let her mind rest. The first thing she wanted to know, she decided as they all took their seats, was why Arianna, a woman carrying a child, had decided that she just had to visit her long unseen cousin-by-marriage, several times removed, now.

Chapter Two

"My husband was married!"

Triona blinked and carefully ate a piece of bread as she studied her cousin. That was not quite what she had expected when she asked why her cousin had come to visit. Nor was the high emotion behind the statement. She was happy to hear that Arianna was actually married, but the fear of an angry husband banging at her gates returned.

The Arianna she recalled from her childhood had always been sweet, calm, obedient, and very learned in all the ways of a well-mannered lady, at least when presented to their elders. When lecturing Triona on how to behave, Triona's mother had often pointed to Arianna as the perfect example of a lady. Once out of sight of the adults, however, Arianna had revealed a bit more love of fun, a hint of spirit, but even then she had still been far more of a lady than Triona had been or had ever hoped to be. It occasionally still surprised Triona that the very rigid, proper, and pious Boyd had chosen her for his wife. Arianna, on the other hand, had always appeared to be the perfect choice for a gentleman's wife.

There was little sign of that sweet, even-tempered, genteel lady now, however. Arianna was scowling at the food on her plate even as she stabbed at it and shoved it into her mouth. During the time since they had seen each other last, Arianna had grasped a firm hold on all of that spirit she had tried so hard to bury beneath courtly manners.

"Arianna, if he was already married, then how could he have married you?" Triona asked. "Are ye telling me that ye are nay truly married to the mon?" It was difficult to believe that Arianna's Murray kin would accept such an insult, or allow the man who delivered it to live for long.

"Oh, nay, Brian and I are truly married. But my husband, the lying swine, neglected to tell me that he had been married before, that I am his second wife."

"Why does that matter? Many men have more than one wife in their lifetimes. Mine was wed before me. Sad to say, many a mon loses his wife in childbed, if naught else. So do women often have more than one husband in a lifetime. Ye were married before him, were ye nay?"

"Aye, I was, but at least I told him about that, and at least I recall my first marriage. All too weel for my liking," Arianna muttered.

There was such heavy meaning behind those muttered words that Triona had to fight the urge to ask her cousin just what she meant by them, and remain fixed upon the matter at hand. "Then why does it matter if Sir Brian was wed once ere he married ye?"

"Because he didnae tell me about it. Nary a word. I had to hear about his first wife from someone else."

Triona opened her mouth to begin a scold, to tell Arianna not to be so foolish, and quickly shoved a piece of bread into her mouth before she could say a word. The first thought that had entered her head was to tell her cousin that she was being silly and should just go home to her husband. Yet the more she thought on the matter, the more she had to wonder why the man would hide the fact that he had once been married. She could think of no good reason for doing so.

"Why would he hide the fact that he was once married?" she finally asked.

"He says he forgot about her," Arianna replied, and nodded at the shocked reaction Triona could not hide.

"He forgot he had a wife?"

It was difficult for Triona to understand, but she found that she trusted her cousin enough, despite how long it had been since seeing her, to trust her word on it. Arianna's word had always been good, and despite how her cousin appeared to have changed, Triona doubted that had. A glance toward the men revealed them torn between disgust and amusement. It was either just a strange manly twist of humor that would make them think that such a thing could ever be funny, or they knew something about Arianna's husband that she did not.

"Aye," said Arianna. "When his father said something about Brian's wife and I kenned he was nay speaking about me, I demanded to ken what he was talking about. He said that Brian had wed a lass five years past. I didnae believe it, but Fingal, my husband's father, was adamant about it. Then his wife, Mab, assured me that it was true, that Brian had had a wife before me. It seems my husband ran off with this lass and wed her, but she died within a month or two."

"Mayhap that is why he forgot. Such a short marriage could easily slip a mon's mind after so many years." Triona ignored the soft snorts of amusement from the men over what even she saw as a weak excuse for such an omission. "There would be so few good memories that they wouldnae linger in his mind."

It was hard not to wince at the gently disgusted look Arianna gave her, her response only adding to the derisive sounds the men had made. Even a short, dull, loveless marriage should linger in a man's mind, if only as a lesson well learned. There had to be some reason, some explanation for it that Arianna had not yet revealed or simply did not know. If not, then her cousin had wed herself to either a very heartless man or a very odd one.

"A mon doesnae forget that he ran off with the bride that had been intended for his own brother," Arianna said.

"He stole his brother's bride?"

"Aye. He did. Slipped off with her in the dark of night."

"And his brother did naught about it?"

"Nay. In truth, Gregor was pleased that the matter of wedding Mavis was no longer his concern. He had fallen in love with my cousin Alanna and wanted her as his wife. So Brian running away with Mavis was accepted by all, including her father, as he was but looking for a good strong mon to give him a grandson. The MacFingals are somewhat renowned for bearing many sons. Sad to say, poor Mavis died but a month or two after they were wed and Brian didnae gain anything, land or coin, from the short marriage, so he came back to Scarglas."

Triona frowned when the men laughed at Arianna's remark about the MacFingals' ability to breed sons but decided now was not the time to ask what was so funny about that. "And promptly forgot all about her?"

"There, now ye begin to see how ridiculous that is. Nay only did he care enough about the lass to take her from his own brother, but she died young, their life together barely begun. How does a mon forget that?"

Triona had no real answer for her cousin. How *did* a man forget such a thing? There had to have been sorrow and loss to mar his heart. No one forgot such things that easily, nor should they do so. Even if it was not the love match Arianna evidently thought it to have been, the loss of someone you had exchanged vows with should stick in your memory. She prayed her cousin was not trapped in a marriage as cold as hers had been.

"Mayhap he just didnae think it was of any importance," she finally said. "It was all in the past and of no concern to what he had with you, and so short-lived a part of the past that he had naught to say about it."

"I am nay sure that is any better," muttered Arianna.

Triona did not think so, either, but she had little else to say. It was hard to offer comfort and advice when she thoroughly agreed with Arianna's upset. Yet she was not sure that it had been wise to just run away. It was evident that Arianna had no trouble telling all of them what had her so angry with her husband, so why had she been unable to stay and tell the man himself?

"Cousin, I agree that that is a grievous thing, something that cries out for explanation and discussion, but why did ye nay stay and confront him?" she finally asked, deciding that being direct was the best way to speak with Arianna. "Your husband is the only one who can really answer your questions."

"I was too angry and hurt. Brian was away, and suddenly I just had to get away as weel. I dinnae think we could have had a reasonable discussion about it. I was afraid I was so angry that I would say things that could not later be forgiven or forgotten. I just needed to go somewhere, away from all his kin, and think about all this. Is it acceptable to you that I stay here for a wee while?"

"Aye, ye may stay as long as ye wish. I will say, however, that it isnae as peaceful as it looks about here, so ye may change your mind soon enough."

"Nay, I doubt I will. It isnae often that peaceful at Scarglas, either."

Before Triona could explain what was wrong at

Banuilt, she saw young Peggy, the nursemaid, enter
with Ella. She welcomed the distraction, for she was
not certain she wished to expose her troubles to these
people, at least not in full. She smiled at her daughter
as the little girl hurried to her side. Ella was newly
turned five and so pretty that Triona often wondered
how she had borne such a jewel. With her wild, dark
red curls and big blue eyes, she was so bright it always
made Triona a little too aware of her own dullness.
She quickly introduced her daughter to their guests,
pleased with the way Ella curtsied and greeted them
all with perfect courtesy.

"Mother, I kenned ye had guests but wondered if
that meant ye willnae be telling me a story ere I go to
sleep," Ella said quietly as she leaned against Triona's
side and lightly stroked her long braid. "I sleep much
better when ye tell me a story."

Coaxing little wench, Triona thought with affection. "Och, aye, I shall be up to see ye to bed verra
soon, love," Triona said and then looked at Peggy.
"Wouldnae settle until she saw who was visiting,
aye?" she asked, and grinned when Peggy laughed
and nodded.

"I told her we could see ye for just a moment for ye
must tend to your guests," said Peggy.

"And I said I should be able to see who has come
into my home," said Ella. "We ne'er have guests and I
wanted a wee peek."

"And ye have had one now, lass, so go on back to
your room and I shall come up soon," said Triona,
and then kissed her on the cheek.

Ella nodded, said good night to everyone, and let Peggy lead her out of the great hall. Triona was still smiling about how her daughter had managed to get herself introduced to the guests as she turned back to Arianna and caught the woman looking wistful. Since Arianna was carrying a child, she had to wonder what the woman was thinking about, as she would soon be gifted with her own child.

"Do ye wish to have a daughter?" she asked quietly.

"I but wish to have a fine healthy bairn," Arianna said. "Your daughter is a beautiful little girl, Cousin. And verra bright. Her father must have cherished her."

Triona grimaced. "I would like to say he did, but I fear he barely noticed her. By the time she grew those lovely red curls and showed a hint of the promise of true beauty, he began to take a small interest in her, but then the fever came and took him. Boyd wanted a son, ye see. He appreciated having a child to carry on his bloodline, but he truly wanted a son to take the laird's seat once he was gone."

"Ah, foolish mon. She is a bonnie, clever wee lass, and he lost something by nay seeing it and enjoying her for as long as he could."

"I ken it but so did she, and that is even sadder." After rinsing her fingers off in the finger bowl, Triona wiped them on her linen napkin and stood up. "Enjoy the food and drink. I will nay be long, but I must tell Ella her story or she will be back here pestering for it soon."

"Go along and see to the lass then," said Arianna.

"We will settle here and be ready to tell ye all the news we have when ye return."

That was something Triona looked forward to, and she hurried off to see to her daughter. She was eager to hear whatever news Arianna and the others had to tell her. She so rarely had had any visitors when married and was forced to be very subdued around them when they came, and no one visited since the fever had devastated Banuilt, so she did not feel guilty when she hurried through her storytelling.

"Weel, what has all of ye frowning and looking so serious?" Arianna asked the men as soon as Triona was gone.

"There is something nay right here, Arianna," Brett said. "We all can see that."

"Aye, I saw it as weel. I saw a village that had lost far too many of its people to a vicious fever only eighteen months past."

"How did ye learn that?"

"The maid Mary loves to talk and is too sweet, and mayhap nay so sharp of wit, that she will tell one anything one wishes to ken. She said near half the people here, including the laird, were killed by the fever. She also said that most of the surviving garrison packed up and went to France to fight for the French and bring home full purses, planning to aid Banuilt in returning to what it once was. There does appear to be a little trouble with the laird to the west of them, but Mary actually grew cautious when mentioning him, which led me to believe that the trouble may be serious and still continues. Mary trying to be cautious was quite a wonder to behold, too. But this laird may be why Triona warned us that all is nay as peaceful as it seems here. I didnae press Mary then, but I will in time."

Brett laughed and shook his head. "Verra weel done. Howbeit, I think it would be a verra good idea if we tried to find out about that trouble young Mary didnae want to talk about."

"Aye, so do I," said Arianna, and frowned. "She grew verra confusing when I asked, muttering something about fields on fire and livestock stolen."

"Mayhap we should find another place for ye to have your sulk," said Harcourt as he grabbed the jug of ale and refilled his tankard.

"Sulk?" Arianna glared at her cousin. "It isnae a sulk; it is a righteous anger."

"Then mayhap this isnae the place to nurse your righteous anger ere your husband comes riding up to find ye."

The way Arianna was looking at Harcourt and gripping her knife made Brett think it was time to divert her attention. "So ye think there is some threat here?"

"I dinnae think it is a big threat," Arianna replied after one last glare at Harcourt. "I dinnae feel that the people here are all afraid and readied for a fight, do ye?"

"Nay," Brett replied after thinking about it for a moment. "Nay, there is no sense that Banuilt is a place under siege. Of course, how much of that is because the men here are so poorly trained, I cannae say. Yet there is nay doubt in my mind that there is trouble here, and I mean to find out what it is. Howbeit, if e'en the maid, who ye think isnae all that quick of wit and far too trusting, grows careful with her words when asked, it may nay be as easy as I thought to find out the truth. E'en Lady McKee's warning was gentle and vague."

"There is one thing ye could do if ye think I am nay as safe as I should be here."

"And what is that?" asked Brett, not trusting the sweet smile she gave him.

"See if ye can give those poor lads out there a little skill. The men who went to France clearly didnae train anyone to take their place."

"That is true enough," muttered Callum. "I havenae seen such lack of skill in a verra long time, leastwise nay in the men who should be guarding the gates."

They all fell silent when Nessa and two young girls came to clear away the remains of the meal and set out fruit and tarts for them to enjoy. Again, unlike the older Nessa, the young girls revealed their lack of training, being hesitant and just a little awkward. Brett decided that the fever Arianna had spoken of had taken a great toll amongst the ones who served in the manor.

"Are ye certain the fever has left the area?" he asked the moment they were alone again.

"Aye," replied Arianna as she cut up an apple. "I spoke of worrying about my child, and Mary was very concerned but assured me that no one has had e'en the smallest of illnesses since the last one died of the fever. It took people quickly and viciously, from all she said. Came into the village and the manor and cut them down and was gone within a fortnight, only the still sick and dying left behind. She said it also hit Gormfeurach, the land to the west. Poor child lost two sisters and her mother. That all happened about two years ago."

"I have heard of such things, but such a fierce, quick, deadly illness is often found in cities or within the ranks of an army. 'Tis odd to hear of one out here where there are nay a lot of people crowded together."

"Mary told me that Nessa thinks it came through with some drovers. After they recovered, a few men found new graves a few miles down along the drovers' route. She also recalls that one of the men didnae look verra hale, but the men came and went so quickly none thought of it until the first one of their own fell ill."

"They must have stopped at the other keep as weel then."

"Or someone from Banuilt passed it on, because Mary said the two wee clans were verra close until recently."

"Ah, something to look into. It may be just that the people at Gormfeurach blame the people here for the sickness, but there could be more to it."

"There may be, for I think Mary would have said if it was just blame for the fever. After all, it could just as easily have been someone from Gormfeurach who passed it to the drovers or one of the people here."

Arianna glanced toward the doors of the great hall and smiled when Triona stepped into the room a heartbeat later. "Just in time for the sweet, Cousin."

"I am sorry I left ye to yourselves like that, but Ella isnae used to our having guests, and it may take her time to understand that she will have to wait for some things," said Triona as she sat down next to Arianna. "I did just explain it to her, but I am nay sure she is old enough to grasp that truth yet. There is also the chance she just may nay wish to grasp it, either."

"Weel, we dinnae mind if ye have to leave to tend to your child from time to time. Ye must nay think that ye have to be at our beck and call. I have imposed my company"—she nodded at the men—"and theirs, upon ye without invitation. I apologize for that."

"Nay need. I fear I have nay thought to invite anyone since my husband died, and in truth, he didnae invite many here before that. He preferred to go to them." He had also preferred her not to mingle with them much at all, but her cousin did not need to know that.

"Weel, allow me to tell ye all the news I have then, as it appears ye dinnae get verra much out here."

Triona poured herself some cider and listened raptly as Arianna told her about France and Scarglas. The tales of the MacFingals, ones the men occasionally added to also, had her both amused and amazed. Arianna had married into a very large and strange family, yet she could hear the affection for them all in her cousin's voice.

A part of her was jealous of all her cousin had done,

and even more jealous of how she had found herself
part of such a large, loving family. Triona recognized her jealousy but found no rancor in it, just
an understandable envy. She had never had such
things but had always wanted them. An equal part of
her was happy for Arianna because, despite her anger
at her husband, Triona could hear the love she had
for the man every time she spoke of him.

When Arianna admitted to being tired and needing to seek her bed, Triona also excused herself. She
wanted to stay and speak with the men, her mind
eager for any conversation that did not have to do
with breeding stock or planting fields, but did not yet
feel comfortable enough with them to linger without
Arianna there as well. Although she was accustomed
to dealing with men, they were men-at-arms, farmers,
and other villagers. The men who had come with
Arianna were knights and men of the world. In some
ways she was intimidated by them, by their greater
knowledge of the world outside the boundaries of
Banuilt.

Alone in her bedchamber, she dressed for bed and
banked the fire. A small part of her missed Boyd, but
only because she now felt as if all the weight of Banuilt
rested on her shoulders, and she could have done
with his sharing at least the small part of it that he had
when he was alive. The fact that she did not miss him
in any other way struck her as very sad. It should not
be that way, and yet she knew he would not have
missed her all that much if she had been the one
taken by the fever. He would have found another wife

with a good dower so that he could have continued to make Banuilt—once little more than a peel tower and grazing land—into a grand fortress.

Triona wondered what it would be like to love a man as she knew her cousin loved her husband. By the way Arianna and the others talked, that love was returned, and the man would soon come hunting for his wife. They had implied that, even if Sir Brian MacFingal had thought to allow his errant wife to stew in her own anger for a while, his clan would push him to go to her, for they would not wish the man to risk losing her. She envied her cousin that, and hoped the woman knew how very fortunate she was.

It did puzzle her that Arianna was so close to her cousins, because when they were younger, she had gotten the feeling that Arianna's parents, though loving, had not often mixed with the very large Murray clan. More than Triona's had, yet there had been expectations placed on Arianna that, from all her grandmother had told her, would never have been placed upon other women in the Murray clan. Arianna had never complained, however, and Triona had known even back then that her cousin was far luckier in her family than she was.

She sighed and stared up at the ceiling. There was a lot she did not have, but she knew she had more than most. It was not good to envy what others had, especially if there was little chance that one would ever gain that for oneself. That way led to a poisoning in the heart and mind. Triona knew she would never have what Arianna did, and would have to accept that sad truth. Her own family had sent her off to her aging husband and had never once checked to see if she was happy to go or even happy to stay. They had seen her marriage as an advantageous one, a connection that would aid her brother in gaining some much needed influence with people who could get him into the king's court and rid them of a lass who would only have been a burden to them as she aged.

"I have friends," she whispered. "I have Ella and I have Banuilt. I have a great deal to be grateful for. I have food enough to keep from starving, a roof o'er my head, and clothes on my back. I have a nice soft bed to curl up in when I need to rest, and women to help me with all the work that needs to be done about here. I am a verra fortunate lass and must cease craving what I cannae have."

Triona nodded. It always helped to remind herself of all she did have, things many another woman would kill to have. Life was not perfect, and she doubted she would ever completely cease to wish for something just a little different, but most of the time she was content with her life. In many ways she had the large family she had always craved. She had all the people of Banuilt.

When thoughts of a man with dark green eyes crept into her mind, she frowned. She did not need a man, she thought crossly, but that did little to push away the image in her mind or the way her heartbeat quickened as she thought of Sir Brett Murray. He was too handsome for his own good, but that did not stop her from appreciating his fine looks, as far too many women undoubtedly did. Neither did reminding herself that she was no beauty, and she suspected he was a man who was all too well acquainted with many beautiful women.

Cursing softly, she sat up and then moved to get a drink of cider. She was too old to be infatuated with some man just because he looked so good. Appreciating his beauty, his strength and manly grace, was acceptable, but letting him invade her thoughts to the point that he disturbed her rest was not. Her marriage had taught her that one did not get much benefit from having a husband. Hers certainly had not made her feel much less alone than she had growing up in her family's unloving home.

Once back in bed, she closed her eyes, determined to clear her mind and get the rest she needed. She growled when she had the sudden thought that Sir Brett would probably give a woman many children, all strong and handsome. He might also cause her to enjoy the making of those children. Triona flopped onto her back and glared up at the ceiling. It was going to be a long night, she decided.

Even as she finally managed to relax enough to reach for sleep, the alarum was rung and Angus burst into her room screaming, "Fire in the blue field!"

Chapter Three

Brett studied the charred ground in the far corner of the field. It had not taken them long to put out the fire, despite the plentiful fuel for it to feed upon. What truly roused his curiosity was why, if the fire was meant to destroy the whole field of crops, had it been set in a place so easily seen from the walls of Banuilt? Not only that, but it had been set in a place easily reached, where there was little risk of many feet and a cart crossing the field and damaging the crop. It was possible that the men who had set the fire were simply witless fools, but he had some strong doubts about that. It was hard to believe any men could be quite that witless.

He looked at Triona, who stood by his side. It troubled him that he had such a fierce urge to brush the loose strands of hair from her face, and he clenched his hands into fists at his sides as he fought it. Despite what his family thought, he had turned away from women. If they ever uncovered that truth, a lot of questions would be asked, and he had no wish to explain why he allowed everyone to think him such a dissolute man when he was far from it. He did, however, need to remind himself of those reasons when he was near Triona.

"Why is the field called the blue field?" he asked, praying that talking to her about the trouble they had just dealt with would distract him from his growing attraction to her.

"Naming the field makes it quicker for everyone to ken which one we must all rush to," replied Triona.

"And ye all have to rush off to tend to a field often, do ye?"

Triona sighed. She was so tired. The first troubles had begun only a fortnight after the well-trained men who had survived the fever had sailed away to France to seek their fortunes fighting for whoever offered them the most coin. Over the following nearly two years there had been few times when it had been peaceful at Banuilt. The people here spent far too much of their time repairing damage and not nearly enough building up Banuilt. She feared they now took more steps back than they did forward, and their lives would never return to the more profitable and plentiful ones they had all enjoyed before the fever had so devastated their people.

"Too often. I will just see to the placing of a few men to guard the field and make very certain the fire is truly out and we can return to the great hall. I can answer any questions ye may have then."

Brett watched her walk away, enjoying the sway of her gently rounded hips for a moment. Underneath her somewhat plain gowns there were obviously curves enough to hold a man's interest. Then he quickly forced his errant thoughts back to the problem at hand. He had a lot of questions about what was going on at Banuilt but wondered how fully she would answer them. His greatest concern was for Arianna. He did not like to think he had placed his cousin in the midst of a very dangerous situation.

"Ye were right," said Callum as he walked up to stand next to Brett.

"Of course I was. I usually am." He grinned at the disgusted look Callum gave him. "What was I right about this time?"

"That something is badly amiss at Banuilt."

"I believe we all agreed on that, and I also believe that I told ye Harcourt was the one to speak that thought aloud first."

"No need to give the mon anything else to be vain about."

"Of course not. Did anyone happen to mention exactly what is wrong here? For this"—Brett waved his hand in the direction of the burned ground— "badly done as it was, wasnae caused by any simple mischief or accident."

"A few started to say something but stopped ere I could hear anything of any worth. I do believe the wee lass has an enemy or an angry, rejected suitor. All I did catch word of was that she should either kill him or marry him."

"This seems to be more the act of an enemy than some angry lover." And the idea of Triona having a lover burned in his belly, much to his dismay.

"'Tis a strange wooing, aye," agreed Callum. "Unless ye are trying to ensure that she cannae survive or care for the people who depend upon her without the help of some mon to rule o'er it all."

"Ah, of course. He isnae doing a verra good job of it, if that is his plan."

"Weel, ye dinnae want to leave yourself naught but a smoldering ruin when ye finally gain your prize, now do ye. It may be, too, that the ones he is sending to do this dinnae really want to, and so they fail."

A grunt of agreement was all that Brett could manage in response. His mind was already crowded with questions he needed answered. If there was any real danger to Arianna, he would have to get her away from here as quickly as possible, no matter how much he suddenly wanted to help Triona, who had looked so sad and weary. Arianna was not only his kinswoman who was with child, but she was now a MacFingal. That was not a clan his family wanted a feud with. In truth, he would be willing to risk angering the MacFingals, would even accept a small risk to Arianna, to help the people of Banuilt, for he believed they were in a fight for their very survival. What he would never do, however, was risk the child Arianna carried.

There was serious trouble brewing at Banuilt, of that he no longer had any doubt, but he could not even begin to guess what kind it was. It had also been going on long enough for the people here to become very well organized in fighting it. He had rushed out of the manor at the first ring of the alarum to find a cart with barrels of water already having its team hitched to it, and men dressed and racing off toward the fields. It had all been done quickly, without hesitation, and with no sign of panic. This had happened to them before, many times, and it was obvious that, in this, they were all very well trained.

When Triona walked past them, signaling that they follow her back to the manor, he and his men did so silently. Brett could tell by the looks upon the faces of his companions that their concerns matched his. What had been idle speculation over the oddities they had noticed only a few hours ago was now a certainty. Something was very wrong at Banuilt.

Triona ordered some ale, cider, and wine to be set out for the men and then hurried off to her bedchamber to wash away the soot on her hands. There was little she could do to be rid of the smell of smoke that clung to her clothes and hair. She doubted the five men waiting for her to explain what was happening would be pleased to wait while she bathed and changed her clothes. They were concerned for what they may have just brought their kinswoman into the middle of.

After taking a quick peek at herself in the looking glass her late husband had given her as a wedding gift, Triona made her way back down to the great hall. She knew her reluctance to tell Sir Brett and the others the ugly truth about life at Banuilt was due less to how it might bruise her pride by making her look like a weak laird, and far more to do with how they might decide to take Arianna and leave. It definitely did sting her pride to admit, even if only to herself, but five skilled knights were sorely needed, and it would be a hard loss if they rode away.

"'Tis your trouble to deal with, Triona," she softly scolded herself. "Nay theirs."

As she entered the great hall, the first thing she noticed was the vast amount of food and drink her women had set out for the men. She would have to speak to the women, for if they continued to offer their guests such bounty, the larder would swiftly be emptied. Triona doubted the others returning from the field would be offered such a feast. It was not that long since they had had a meal, and it was a bit early to be breaking their fast.

Glancing around as she made her way to her seat, she also saw that no one had brought Arianna down from her bedchamber to join in this discussion. She doubted that was because they all felt a woman with child needed a lot of rest, which she did, and was more because they knew Arianna would immediately offer her aid without much thought for her own safety. For one brief moment, Triona considered sending for her cousin but quickly shook that thought aside. It would not be honorable to interfere with the men's decision in such a way. They had a duty to their kinswoman and the child she carried. Triona would not try to undermine that duty in such a sly way.

"What is it ye would like me to tell ye?" she asked as she sat down and poured herself a tankard of cider, wondering if there was any way she could calm their worries without telling them everything.

"That fire was no lad's prank, some simple mischief, or even an accident, was it?" said Brett, watching her face closely in the hope that he could detect it if she lied.

"Nay. It was yet another attempt to keep Banuilt from reaping a harvest good enough to stave off hunger this winter," she replied, hating that she had to tell these men how bad things were at Banuilt and how little she had been able to do to stop the constant harassment.

"Ye have an enemy."

"Nay as ye mean it, I am thinking. There are no direct attacks upon us and no bloodshed." *At least not yet*, she mused as she sipped her cider. She could see by their expressions that the men were thinking much the same.

"Weel, no need to do so if they starve ye," said Sir Callum.

"Verra true." For such a handsome man he could look impressively fierce, she decided.

"Who does this to ye and your people?" asked Sir Brett.

"My neighbor to the west, Sir John Grant, laird of Gormfeurach."

"And he has been doing it for a while, hasnae he? Ye were too weel organized for such an event, too quickly readied to go and put out the fire, for it to have been something rare."

"We began to practice a swift response after the third fire in the fields. 'Tis when I also named each field a color. It allows us to get to the right one quickly.

There are two wagons always readied with barrels of water and buckets, one in the village and one here. Everyone in the village who can run comes to the field to help, so that whatever fire has been set can be put out with as little damage done as possible. It has still cost us dearly but nay enough that we have all gone hungry." She sighed. "If we had not lost so many to the fever, we might have faced starvation, though. There are now a lot fewer people to feed at Banuilt."

"And a lot fewer at Gormfeurach?"

"Aye. They fell ill at nearly the same time. We think it came with the drovers, but we cannae be sure. Nor are we sure who had the illness first or who gave it to whom. It doesnae matter. It killed a lot of us. We had more women survive it, and Gormfeurach had more men survive it. For a verra brief time, that appeared to bring us e'en closer than we had ever been, but it was a short-lived peace. Sir John saw to that."

"Because ye became the laird here when your husband died?"

"That is some of it. Sir John doesnae believe that is right. This isnae some clan stronghold as ye get in the Highlands, but a part of a much larger holding. 'Tis mine, but there is an agreement of sorts with a richer, more powerful laird to the north of us. He is our liege and he is the liege of Sir John, as weel. He allows me to rule here, although I think he doesnae truly like it, but Sir John is verra unhappy about it."

"Why has your liege laird nay done anything about what Sir John is doing?" asked Callum. "Ye have complained to him, have ye nay?"

"Oh, aye, many times. I only recently gave up doing so. Sir John is far closer to the mon than I am," Triona replied. "I am but Sir Boyd McKee's widow. The mon believes Sir John's denials and feigned sense of saddened insult. He undoubtedly believes I am naught but a silly woman trying to find someone else to blame for my own incompetence. Since I have nay actual proof of Sir John's crimes, only my word against his, I ceased to complain for I feared the laird would decide that someone else should hold this land. I am nay sure he could hand it over to someone else, but I have nay wish to test that."

"Do ye have papers concerning the rights to all of this land?"

"Aye. And that is another thing that troubles Sir John. Back before my husband's first wife's grandfather's time, one of my husband's first wife's kin did a mighty favor for the king and the ruler gave a piece of the Grant land to Banuilt. The king wasnae verra happy with the Grants at the time. They owed him money, and some of their kinsmen had been traitors to the Crown. So the land was the payment and was then handed over to the McKees as a reward for their help in the matter. Sir John wants it back. 'Tis good land. Fertile and weel watered. Our liege cannae fix that, for it was a king's grant—so that has only added to Sir John's unhappiness."

"Might I see what papers ye do have?"

"Of course. Any time ye wish, I shall show them to ye. But why?"

"I may find something that can settle your worry

about losing this land and thus give ye the confidence to press your complaints about Sir John."

She smiled at Callum. "That would be verra helpful. Thank ye."

"Are Sir John's men incompetent?" asked Harcourt.

Triona frowned. "Nay. Why would ye think so?"

"Because that fire was poorly set, if it was meant to destroy the whole crop."

"Ah. We believe that Sir John's people are nay fully behind his attempts to destroy me. The people of Banuilt and Gormfeurach have been allies for many, many years. There are so many connections among the people through marriages and all, that there has always been easy, open passage between the two lands. They all have kin in each place, or good friends. They also believe the land was given fairly, and by royal decree, so Sir John really doesnae have a right to cry foul. They ken the history of it all far better than he does, I am thinking. We have also helped them as often as they have helped us in the past."

"Firmly joined then."

"Aye, in so many ways. I dinnae understand why Sir John has taken it into his head that he should have this land. None of the previous lairds of Gormfeurach bothered. There was ne'er any trouble. I begin to think Sir John has nursed his sense of injustice for many years and, once Boyd was dead, felt he had a chance to put things back to what they were."

"So he sends men to burn your fields?" Brett frowned, thinking that she was not telling them everything, but decided he would just let her tell them what she wanted to now, and press for more later.

"Burn our fields, steal our harvests, steal our livestock, and such as that. He wants me to give up. He wants me to walk away, I am thinking."

He also wanted her to marry him, but Triona was reluctant to admit that. Something told her that these men would find Sir John's insistence that she marry him so he could take Banuilt as his own as appalling as she did, but she could not be sure. The very last thing she needed at the moment was men telling her to do as Sir John wanted so that her people would not suffer. It was what most men would do, and she did not know these men well enough yet to be certain they would not do the same.

Guilt often made her consider giving in, but she could still banish it easily. She knew Sir John and she knew he would be a bad laird for her people. His own people were not fond of him, but loyalty to the clan and love for their home kept them under his thumb. He was a vain, greedy man, and she knew without any doubt at all that he would be very bad for Banuilt. Unfortunately, his attempts to beggar them and starve them were also bad for them all.

"He has ne'er openly attacked ye or any of your people, has he?" asked Brett.

"Nay. He has spilled nay blood o'er this. He wants us to bend to him, to come to him because we are broken and starving. Then he, in all his gracious charity, will take the reins." She winced, knowing she sounded as angry as she felt, her bitterness over the situation leeching into her words.

"Go and get some rest, m'lady. Ye have told us enough."

"So ye will be taking Arianna somewhere else?" She tried not to show her disappointment, understanding that they had to think of her cousin first.

"Nay. We will stay. As ye said, nay blood has been spilled, nay direct attack against the people has occurred, so there is nay real threat to our cousin. I think Sir John Grant needs ye to hand the land over to him, there being nay other way he can get it without bringing trouble down upon his own head. We will stay and we will do our best to make him change his mind."

She blinked, unable to believe what he was saying. "Ye mean to help us?"

"Aye, we do," he said firmly, and all his companions nodded in agreement. "We shall stay until this is settled. One of the first things we shall do is begin to train your men. Mayhap a strong garrison will help. After all, Sir John didnae cause ye trouble ere the garrison left, did he?"

"Nay, but they left soon after Boyd died, when the fever had finally waned, so I cannae say for certain that their presence would have made any difference."

"They should ne'er have deserted their posts."

"I understand why they did. We have ne'er had any troubles here, nay for a verra long time, so the need for their protection of the land was nay one that was clear to see. And, during and right after the fever struck, we lost so much that the temptation of gaining some coin to bring back the life they had kenned was more than they could resist."

"So they stole your horses and emptied your armory and went away."

"Weel, it wasnae truly theft. I didnae tell them nay to take the things, and they were doing what they thought would help Banuilt. I but wish I could ken how they are all doing, for they have been gone, oh, eighteen months or so, and there hasnae been any word."

"Mayhap we can think of some way to find out how they fare. Go rest, m'lady. We can tend to ourselves."

She nodded and went to her bedchamber. Her whole body ached with weariness, and even the fact that five strong men had just said they would stay and help her battle Sir John did not ease it. Morning was going to come all too soon, and she had so much work to do. A few more hours of rest was more important than thrashing out a plan at the moment.

"There is something she isnae telling us," said Harcourt as soon as Triona was gone, the doors to the great hall shut behind her.

"I ken it, but she will eventually, or we will discover what it is," said Brett. "I have a suspicion or two."

"Care to share what they are?"

"What is the easiest way for a mon to get his hands on a woman's lands?"

"Ah, of course. Ye think he wants her to wed with him and thus make himself laird of it all. Why wouldnae she just say so?"

"Many men would tell her, bluntly, to cease making her people pay for her reluctance and marry the mon. I suspect she has been told just that, too often, since her husband died. She doesnae ken us weel enough to ken if we are of that ilk or nay. Most of the people here are young or female, so her resistance doesnae trouble them. Mayhap they agree in part because they dinnae like Sir John. It may be an idea to try to get some knowledge of the mon. She could be fighting to keep her people out from under a bad laird's bootheel as much as she is fighting an unwanted marriage."

Uven nodded. "I think he would have to be a mon that would make a bad laird, simply because of what he is doing to get what he wants. Especially since what he wants isnae due him, as he believes it is. But working to starve people, mostly women and children, into making the lady wed him? Cannae think that any mon who would do that could be a good mon."

"I think she forgives her garrison a wee bit too quickly as weel," said Harcourt. "They deserted her and took horses and weaponry she could have made good use of."

Brett nodded. "I wouldnae be so forgiving, either, but they may have done it for just the reasons she said. After such a disease devastates a place, things can be verra bad. When so many fall ill there are a lot of tasks that cannae be done, and if many die, then there are nay enough people to ever catch up. The idea comes along that money could be made by selling one's sword for a while, and there is the solution to the trouble, the hunger, and the care their families need. Foolish, mayhap, and nay so weel thought out, but nay such a crime. I just wonder if that is what truly happened."

"What do ye mean?"

"I ken that a lot of men cannae write, but they always find a priest or monk to pen some word to their kin when they travel. These men have been gone for near to two years and there hasnae been a word? There hasnae e'en been a body sent home to be buried, or wounded sent home to be tended by their kin? Or e'en gifts bought with the coin they are supposedly earning?"

Harcourt rubbed his chin and frowned. "That is odd. Nay e'en word that they arrived safely and found work. Aye, ye are right. There is something verra odd about that."

"And who would benefit from the loss of the weel-trained garrison?"

"Dear Sir John, although he hasnae attacked the place, so that cannae be why he would want them gone. As Lady McKee said, he cannae just take the place by force or he will bring a fair load of trouble down on his own head. It has to be given, sold, or married into."

"But no garrison means it is easier to play this game of burning fields and stealing stock and trying to starve the people into submission. Who is here to stop ye save women, bairns, the old, and the completely untrained?"

"But if they didnae go to France, where are they? Ye dinnae think the mon had them all slaughtered, do ye?"

"I dinnae ken. It may be naught and I have just let

my mind weave wild tales, but I just cannae shake the feeling that all is nay as it appears."

"Another matter to look into," Callum said.

"Nay sure how to do that, but, aye, it should be looked at most carefully," agreed Brett, and then he yawned.

"I think it best if we catch a few more hours of rest, too," said Harcourt as he stood up. "If naught else there are men to start training, and from what I have seen, that will take all the strength we have."

Brett laughed as he followed his brother out of the great hall, Uven, Callum, and Tamhas coming after them. He briefly wondered if he was right to think it was safe for Arianna at Banuilt and then shook aside his concern. Sir John had not spilled blood in almost two years. He doubted the man would start now. He wanted capitulation, and he did not want to anger their liege laird, an obvious ally, by trying to steal Banuilt by force. The man probably also saw the keeping of the people who worked the land hale and ready to begin working to his advantage when he took hold of Banuilt.

Proof of the man's crimes was needed. That was what they had to work toward as they helped Lady Triona keep Sir John's vicious little games from bringing Banuilt down. With proof, she or some representative of her choosing could go to their liege laird and demand justice. It would be easier to just kill the fool, but Brett decided watching the man brought down would be almost as satisfying. He fully intended to show Sir John Grant that sometimes giving in to greed could lose a man everything he had.

Chapter Four

"This weaving is beautiful, Joan."

Triona stroked the wool cloth Joan held out for her to study. Joan was an excellent weaver, her work much coveted at the marketplaces in the larger towns. The shearing had been good last year and looked to be even better this year, if all continued to go well. Soon they would not only have enough wool for all of Banuilt's needs but a goodly amount to take to market as well. It was one of the few things that had not yet suffered from Sir John's continued attempts to beggar them. It might even prove enough to make up for all he had cost them, for it would give them the coin needed to buy supplies.

"'Tis going verra weel, m'lady. The shearing is coming along weel and it looks to be a finer lot than we had last year. The flocks are weel guarded and there has been no trouble. We move them around more often, too, just as ye ordered, so that they are nay so easily found."

"Good. I think we need to try to do the same with

the cattle. Will says we lost six head last week. Poor little Donald was so upset that he had failed as a watchmon, he was close to crying, but I cannae fault the lad. He is young and he fell asleep."

Triona looked around the village as she fought down her anger over that loss, and idly noted that a few of the buildings needed some repair. It was sad to see how very empty the village now was. With so many of the surviving men having gone to France, it was mostly women and children who remained. A lot of them had moved in together, finding it much easier to manage the work and their children with other women right at hand. It was a good idea, undoubtedly made the women feel safer as well, but it left a lot of empty cottages, and there were not enough skilled hands to keep those empty buildings in good repair. It hurt her heart to see the once thriving village in such a state, and she knew that the longer the lack of repair continued, the harder it would be to return it all to what it had once been.

"There be only two cows missing now, m'lady," said Joan, breaking into Triona's thoughts. "Four wandered home."

Looking back at Joan and nearly gasping in surprise, Triona asked, "They wandered home?"

"Aye, m'lady." Joan grinned, giving a beauty to her plain, round face, which had undoubtedly been what had captured the heart of her tall, handsome husband, a man who was now running about France with far too many other Banuilt men.

"What amuses ye?"

"Weel, either the men who stole them were a witless lot, or they let a few come back here apurpose. I be thinking it was the latter. I have kenned enough Grant men o'er the years to ken that they are nay a witless lot. And some of them are nay so far removed from their reiver ancestors."

"Ah, so ye, too, are thinking that Sir John Grant's men are nay in favor of his tricks. 'Tis something I have begun to believe and Sir Brett and his men suspected. E'en Nessa believes it."

"Aye. There be a lot of ties atween people here and the people there. Sir John's father was a fine mon though nay a great laird, and ne'er a bother. I dinnae ken what went amiss with his son. 'Tis sad and all, but Sir John isnae the mon his father was, and his people ofttimes complained on the fact. They say he is a harsh laird and given to fits of temper. Weel, they told us such things afore this trouble started, and, once the harassment began, we ceased speaking to each other."

There was something in the tone of Joan's voice and the way her gaze briefly drifted to the right that told Triona there was a lie being told. Obviously not all ties had been broken. For a moment she considered pressing the woman for the truth and, if there were some meetings between her people and Sir John's, demanding that they cease immediately. Then she inwardly shook her head. As of the moment, no blood had been spilled, something she suspected was aided by those ties that had not been completely broken. Until this fight with Sir John turned bloody, she would simply ignore it all. Thus far, communication between the people of Banuilt and those of Gormfeurach had really been to her benefit, such as in the mysterious return of four of the six stolen cattle.

It was sad that the two clans had to remain apart, thought Triona as she looked around the village again. The fever had hurt the Grants as much as it had hurt her own people. There were far too many widows and widowers in both places. Somehow Sir John had kept hold of enough supplies and coin to keep his remaining men from going off in search of it as hers were forced to, but he had not been able to replace the women they had lost to the fever. For reasons she knew she would never fully understand, the fever had hit the women of Gormfeurach the hardest. In Banuilt it had struck harder at the men. Instead of pulling apart, the people should be pulling together to rebuild both places. The way Sir John wanted that to happen was not one she could accept. The mere thought of being forced to marry him made her shudder with revulsion.

"Do ye think our men will soon return from France?" asked Joan. "It has been near eighteen months."

"I dinnae ken, Joan," Triona replied. "In truth, I dinnae really understand why they left at all. We were nay in any danger of starving. Mayhap they thought they couldnae abide being ruled by a woman." Triona did try to understand why the men left but could not fully stop herself from fearing now and again that it was her becoming laird that had done it.

"Och, nay, they didnae care about that. My Aiden was all excited after talking with a mon o'er an ale.

Man's name was Birk. Aiden said the mon was going to fight in France and that there was a lot of coin to be made in the doing of it. He told our men of others who had gained riches doing the fighting for the lairds and the king o'er there, and that they welcomed the sword of a Scotsmon. Threw in a few tales of fighting the Sassenach and getting paid to do it, and nay one of those fools would heed us women when we asked them nay to go. Nay, they set off all cheery and promised to return with purses heavy enough to buy us all fine linen gowns and bonnie slippers and all. Things we ne'er said we wanted, nay once. I am just a wee bit concerned that we have heard naught from them since the day they rode away."

Triona was not sure why, but a chill of suspicion ran through her veins. No matter how foolish she told herself it was to think it, she could not stop wondering if Sir John was somehow responsible for the loss of all her fighting men. The fact that those men included the ones skilled in hunting, woodworking, thatching, and nearly every other skill a village desperately needed to survive, would only make such trickery a greater success for Sir John. Yet, she wondered, if the men of Banuilt were not really fighting in France, where were they? It was the question she asked herself whenever the thought of treachery slipped through her mind, and the reason she had so often shrugged aside the suspicion. She simply could not believe Sir John's people would stand silent as he slaughtered thirty men, nor would they have helped him do it.

She tried to tell herself that she was being foolish, that she had just never heard the whole tale of how the men had decided to go to France because of the confusion and deaths caused by the fever and was seeing more in it than there was. How could Sir John lure away so many men and the men never guess at his game? They had to be in France. All reasonable questions, but this time her suspicion was not being so easily dismissed.

"Weel, isnae he a bold bastard to come ariding right into the midst of the people he torments."

Joan's muttered words drew Triona out of her confused thoughts. She looked in the direction of Joan's scowl and nearly cursed. Sir John was riding toward them, six armed men riding guard, and he was looking around her village as if admiring all the signs of the results of his trickery. The man knew she had no firm proof that her troubles were his fault, just as she knew that without such proof she could not demand that he stay off her lands. His friends were far more powerful than the few Boyd had had and would not look kindly upon her if she was seen to have insulted Sir John in any way.

As he rode up to her, she had to admit that he was a fine-looking man. Not tall, but strongly built, and with a face most women would find attractive. His hair was the deep brown of a chestnut and his eyes were an interesting hazel color. He also dressed very elegantly, yet all she could think when looking at his finery was to wonder just how much it had cost him. Everything about him would suit many women, and probably had. Yet, not once had he made her heart flutter.

His nature, however, was one that she utterly despised. He was cocksure, so arrogant that it made her teeth hurt from clenching them against all the words she wanted to say to him. The man also made his opinion all too clear, in his every look and word, that women were far beneath him. Whenever his words stirred her anger, making her ache to spit out that fury at him, she simply reminded herself that, without a woman, he would not even be alive to strut around as he did. It always gave her the strength to let his words just flow around her, never touching her.

"My laird," she said, and curtsied, ignoring the fact that his returning her curtsy with little more than a slight nod of his head was an insult. "Why have ye come to Banuilt?"

"I but ride through on my way to dine with our liege laird," he answered, and smiled.

A smile meant to keep her keenly aware that their liege laird, the man they all vowed allegiance to, had never once asked her to dine with him. She and Sir John were but small septs within the larger clan, minor landholders with only a few men to spare for any battle and no vast riches to draw a covetous eye. Boyd had gone to dutifully pledge himself to the laird, even occasionally sending some of Banuilt's men to increase the size of the laird's forces, but she had been mostly ignored. Once Boyd was dead, their liege laird had only requested she sign a promise to continue the allegiance the men of Banuilt had always pledged. He had decided not to extend her the courtesy of inviting her to his keep to offer her pledge face-to-face.

It had been an insult in a way, indicating that she was simply not important enough for the laird to see in person. At the time she had been so busy with the sickness gripping the people of Banuilt, fearing for her daughter's life, and seeing to the burying of far too many people, that she had ignored it. When one is burying people one has known and liked for years, the lack of a proper invitation from one's liege laird is of little importance. Now and then it still stung, however. The man had not even granted her request for a new priest.

Not that she missed the old one. If that man had survived, he would have been following her around day and night, telling her that it was her place as a woman to have a husband, and how Banuilt would be better for it. He had died still cursing her for dragging him to every man, woman, and child in the fever-ridden town and manor to give them what was needed so that none would die unshriven. Triona suspected she would be quite happy to live without another man like that around, but people needed a priest, and she would have to write the laird about it again.

She noticed Sir John glaring at her and realized she had been expected to reply to his statement. "I wish ye a safe journey, m'laird."

"Banuilt is looking a wee bit worn," he murmured as he glanced around. "It needs men here to mend what is broken."

"We are doing weel enough, m'laird, and will do better still when our men return from France."

"Those who go to France dinnae always return, m'lady. 'Tis a fine country and the weather much fairer than ours, and it can sore tempt a man to settle down in it. Bonnie lassies, too. Ye shouldnae hope too much for them to come home and rescue ye from this."

"Many of them left behind wives and bairns, m'laird. I suspicion they will wish to return to them if naught else."

The smile he gave her was so condescending that Triona's palm actually itched from the urge to slap it off his face. From behind her she heard Joan softly curse and knew the woman felt the same. Sir John thought her naïve to believe a man would come home simply because he had left behind a wife and a child or two. Some might act with such dishonor, but she had more faith in her men. She also knew that most of them truly loved their wives and children.

"A wee cottage in a French village with a bonnie French wife could be equally tempting," he said.

"Then I hope such a mon stays there, for I would want none who thought so little of their promises given to another to serve me." The fact that he could find such a possibility something to smile about was just one more reason to never accept his offer of marriage.

"So naïve ye are. It would be good if I could tell your liege that ye have agreed to allow me to take this place in hand, my lady."

"I have it in hand, thank ye kindly."

"Do ye? It appears to be slowly rotting beneath your touch. A strong mon at your side could make all the difference."

He was about as subtle as a rock to the head, she thought. It was hard not to spit out her accusations against him, to tell him that she knew well who caused her to have trouble keeping Banuilt's larders filled and its cottages in good shape. She had tried giving voice to her suspicions in the beginning, and it had done nothing but gain her Sir John's feigned show of hurt and insult, as well as a letter from their liege telling her to be more cautious in her speech.

"It but needs to recover from the loss of so many of its people," she said.

"Ah, but if the people from Gormfeurach and Banuilt were united, that repair would move along much more quickly."

Brett paused in his approach to study Sir John Grant. He was a healthy man of Brett's own age or thereabouts, but despite his good looks and fine clothes, there was something immediately disquieting about the man. Brett had seen the men ride into the village and had begun a cautious approach, his companions spreading out and doing the same, but noticed no alarm amongst the women. In fact, he had caught the exchange of flirtatious looks between some of Sir John's men and some of Triona's women, and relaxed his guard just a little.

Once close enough to hear what was being said, however, his caution rapidly returned. This man was the one responsible for trying to keep Banuilt in a state of near starvation, and only Triona's skills had stopped him from succeeding. Sir John sat there on his mount, looking down at her with a look of such arrogant condescension that Brett was astonished she had not told him to leave and never return. She showed more restraint than many of his kinswomen would have.

What he gathered as he slipped closer and listened carefully was that Sir John wanted Triona, not just the land. Just as he had suspected, the man had hoped to simply marry his way into the laird's seat at Banuilt. He doubted the man did more than lust after her, for no man who actually cared for a woman would speak to her in such a way, but it was clear that he wanted her to give in to his wishes to become the laird of Banuilt through a marriage between them. The man was also a fool not to at least attempt to woo Triona. He was not making her more inclined to give in, with his tricks and not-so-subtle insults, only making her stand more firmly against him. And, he thought as he glanced around at the other women, making her women stand more firmly beside her as she refused him.

Deciding he had heard enough, he moved into the open and walked the last few feet to stand beside Triona. He smiled faintly when Sir John scowled and his hand went to his sword. Brett would welcome a fight but knew now was not the time for one. He just crossed his arms over his chest, not showing any overt threat to the man. Brett swore he could see his men all bristle with badly hidden outrage each time the man opened his mouth.

"The lady has help now," he said.

"And who are ye?" Sir John demanded.

Triona hastily introduced the men to each other, thinking that they looked a little too much like male dogs bristling in preparation for a battle over a bone. Looking from one man to the other, she decided that Sir Brett was by far the better specimen of manhood, and Sir John would easily lose to him in any fair battle. Something about the way Sir John glared at Sir Brett told her that he also thought that he would lose a fight with the man.

"They came with my cousin Lady Arianna MacFingal, who decided to visit with me for a while," she explained, but it did nothing to ease the tension between the two men.

"How long do ye mean to stay at Banuilt?" Sir John demanded.

Before Triona could reply that it was none of his business how long her visitors remained, Brett said, "For as long as it takes to be certain that Banuilt stands strong and untroubled again."

And that was a gauntlet thrown down if ever she had heard one, thought Triona. She had to fight the urge to kick Brett. This was not how she had wanted Sir John to find out that she had strong fighting men at Banuilt. This was a challenge to Sir John, but she suspected that, at heart, he was too much the coward to take it up directly. He would just increase his efforts to cause her misery. She had welcomed the addition of fine, strong fighting men, but knew they could not watch over everything at Banuilt if Sir John decided to try even harder to beggar her and her people.

Worse, he might think Sir Brett or one of his men could become a threat to his own plans for her. How was he to push her into a marriage she did not want if she had men of equal rank around her at all times, men who might decide they would like to be laird of Banuilt? Since Sir John wanted to marry her so he could set his backside in the laird's chair at Banuilt, he would no doubt suspect that any other man near her coveted the same thing. Triona did not want to even think of what Sir John might do then.

It also annoyed her that Sir John saw Sir Brett as an equal and a threat, yet had never considered her to be. He had seen her only as a nuisance, one he simply had to push to do his will. She had held out longer than he liked, but she doubted he had ever considered that he would fail, until he saw Sir Brett walk up. Triona was deeply insulted by that and wondered why the man could not acknowledge that it was her and her people, most of them women, who were holding him back from getting what he wanted.

"Banuilt suffers because it is too much for a lone woman to manage," said Sir John.

"I suspicion she would manage weel enough if the fields didnae catch fire and her stock stayed where she put it."

There were a few snickers from the women listening to the exchange, and Triona saw Sir John flush with anger. "Sir Brett and his men have most kindly offered to give my men some training," she said quickly, hoping to ease the sudden tension between the two men. "They must take the place of the garrison lost to France, and training by belted knights is an offer I would be foolish to refuse." She watched him closely to see if he had any reaction to her mention of her garrison, and wondered why she was not relieved when she saw none.

"Ye could have asked me for some men to do that," Sir John said. "I would have sent ye a few of my best to see to the training of yours."

Which would have given him armed men right inside the walls of her manor, she thought, but just smiled. His one true weakness was his utter disregard for the wits and strength of women. She knew he thought her foolish enough not to see how such an offer would aid him in taking hold of Banuilt, but she would say nothing to make him question his own opinion. There was also the chance that he would send men who would not be such a great help to him because they might simply be reunited with the women of Banuilt who were heartily missing them, but she doubted he noticed enough of the goings-on amongst his own people to be aware of that. Triona had no intention of enlightening him, either.

"That would have been most generous of you, my laird, and I thank ye for the offer. Howbeit, as Sir Brett is a cousin by marriage . . ."

"Many times removed," Brett said, and met her quick glare with a grin.

"I think it best if I allow him to do the training," she continued. "If he and his men are forced to leave ere the men are fully trained, I will give due consideration to your offer and let ye ken what I think."

Which she would never do, she mused, for if she told the man what she really thought, he would probably beat her and then drag her before a priest. Triona could see the brute beneath his fine clothing. From the gossip she had heard from her women, his men thought him a harsh laird, nothing like his father or grandfather. They called him vain and spoiled, his temper flaring at the smallest thing. Since Sir John had so many highly placed friends, she had to assume that he saved the revelation of that side of his nature for those he thought beneath him. Since those included women, that was another reason she had never even considered the marriage he offered.

"As ye wish, m'lady, although I think it a mistake," said Sir John. "Always best to stay with those closest to ye. I have ne'er heard of any of your kin coming to visit ere now, so pardon me if I am concerned just a little about this."

"My cousin resided in France until recently, my laird. She was a close friend of mine before then. Naturally, when she returned home to Scotland she wished to renew our friendship. I am certain all will be weel."

"Ye ken how all can be weel, my lady, but ye continue to refuse to see the wisdom of our uniting."

"I am still in mourning, my laird. Considering anything more than honoring my husband's memory would be wrong."

Triona was amazed those words had not burned her tongue. She had barely thought of Boyd after he died, missing him only in passing and in an odd, unemotional way. She had buried him and just continued on as she always had, only without the tedious business of his trying to breed a son on her. There was a hard look in Sir John's eyes that told her he might have some idea of how little she grieved for her husband, but she did her best to continue to look sweet and innocent.

She did wonder why he felt so at ease delivering what was a less than subtle insult to Sir Brett. Sir John had implied that she was wrong to trust the man, and many a fellow would see that as a slap against his honor. A peek at Sir Brett, however, revealed him just calmly watching Sir John, apparently unmoved by the not-so-well-hidden slur.

"Please wish our liege my best when ye see him, Sir John," she said, hoping to move the man on his way.

"Oh, I intend to speak to him about ye and Banuilt, have nay fear of that. I do my best to keep the mon weel informed of all that goes on here, and the sad state of the village." He looked at Sir Brett and frowned at the four men who had silently come out of the shadows to stand behind him. "I will also speak on your new guests."

"Ye do that, Sir John," said Brett. "Be certain to mention that she is kin to the Murrays of Donncoill."

"Through marriage many times removed," Triona murmured, but was not surprised when Brett ignored her as completely as she had ignored his reminder of that fact.

". . . and the MacFingals of Scarglas, and the MacMillans," Brett continued. "He may have heard of some of us and be able to put your concerns to rest. Many of my kinsmen spend time at the king's court, as I suspect your liege laird does. I also have many kinsmen I can call upon to help me in aiding Lady Triona if she should have need of it."

Triona was not sure what good that would do, but Sir John did look briefly disconcerted. Perhaps the confidence behind Sir Brett's words made him worry that there was something about those clans he should know but did not. He simply jerked his head in a nod and rode off, his men scrambling to follow him.

Chapter Five

The dust stirred up by Sir John's retreat was still clouding the air when Triona turned to glare at Sir Brett. "Was it necessary to goad him? Aye, e'en threaten him?"

"I didnae threaten him," Brett said.

"Och, aye, ye did. It was more like a pinch than a blow to the head, true enough, but the threat was still there, and all heard it."

"Good." He crossed his arms over his chest. "I wouldnae have liked to have to repeat myself."

If it had been at all possible, Triona would have grabbed him by those muscle-taut upper arms of his and shaken him until his teeth rattled, but she had to content herself with as fierce a glare as she could manage. "Ye made him verra angry, especially when ye so kindly told him that ye were staying to aid me and the people of Banuilt. I didnae want him to ken that."

Brett knew it would have been far better if the man had remained ignorant of that fact for a little while longer, but he did not regret what he had said, either.

He did not believe the man would have remained ignorant of his plans to help Triona for much longer anyway. In a place as devoid of strong fighting men as Banuilt, he and his companions would quickly be noticed. It would not surprise him to learn that Sir John had come to Banuilt to see the men he had already been told about. Since there was no hiding the presence of him and his men for long, he had also decided it would not hurt to let Sir John know exactly how much aid Brett could call on to help the people of Banuilt.

He found an angry Triona beguiling but knew it would be a grave mistake to tell her so. The women in his family had taught him that lesson well, at an early age. Brett could not clear his mind of thoughts of her, however. Her blue-gray eyes had darkened to the gray of storm clouds. The sunlight brought out the red and gold streaking her brown hair, making it glow with warm color. Her full lips were turned down into a scowl that he ached to kiss off her mouth.

Forcing his thoughts away from how that tempting mouth would taste, he said, "He kenned we were here. I am fair sure of it. That is exactly why he rode through the village. He was hoping to catch a glimpse of us for himself."

"Catching sight of ye doesnae tell him much."

Triona watched one of his neatly curved dark brows cock upward and the corners of his mouth lift just enough to hint at a smile. It was an arrogant look and one that gently scolded her for saying something so foolish. It irritated her, made her palm itch to slap it off his handsome face, but she knew it was also deserved. Sir John did need only one look at Sir Brett and his companions to know exactly what they were: the strong warriors that had been missing from Banuilt for so long.

She had needed only one look to know it. They had not even had to display their fighting skills for her to know exactly what they were from the moment they rode into her bailey. It was revealed in the way they held themselves, in the way they moved, even in that arrogance that was so irritating her at the moment. It was certainly revealed in the movement of the four men who had suddenly appeared behind Sir Brett while he had confronted Sir John and now disappeared with equal stealth at just one flick of Sir Brett's hand. Triona just wished Sir Brett had not informed Sir John of their intent to remain at Banuilt to give her aid.

"He didnae ken for certain that ye were staying here," she grumbled. She noticed that at some point during their talk, all the women had slipped away and started to walk back toward home. "He could have been left to think ye were naught but guests who would be leaving soon. Ye didnae have to tell him ye were here for more, and ye certainly didnae have to throw that bit of information about your horde of kin at him."

"Why does it trouble ye so that he now kens that we mean to aid ye?" Brett asked as he fell into step beside her. "For all he kens now, that aid could be

nay more than a wee training of your men. 'Tis what
we told him we would do."

"Something he doesnae want to happen. He is
better served if my men stay just as they are—good,
fierce fighters if they are pressed to be, but verra few
having had any real training at all. If I soon have a
weel-trained force of men, Sir John will find it a lot
harder to weaken us little by little, as he does now—
weaken us until we have nay choice but to do as he
wishes, just to survive. Once I have weel-trained men,
he could see us as a true threat to him and then the
blood will flow."

"Have ye considered simply selling him the land he
covets so much?"

"Only for a moment. I dinnae want to, and e'en if I
decided that it was the only way to put an end to this,
I am nay sure I can do that. I would have to closely ex-
amine all the records Boyd had. Mayhap Sir Callum
will find something when he looks them all over." She
rubbed a hand over her forehead as the hint of a
headache began to form. "That wouldnae make him
leave us alone anyway. 'Tis nay all he wants."

"He wants ye." Brett was astonished at how angry
that knowledge made him.

Triona frowned and turned to look at him. The
hard, cold anger behind those three words surprised
her, as did the look of fury on his face. She firmly told
herself that it meant no more than an honorable
man's outrage over Sir John's attempts to force a
woman to his will. It could even be an anger stirred by
the manner in which Sir John was doing it, through the

harming of her people. Many men would consider marriage to Sir John a reasonable outcome, and would wonder why she, a lone woman, would be so foolish as to believe she could rule Banuilt without a man at her side. And not just at her side, she thought crossly, but telling her each and every thing that she should do, and just how to do it.

Once the trouble with Sir John had begun, a few people at Banuilt had suggested that a new laird might end it, that she might consider finding herself a husband to stand up to the man. Behind their words, however, had been no hint that they thought she could not care for Banuilt or its people very well, if not better than many a man could. There had also been no hint that the man she chose to help should ever be Sir John. Her people all knew who had done most of the work managing Banuilt since not long after she had married Boyd. He had had little interest in such things as the fields, the stock, or the need to send something to the market every year. The people of Banuilt were content with her as their laird, even if few others would recognize her as such. Even the very few who were uneasy with a woman sitting in the laird's seat preferred her to Sir John.

It was now evident that Sir Brett saw no harm in her sitting in the laird's place. The more she thought on the matter, the more she realized that none of the men with him did, either. Triona recalled tales of the Murray women told to her by her grandmother, whose aunt's husband's sister's marriage to a Murray had given the family their tenuous connection to the clan. Every single tale had shown the Murray women to be strong, standing beside their men rather than merely bowing to their authority. It would explain why Sir Brett and his men did not hesitate to accept her authority at Banuilt. Sir John never had and never would.

"Sir John believes we should be married, rejoining the lands and placing him as laird over it all," she said, seeing no reason to deny the truth. "I suspicion that he sees that as the easiest way to retrieve the land the king gave to that old laird of Banuilt. And Banuilt's ancient lands as weel, lands far more fertile than the ones surrounding Gormfeurach."

"And he gets ye in his bed. I suspicion he has wanted that for a verra long time as weel."

Triona shook her head and started walking again, idly studying the trees as she walked the road that ran through them, noting that work was needed here as well. The undergrowth had been left to grow too thick, and there were trees that could be harvested, new ones planted. Boyd's first wife's grandfather had left very precise records and advice on caring for the woods, ones that she had followed closely. Boyd had found her diligence amusing, and acted as if he kindly indulged her when he allowed her to follow his first wife's grandfather's teachings. She was abruptly pulled from her thoughts when Sir Brett grabbed her by the hand and forced her, gently but firmly, to halt and look at him again.

"Is something wrong?" she asked.

"Aside from this matter with Sir John, who tries to

beggar Banuilt and force ye to wed with him?" Brett did not like how angry that made him, for it meant that she had touched him in some way in which he had not been touched in a very long time, and done so in but two days. But he could not smother the anger churning within him. "Ye dinnae see it, do ye?"

"Of course I see it," she snapped. "I see it every time we put out another fire or lose more of our cattle or sheep. I am nay blind."

"Ah, but ye are. It isnae just this land that mon is trying to steal. As I said, he wants ye, too."

"Only because it is the easiest and most thorough way for him to grab hold of Banuilt. It may be mine, but once a mon lays claim to me, he will have a claim to Banuilt in most people's eyes. Sir John sees it as a way to get all he covets without making anyone question him or grow angry with him."

"Anyone being your liege laird."

"Aye. That mon may nay like the fact that a woman now rules here, but so long as I maintain the alliance we have with him, sending him men and supplies when he needs them, he willnae move to change things. Sir John found that out quickly enough."

"He asked your liege laird for permission to wed ye, and take hold of Banuilt?"

"Aye, but I gather it isnae a thing he can grant, or he just didnae want to. He told Sir John that Boyd had named me his heir, and that was agreed to so long as I upheld the agreement between Banuilt and him. I was surprised and I am nay sure I trust in that reason, but until I can see exactly what is said in

Boyd's papers, or your cousin Callum—who may have more expertise than I do in checking the contracts made and legalities of my rights as laird of Banuilt— finds out, I must accept that."

"Ye seem surprised that your husband would name ye the heir."

"Och, aye, as he ne'er appeared to think me worth all that much because I didnae give him the son he craved. He did leave a verra fine dower for Ella, too, or rather made certain I understood that there should be one. 'Tis evident that Banuilt is one of those places that can go where the owner wishes it to. I would like to think my husband left it to me because he recognized the work I did here, but I think not. He just did as has always been done here, or mayhap to pay me back in some way for the money I brought him. There was no son to name heir and he would ne'er have considered leaving it all to a wee girl child, so he left it all to me."

"Did ye nay consider that Sir John may recognize the work ye have done here and want your skill as weel as your land? His is a poorer keep, aye?"

"Only a wee bit poorer. Weel, when all is weel and we dinnae have to deal with fields burned and stock stolen." She frowned. "I just cannae see Sir John recognizing my work, either. He has that same ill opinion of women that my husband had to some extent and our priest certainly had. If he thought what was good about Banuilt was my work, he would have to believe I was capable of more than planning what to set on the table and making a bairn or two. I dinnae think he does, nay about any woman."

She was right in one way, but Brett did not completely dismiss the idea that Sir John was aware of the work she had done. The man might accredit it all to guidance by her husband or lessons taught by her father or some other man, but Brett could not believe even the man's prejudices concerning women could completely blind him to who had done most of the work at Banuilt. If nothing else, Sir John would have known Sir Boyd well enough to know the man's failings and strengths.

Sir John's insults needed answering, but Brett had held his tongue. Despite presenting himself and making it clear that he and his men were helping Triona, he knew pushing too hard could cost her. Her men were not ready for a true fight with Grant. Nor were they prepared to protect Banuilt much more than they were now, from damage to their sources of food. Until some work had been done to get her men stronger and better able to fight, he had to be careful. That did not mean he could not continue to search out any and all information about the man.

Brett carefully moved closer to Triona, nearly smiling when she stepped back and ended up against the trunk of a tree. "I think he kens that ye are the one doing the work here and have been for a while. He may make many an excuse for it, giving credit to some mon for most of it, but he kens it. I suspicion he has wondered how ye might help Gormfeurach to prosper."

"Weel, now that ye have told him what ye mean to

do, he will be wondering how to end that," she said, growing angry all over again. "I truly think it would have been best if he had remained ignorant of your promise to help us, at least for a little while longer."

"Mayhap, but I dinnae think so. He was here to see us, to see me and my companions and get a closer look. I would wager his men mentioned us and that stirred his curiosity. It matters not. What's done is done. Ye couldnae have expected me to stand silently in the shadows whilst he insulted and nay-so-subtly threatened ye, could ye?"

"Aye, I could. He does that all the time."

"Weel, he can stop now!"

There was a hard note to his voice that made her shiver. The way Sir John had spoken to her had angered this man, and she found that both strange and intoxicating. She could think of no other man who had ever gotten angry on her behalf. Triona was a little surprised that she could find something like that so deeply attractive. It was not something she should become accustomed to, however, or depend upon. Sir Brett would not be a part of her life for long.

"I doubt he will. He thinks like too many other men do and he willnae change. 'Tis why I will do all I can to ne'er have to marry the fool."

Brett placed his hand on the trunk near her head, lightly caging her between him and the tree. "Did ye ne'er consider it? It must have made ye pause for but a moment, to think on how much easier it would be for ye if there was help from another, from him and his men."

"Nay, not even for a moment. I ken the mon. He visited Banuilt many times when my husband was still alive. I have also heard what has been said about him by his own men. My husband may have been passionless, humorless, and so pious he would make a nun feel like a sinner, but he was e'en of temper and ne'er raised a hand to me. I kenned, from the first moment I met Sir John years ago, that he would think nothing of beating his wife. Most of what his men say about him confirms my first thought—that Sir John is quick to anger and quick to inflict pain when he is angry."

She had grown into womanhood under the rule of such a man, and she refused to step back beneath the hard rule of another. It was not something Sir Brett Murray needed to know, however. Triona had to admit she would also feel a little embarrassed if he knew how she had suffered under her father's rule.

Triona looked to the side when Brett rested his other hand beside her head. It brought his body so close to hers that she could feel the warmth of him. She looked from his hands to his face, frowning in response to the gleam of amusement in his eyes.

"I think we had best return to the manor now," she said, yet did not seem inclined to move despite how much she told herself she should.

"In a moment."

He did not wait for her to think long on what was about to happen but just kissed her. Brett brushed his lips over hers, savoring their soft warmth. He quickly recognized that she was not a woman well experienced in kissing, and silently cursed her husband. For her sake only, however, for a part of him was pleased that he might be able to give her something her husband never had. A woman married to a man for six years who did not know how to kiss was a woman who had suffered a cold bed, and he could show her heat, he was certain of it.

Triona trembled and then fought to go still. His mouth on hers was so warm and surprisingly soft for such a big, hard man. The way he stroked her lips with his, teased them with his tongue, had a fire starting low in her belly. Before she even thought about what she was doing, she grasped his jupon in her hands to cling tightly to him. The way he nudged at her lips with his tongue confused her for a moment, and then she cautiously parted her lips.

Shock swept through her when he plunged his tongue into her mouth and began to stroke the inside. Nothing had ever made her feel so alive, so excited yet afraid at the same time. She wanted more, wanted to get even closer to him, and yet also wanted to pull away and run. It was almost too much to endure.

When he pulled away, she stared at him, dazed. Then he tilted his head a little and smiled. It was such a satisfied, manly smile that she was torn out of her bemused state quickly enough to make her head spin. Triona fought to pull her dignity together, stiffened her spine, and pushed him back away from her.

Giving him a look she hoped told him exactly how improperly he had behaved, Triona marched off toward the manor. She would have liked to have left him with some sharp, scathing words, but she feared her voice would reveal how very far from angry she was. The fact that she could even walk steadily astonished her, because her whole body still trembled from the force of all that his kiss had made her feel. Triona had never been kissed like that. Boyd had pressed his mouth to hers from time to time, especially when he was wooing her, but he had never put his tongue into her mouth. She would have wondered what the man was about, except that she had seen others kiss like that.

She arrived at the manor and was nearly to the door of her bedchamber before her heart stopped pounding and her blood cooled. She went inside and walked straight to the bowl of washing water. It was cold, but that was just what she needed. After splashing some of the chilled water on her face and pushing away the last of the heat in her blood, she wiped her face and then flopped down on her back on the bed.

The sensible part of her told her that any kissing of Sir Brett could not happen again, that anything that made her blood run so hot was dangerous and should be avidly avoided by any woman who wished to remain pious. A greater part of her wanted to do it again. That had been passion. That had been what made Joan blush like a maiden whenever her Aiden winked at her. That was what she had hoped to find in her own husband's arms, only to be bitterly disappointed.

She was going to have to think about this, Triona decided. Think long and hard. The man was not going to stay at Banuilt forever, was not wooing her for a wife, and so she had to consider how kissing him would appear to her people. Joan seemed to think she worried too much about appearances, yet it was important. For her to be the laird the people of Banuilt needed, they had to respect her, and people often showed very little respect for women who went about kissing men who were not their betrothed or their husband.

And that kiss had made her want far more than just another kiss. There was an ache in her body that cried out for more. Triona was astonished that she would ever want to try bedding a man again, and yet she was sure that was what her body craved. She also could not stop wondering how it would feel to bed down with Sir Brett. What she needed to do was decide just how much she was willing to risk to enjoy another kiss, or more.

Brett grinned as he watched her walk away, her nicely rounded hips swaying with each angry step. Her kiss had been sweet, all he could have imagined it would be. Even better, there had been no ghost, no hint of Brenda's specter. He had not even scented his old love's perfume.

He took a few deep breaths to clear away the lust clouding his mind and began to walk toward the manor. Triona McKee had a lot of passion hidden inside her body, and he wanted to taste it all. Brett began to wonder just how long it would take to seduce her.

His conscience suddenly reared its unwelcome head and he softly cursed. Lady Triona McKee was a respectable widow, a laird, and a woman troubled by a neighbor who was trying to force her into marriage so that he could grab her lands. It would be unkind of him to play the game of seduction with such a woman. Triona had more than enough trouble to deal with.

The problem was, his body wanted her and did not care about such considerations. Brett doubted he would ignore any other chance he found to kiss her and hold her nicely curved body close to his. He tried to comfort his conscience by reminding it that he had no designs on the woman's lands, would never force her into marriage to steal the laird's seat from her, but he knew it would still be wrong to try to seduce her.

Despite her years of marriage, Brett was confident that Triona was innocent of a lot that could be shared between a man and a woman. That, too, tempted him. He wanted to be the one to show her all the pleasure they could share, pleasure he was certain her pious, passionless husband had never given her.

"And wasnae that a waste," he muttered as he walked through the gates.

"What is a waste?" asked Callum.

Brett turned to see the younger man leaning up against one of the open gate doors watching him. There was a look in Callum's eyes that told Brett he might well have seen him kissing Triona. There was a hint of anger there. It annoyed Brett to be condemned for his actions, even silently, and yet he also appreciated how Callum already felt the need to stand as Triona's protector.

"I was just thinking that m'lady's husband wasted his years with his wife," Brett said. "She called him passionless, pious, and humorless. I suspect that describes not only her husband but her whole marriage.

The man was a fool if I am right. He was wed to a fair wee lass who is none of those things."

"She is, however, a good woman, one with a heavy burden to carry," said Callum.

"I ken it." He sighed and stared at the heavy wooden doors leading into the large manor house. "I ken, too, that she had a cold marriage and now has a bastard trying to force her into what would be a hard marriage with a hard mon."

"Yet ye try to seduce her."

"Nay, not yet. I but kissed her. I want to seduce her, but it appears my conscience is wrestling with my desires and I am nay sure which one will win yet."

"At least ye ken it would be wrong."

"By most people's thinking, aye, but I am nay sure it would be wrong. She is, after all, a widow of five and twenty."

"True enough, and such a one is often just the sort of woman a mon could comfortably sate his lusts on, but I believe Lady Triona is no worldly widow who could take a lover and be at ease with it."

"I believe she worries over losing the respect of her people if she does take a lover, nay her own heart. She doesnae see that the people here all love her. To them she is Banuilt. She may have been little more than a child when she came here, but she quickly became all to these people. What happened during and after the fever tore through the village and manor only confirmed that in their minds and hearts." He held up a hand to silence the words Callum was about to speak. "I will nay put that at risk for her, so I will make sure of my opinion ere I decide what to do. Just ken this—I badly want the lass and she wants me. Neither of us is too young or too innocent to nay ken our own minds. I will also ne'er promise her anything I cannae give and will make her understand that ere I do anything."

"Fair enough, for ye are right. Ye are both grown and she isnae some virgin lass."

Brett started for the manor and Callum fell into step beside him. "What did ye think of Sir John?" he asked.

"Arrogant bastard, and ye are right. If she is forced to take him as her husband, to save these people, she will find herself wed to a hard mon and one, I think, who will fully try to break her to his will. He will probably have nay trouble bedding her, but he sees her as nay more than a key to these doors."

"Find out all ye can about him. He has powerful friends and she cannae get their liege laird to take her word over Sir John's. He has to have a weakness, something we may be able to use to change their liege's opinion of the mon. Proof of his crimes would be better, but anything to lessen his advantage o'er her will help."

"That I can do. Dinnae worry. I needed but one look at the mon to ken that he would be poison for Banuilt and e'en more so for Lady Triona."

Brett thoroughly agreed with that assessment. Sir John would crush Triona's spirit until she was no more than a shadow of what she had been. He may not have the most honorable intentions toward Triona and her lush little body, but he was determined to see that she never had to suffer the hell that would be marriage to a man like Sir John Grant.

Chapter Six

"Tri, I have been talking to ye for nigh on ten minutes and I dinnae think ye have heard a word I have said."

Triona blinked as she looked at Arianna. Her cousin looked amused, not angry or insulted, and that was a relief. She knew she had been lost deep in her thoughts. The way Sir Brett's kiss had made her feel continued to unsettle her, and she could not stop thinking about it. She could still feel the hot press of his mouth against hers, even though it had been three days since he kissed her. Such passion was unknown to her, and she was not sure she liked it. Yet, while her mind fretted over the alarming strength of the feelings his kiss had stirred within her, every other part of her savored them and wanted more.

Her confusion was not something she particularly wished to confess to. It was bad enough that Arianna already had a good idea of how carefully Triona had to watch her resources. They were in the great hall doing mending because the fire had already been lit. It was more practical to work where there was a fire burning than to waste good fuel by lighting a new fire in her sewing room. Arianna said nothing, but Triona knew her cousin noticed those small attempts to save resources. That and the serving of hearty stews instead of plain meat. Every woman knew how much that saved the contents of a larder.

"I am sorry," she said, and carefully folded the shirt she had been mending. "Matters are so unsettled at Banuilt, as ye ken weel, and all those troubles ofttimes consume my thoughts."

"I am nay surprised. These are verra fine lands ye have here, and 'tis distressing that one greedy mon would act so, just to steal them from ye and wee Ella. For this must one day be hers, aye?"

"I believe it should be, but Boyd left it all to me with a command that I see to a hearty dower for Ella. It was his to do with as he pleased, and as long as I swear fealty to our liege, I can sit here as laird. I brought a heavy purse to him when we were wed, and he used it to better what was nay much more than an old peel tower with a few additions. Naught too grand, but weel enough. The village was as it is now but nay truly thriving. If I had had a son, I suspicion that this would all be his, but I didnae." She reached across between their seats before the fire and lightly touched Arianna's stomach. "I ken I asked ye this once before, but do ye wish for a son?"

"I truly only wish for a healthy, living bairn," Arianna said quietly as she stroked her stomach. "I cannae believe I have put the bairn at risk with my flight from Scarglas. 'Twas most foolish, but I was so angry and so humiliated that all I could think of was getting away from there, away from a place where I was certain everyone thought me the greatest of fools."

"I dinnae think ye have risked the bairn, Arianna. Ye must be several months along, and I suspicion ye didnae have a hard ride to get here. Those guardians of yours would not have allowed it. It takes a lot to shake a bairn free of the womb once it is settled in."

"I lost a bairn once when I was wed to Claud." Arianna sighed. "There was ne'er another. I thought I was barren, that mayhap losing the bairn had hurt something inside of me."

"'Tis obvious that it didnae."

"True, but that doesnae mean I should go riding about the countryside when I am with child. The fear of losing this bairn has been strong, but my fury at Brian wiped it from my mind."

Triona smiled. "Nay, ye probably should not have come riding o'er hill and dale to come here, but if ye had hurt the bairn, ye would surely ken it by now, and truly, it isnae easy to shake one free of the womb. If ye had trouble breeding when ye were wed to Claud, it could have been his fault. He may have had a weakness."

"That is what Sigimor's wife, Jolene, told me when I was fretting about ne'er being able to give Brian a child." Arianna saw Triona frown in puzzlement and explained the relationship of the Camerons and the MacFingals. "I am certain that, if I had e'er spent time thinking on who my husband would be, what his family would be like, and how a life with them would be, I would ne'er have pictured anything akin to the MacFingals and the Camerons. They are an odd lot. Ye just cannae imagine how odd at times. They do make life verra interesting, however."

"Aye, I imagine so."

"So, what is to be done about this Sir John Grant?"

"Struth, I dinnae ken what to do, and that is the trouble with it all. What he does is impossible to fight and impossible to prove. 'Tis all sneaking about and breaking things like some angry, spoiled bairn. We ne'er catch his men at it, so we really cannae go demanding justice. Despite how much his own people dislike him, I dinnae think they would betray him by giving us the proof we need. So for almost two years we have done naught but fight to get enough work done to survive, e'en as we spend far too much of our precious time fixing what new damage he has done."

Arianna frowned. "Is it because he cannae abide a lass holding this land?"

"I am certain that is some of it, aye. He has verra little respect for women and thinks them weak-minded. And though I may be called the laird, we are nay fully a clan, nay like the ones to the north." Triona set aside the rest of her mending and sighed. "Nay like the Murrays or the MacFingals. I am laird simply because I hold this land. Banuilt is close to the Lowlands and the Borderlands, so we also have a fair mix of people who call this land home. E'en a few true Highlanders. From what history I learned of this land, that has always been so. Many of the villagers are descended from drovers who passed through, liked it or found a lass, and once they had completed the business that had brought them this way, returned and settled in. There were even a few reivers who fled here and just stayed."

"As I said, it is a beautiful place and has all that is needed to be a rich, fertile land. That is such a blessing."

Triona nodded. "Boyd's first wife's forefathers kenned it. They also kenned ways to make what wasnae quite so perfect here even better. I have studied their writings verra carefully. Sadly, Boyd's first wife's father wasnae quite as clever, and Boyd had no interest in such things. None at all. The only thing he did care about was training with the men, hunting, and going off to dine with our liege laird or e'en to the king's court."

"But ye did care and ye did the work, aye? Mayhap that is also why he left it all to ye. It might also be why Sir John wants ye bad enough to do all this trickery and sabotage, to try to force ye to wed him."

"I see that Nessie has been talking."

Arianna grinned. "She was ranting about it all as she helped me with my clothes," she said and then grew serious. "Ye must nay let him force ye into a marriage."

"Were ye forced to marry Claud?"

"Nay, not as Sir John is trying to force ye. It was a marriage my family badly wanted me to make, and when I first met Claud, he was handsome and verra charming. I truly thought we could have a verra good marriage, e'en a loving one, in time. No one kenned about his wife, or e'en heard the talk of her being his mistress for years. His family hid that verra weel. They needed the dower I brought to the marriage."

"As Sir John wants what I would bring to a marriage." She grimaced. "And as Boyd wanted that coin I was bringing when he wed me. It would be nice to be wanted for oneself just once, to be taken as a wife simply because the mon cannae think of life without ye in it."

Before Arianna could reply, Angus rushed into the room, stumbling to a halt in front of them. "Men at the gate, m'lady."

"Grant?" she asked as she stood up.

"Nay. Sir Brett says it be her husband," he replied and pointed at Arianna. "The mon isnae verra happy."

"Och, nay?" Arianna stood up and put her hands on her hips. "Weel, ye can tell him that I am nay verra happy, either. Ne'ermind, I shall tell him myself."

"Wait!" Triona grabbed her cousin by the arm when she started to march out of the great hall. "I think ye shouldnae meet him outside, where all can hear what ye may have to say to each other." She waited until Arianna took a few deep breaths and calmed a little. "Go to the sewing room. I will send him to ye. Then ye may have privacy to sort this out."

Arianna nodded and Triona walked beside her as they left the great hall, Angus following close behind them. Triona's plan to keep her cousin's marital discord private ended just outside the doors of the great hall. A tall, black-haired man strode in, coming to a halt the moment he saw Arianna, and then he glared at her.

Triona's first thought was that her cousin had married a very handsome man. Then she saw the anger in his dark blue eyes. Afraid for her cousin, she looked at Arianna only to find the woman glaring right back at her husband, no hint of fear in her stance.

"Have ye lost all your wits, woman?" he demanded in a voice that echoed throughout the hall.

"Woman? Did ye just call me *woman*?" Arianna responded in a voice that was not much softer, yanking free of Triona's grasp and walking right up to her husband.

"Why did that make her so angry?" Angus asked Triona, leaning in so he could be heard over the yelling that Arianna and her husband were indulging in. "She *is* a woman."

"Angus, it wasnae the word, it was the way he said it," Triona replied and sighed, wondering how she could get the furious couple out of sight of the people now gathering in the doorway or slipping up into the hall from the kitchens. "E'en the most sensible word can become an insult if ye say it in the right way, and he did." She was a little surprised to see Angus look thoughtful as he slowly nodded.

"Och, now that is odd." Angus frowned. "How can a mon forget a wife?"

"A very good question, but I think they shouldnae be discussing that right here." She moved quickly to grab her cousin by the arm. "Arianna, this should be private." She shook her cousin a little when the woman ignored her.

"What?" Arianna snapped, and looked at her. "I need to make this fool understand a few things."

"I am sure ye do, but mayhap ye should make him understand in a place that is a wee bit more private. Ye are drawing a crowd," she added more quietly.

Arianna looked around at the people avidly watching her and Brian fight, and then blushed. "Where is the sewing room then?"

Knowing the angry man staring at his wife would follow, Triona led Arianna to the sewing room, opened the door, and pushed her inside. Sir Brian followed just as she had known he would. Triona wondered if that grunt he made before shutting the door after him was the way he thanked her for showing them to a more private place. Then the shouting began and she sighed. They might be behind a closed door, but privacy was lost unless they finally lowered their voices.

"Ne'er seen Brian so furious," said Brett as he stepped up beside her.

Triona looked at him and then looked at the door, frowning in sudden concern for her cousin. "He willnae hurt her, will he?"

"Nay. I would ne'er have let ye send them in there alone if I thought he would. The mon would ne'er raise a hand to her." He winced when Brian bellowed something about foolish women not giving a man a chance to defend himself. "'Tis clear he has no trouble raising his voice to her." His eyes widened at Arianna's somewhat coarse reply. "Nor does she have any problem shouting right back. Marriage to a

MacFingal has certainly given my cousin a lot more spirit than she used to have."

"Weel, emotions are running high, I believe."

"Och, aye, they certainly are."

Triona turned to see a lot of her people plus Brett's men and six new warriors all crowded around. "They may nay have the sense to keep their voices down, but this is a private matter between husband and wife. It would be nice if we left them to it, dinnae ye think so?"

Callum grinned. "Nay, but for ye we will do so."

She watched everyone move away and then looked at Brett. "Is Callum your cousin?"

"Nay by blood. The connection comes through my father, who was fostered, and Callum was found and taken in by my cousin when he was but a boy. A long, sordid tale, but it turned out verra weel for the boy."

"He is verra good to children. It has been a long time since I have seen the children here so taken with a mon they were nay kin to, and see that mon return all their attention and affection."

"Aye, Callum loves them. When he was a lad he made an oath to be a protector of all children. His keep, left to him by his grandfather, fair swarms with them. 'Tis rare that we pass through any village or town where he doesnae collect another poor waif. And God help any mon or woman he finds who is being cruel to one."

Triona began to express her admiration for Callum's kindness when her cousin suddenly wrenched open the door and marched out. Arianna looked as furious as any woman she had ever seen, her skin flushed with anger, her eyes alight with it, and her small hands clenched into tight fists. It suddenly occurred to her that there was more behind her cousin's anger than hurt that her husband had not told her everything about his past. Arianna was smart enough to ken that few men told their wives everything they had done before meeting them, and while forgetting to mention a previous wife was a bit extreme, it should not be tearing Arianna up as it was. Triona did not think all this high emotion could be fully blamed on the fact that Arianna was with child, either.

"We are nay done talking," said Sir Brian as he stood in the door.

"We are for now," Arianna snapped. "I just cannae talk to ye anymore."

A look of something that resembled fear went through the man's eyes as he watched his wife stride away. Triona had the strange urge to pat him and say something soothing. Then he scowled at Brett.

"She isnae listening to sense," he complained.

"I think ye both need to take a wee breath," said Brett. "Tempers are too high right now. Ye should step carefully, Brian. The lass is carrying your child, and raging at each other cannae be good for her."

The man actually paled and Triona was compelled to say, "'Tis nay so verra dangerous, either, Sir Brian MacFingal. Just nay verra good, as it could cause her to feel a wee bit ill or the like."

"She lost a bairn once, and she is terrified that she

will lose this one. 'Tis why I cannae understand why she did this."

"This is nay my business, but since ye are here in my home, if I might just ask ye something?"

"Ask," he said, cocking his head to the side and studying her carefully.

"Arianna was wed before, and I ken that he was a bit of a liar." She ignored the way both men snorted in amusement at her understatement. "And that lie concerned another woman in his life." She nodded when Sir Brian's eyes widened. "Watching her just now, I thought it seemed that she was far too upset about this, and I couldnae think it was just because she is with child. I wonder if there is something from that past, that mon and what must have been a miserable marriage, that has added to her upset. I am nay sure but . . ."

"Ye are right," he said. "I was so angry that she left, put herself and the bairn at risk when she should have just stayed and talked to me, that I wasnae thinking clearly. I must think on this." He started to walk away and then stopped to look at her. "That is, if we are welcome to stay for a wee while."

"Oh, aye. I will see to finding ye all some place to sleep."

As she watched Sir Brian walk away, part of Triona had to fight the urge to do a little dance at the thought of having seven more big, strong warriors at Banuilt. Her more sensible side began to wonder how she would feed so many men. It also wanted her to pause and think of how angry this would make Sir John.

"This willnae please Sir John," murmured Brett.

She frowned at him. "Just what I was thinking, but I would rather ye didnae remind me of it. For just a wee while I wanted to be happy to have a few more big, strong warriors about." She sighed. "But, aye, and he will hear about it soon. I have no idea how he will react to it, either, so no way to protect myself from whate'er he decides to do."

"Increase the watch."

"Aye, that is at least something."

"And I believe I will gather up a few men and go hunting. Big, strong warriors can empty a larder verra quickly."

"Oh, thank ye. Thank ye so much. I was a wee bit worried about that."

Brett reached out and pulled her into his arms. "I think it would be nice if ye thanked me with a kiss."

"Ye havenae caught anything yet." She grinned when he laughed.

He kissed her before she had even stopped laughing, catching her with her lips parted. Triona had to cling to him to steady herself as he kissed her with such passion it made her head spin. She was still clinging to him when he began to pull away. It took her a moment to clear her head enough to realize she still clutched his plaid, and she quickly released him. Her only comfort was that he was breathing as heavily as she was. Then he gave her a grin and walked away.

"That be a verra fine mon, lass," Nessa said, and then laughed when Triona squeaked in surprise at her approach. "That one be a mon a lass should try to hold on to."

"He is only here because of his cousin, Nessa," Triona said, fighting down the embarrassment she felt over being caught kissing a man.

"Doesnae mean he might nay be persuaded to stay when she leaves. Ye should work on that."

Triona watched Nessa walk away and sighed. Aside from the fact that she was not even sure if she wanted another husband, she had no idea how to *work on that* as Nessa suggested. She had known no men before Boyd, and he had not taught her anything about how a man and woman flirted or played lovers' games. Despite having been married for six years and becoming a mother, she had all the experience in love of a sheltered virgin. And, she confessed only to herself, it was love she wanted if she ever let a man into her life again.

Shaking aside all thoughts of the handsome Sir Brett Murray declaring his love for her, Triona went to find her cousin. It did not surprise her to find Arianna sprawled on her bed, a linen cloth clutched in her hand and tears trickling down her cheeks. Finding a woman who was with child, crying, was all too normal.

"Cousin," she said as she sat down on the edge of the bed, "ye should try to keep in your mind that the mon came after ye, hunted ye down."

"MacFingals are verra skilled at hunting people down," Arianna murmured.

"Did he explain why he ne'er mentioned his first wife?"

"Aye, he forgot." She nodded when Triona grimaced. "He said there was naught to tell. He wed her, moved to her clan's lands, they had a verra short marriage, she died, and he came home empty-handed and then decided to make his own fortune."

"Nay the best of answers for all your questions, true enough. I did have the thought, however, that ye may be letting some of what happened in your first marriage disrupt this one."

Arianna frowned. "I do my best to try to forget that marriage, as it was a miserable one and a lie."

"Exactly. It was a lie. He already had a wife before he e'en wed ye."

Triona waited as she watched Arianna think about that for a moment. She hoped her cousin was as sharp of wit as she thought, because it would be hard to try to explain what she thought the woman was doing. And if Arianna did not see how she was letting the lies of her first marriage affect her judgment of her new husband, it would be difficult to get her to believe it. Yet, Triona was sure that was exactly what Arianna was doing.

"Weel, aye, but his wife was still alive," Arianna grumbled and then blushed. "Aye, I ken what ye are saying. And ye may weel be right. It was the lie, but, even more important, it was a lie about a first wife. I can see now that that may have been part of what made me so blindingly angry."

"It may have also made ye see it as far more humiliating than it was. Mayhap made you think those who care for ye see ye as a blind fool, when they ne'er did."

"Oh, be quiet." Arianna laughed and dried her face. "Aye, it was a bad memory as much as anything. The MacFingals are probably wondering if I have gone mad, running off as I did. They certainly wouldnae have seen anything truly wrong with Brian forgetting about his first wife or simply nay thinking it worth mentioning."

"I will admit that I think the mon deserves some scolding simply because he forgot his first wife and she deserves some sort of place in his memory, nay matter how brief or rare it might be. On the other hand, it does tell ye that e'en though he ran off with a woman meant to be his brother's bride, something we women would see as romantic and passionate and all, he didnae truly love her, did he. A part of me would find that verra acceptable."

"And now that ye mention it, I can see that, and, aye, a part of me finds that verra acceptable indeed. Poor Mavis. Forgotten and ne'er truly loved, either. Verra sad. But, as for that fool of a husband now stomping about your keep, I willnae let him just come and take me home. He needs to suffer just a wee bit, I think."

Triona nodded. "He does indeed."

"And I will keep in mind that I am making him pay

for things Claud did. Brian isnae anything like Claud. I do ken that my Brian loves me, but he needs to ken that that means I shouldnae find out about things like a first wife from others. He should tell me such things."

"Weel, he will be staying until ye forgive him, so I had best go and sort out places for him and his men to sleep." She stood up and brushed down her skirts. "It might help to nay call him a dimwitted, rutting bastard whose brains are all in his braes, too." She laughed along with Arianna.

"Thank ye for watching out for her," Brian said to Brett as they stood on the walls of Banuilt and looked out over the land. "I was stunned to find her gone. She has been so afeared of losing this bairn, I just didnae believe she could ride away like that."

"Forgetting a first wife can leave the second wife feeling a wee bit uncertain," said Brett.

"And that lass of yours has it right. My Arianna has already been cursed by one mon who lied about having a wife. I should have thought of that, should have remembered that, for it was a sore hurt on her pride that took a long time to heal. It explains how out of reason angry she is."

"I am nay sure I would tell your wife that she is being out of reason angry. Lassies dinnae usually appreciate that."

"I am nay a complete idiot."

"I have to say, it surprised me that ye could forget a first wife."

"It was five years ago and lasted but weeks. And I didnae love her. Lusted after her and lusted after all she could give me if I wed her. I could see that Gregor didnae want her, so I took my chance. Didnae work, and I swore I wouldnae try to gain land or coin that way again. I was done with that game. So, I fixed my poor wee mind on trading, and that was near all I thought on until I met Arianna. And what I have with her, weel, let us just say that Mavis wasnae e'en a shadow in the back of my mind when I looked at Arianna. Mavis deserved better, but there is the sad truth of it."

"And that is exactly what ye should say to your wife when she decides to speak to ye again. Truly, Brian. Tell her just that."

"I will then. So, tell me what the trouble is here."

"How do ye ken there is trouble here?"

"I looked about as I rode here to find my foolish wife. 'Tis clear to see. Just nay sure how bad it is. Now that I am here and may be staying for a wee while, I would like to ken what is happening. I trust that ye would ne'er put Arianna in danger, so 'tis something else. Ye now have me and six MacFingals, so tell me and we will see how we can help."

Brett nodded and proceeded to tell Brian everything. The kind of skills and knowledge the MacFingals had would indeed be very helpful. There might now be a chance to truly put an end to all the trouble Sir John was causing. Only a madman would keep trying to ruin Banuilt and starve its people when faced with the force Triona could now call upon. What Brett feared, though, was that Sir John was not exactly sane when it came to possessing Banuilt and Triona.

Chapter Seven

Brett was impressed by Triona's skill on a horse. She did not slow them down at all, leading them with a swift grace to the pasture where the sheep had been grazing. It surprised him that the Banuilt men with her were nearly as good as she was, for he knew that they were just villagers, not born into a life of horses and weapons. However, the way they had all responded to the report of the theft of their flock revealed that they had skills that he could hone as he trained them. It had also surprised him that it had taken Sir John two days to try anything after the arrival of even more men at Banuilt, for he had been sure the man would have immediately tested the new, added strength of the place.

When Triona halted and quickly dismounted, Brett moved fast to reach her side, his sword drawn as he watched for any threat to her. She grabbed a bag from her saddle and rushed to where two men were sprawled on the ground. Brett told her men to guard them well and then told his own to have a good look around the area. If there was any sign of the thieves, Harcourt and the others would find it. He could see that the MacFingals with them were already tracking the thieves, as well. The best discovery they could make would be a trail that led straight to Sir John Grant's gates, for it would give them hard proof of his crimes against Banuilt.

"Alive?" he asked Triona as she knelt by the two unconscious men and looked them over.

"Aye," she replied. "Naught but a sound knock on the back of the head for Ian and what looks to have been a hard blow to the jaw for Robbie." She took a rag from her bag, wet it with some water from her wineskin, and began to gently clean off the men's wounds. "I think they will rouse soon."

"So the thieves may still be close at hand."

"We always seem to be too late to catch them. We wouldnae have kenned about this attack so quickly if I hadnae started to put a watch o'er the fields and stock."

Brett thought on the young boy who had run to them with the news about the theft of the sheep. "Ye use the children." She blushed, looking distressed and guilty, and he hastened to add, "I meant nay criticism of it."

"I cannae help but think that I deserve some. About a fortnight ere ye arrived, I had the thought that a warning of some kind might be enough to gain us a chance to catch the ones doing this to us. Yet I have so few men to defend the manor and village, I couldnae think of how to do that. That was when I thought the children could help. Only the older children, with the youngest amongst them watching the land nearest the safety of the walls. Poor Donald fell asleep, or we would have already learned that e'en a quicker warning wouldnae help. He was watching o'er the cattle that were taken."

She sighed and sat back on her heels, waiting for the men to wake. "Since it hasnae worked as I had hoped it would, I might as weel end it and send the children home."

"But it has worked," said Brett. "If luck is with us, we may e'en catch the men who did this. I do think we have a verra good chance of retrieving many of the sheep that were taken, e'en if the thieves get away. We arrived here but moments after the thieves fled with the sheep."

"How do ye ken that?"

Brett pointed to the marks upon the ground all around them. "This is all but newly done. And the wounds the men have shouldnae keep them asleep for verra long, yet they dinnae show any sign of rousing yet. I suspicion the men who did this are nay too far away, especially as they are herding sheep as they flee. Or attempting to."

Triona laughed shortly and shook her head. "I was so concerned about my men that I didnae think about the sheep." She looked at the dog that was resting its head on Ian's narrow chest. "Those men certainly willnae get verra far with ease, without the help of Dun here. E'en if the men escape us, they will be leaving many if nay all of the sheep behind." She crossed her arms over her chest and frowned down at the two unconscious men. "Yet, in its way, this is blood spilled, isnae it. And I placed a child near all this."

"This is naught of any true importance. This was but a way to keep from hurting these men e'en more than this. I ken that, looking at them lying there like that, ye may find this hard to believe, but this really isnae blood spilled. This is trying verra hard to nay spill any blood. The thieves didnae ken about the lad watching them. It would have been quicker, safer, and would have better ensured a successful escape if they had killed these men. E'en if they had seen the child, I doubt they would have hurt him, so ye got the warning ye so needed."

"Weel, ye may be right, but I still believe I shall think hard about any continued use of the children."

"While ye think on it, keep in mind that Callum has said nothing. If he thought the children ill-used or placed in danger, he would have told ye so."

"Ah, I hadnae thought on that. Aye, he would have."

"And I will now go and help my friends with their hunting, as 'tis easy to see that there is no threat here for ye. We may be fortunate and finally gain ye the proof ye need to point the finger of blame for all your troubles right at Sir John."

Triona watched Brett leave and sighed again. It would indeed be good if they caught some of Sir John's men, but she was not sure that would give her the proof she needed to openly accuse Sir John of causing all the trouble at Banuilt. Whoever they caught could simply claim that they had done all of it without their laird's knowledge. Sir Brett did not appear to understand just how hard it would be for her to accuse Sir John of anything without bringing more trouble down upon her shoulders. Not only was the man close friends with their liege laird but he had many friends, and even some kinsmen, in the king's court. Sir John's kin might be distant, the blood tie thin, but they would stand behind him before they would ever listen to her. Their liege laird had already shown her how little weight her word carried in comparison to Sir John's.

Ian groaned, drawing her attention. She quickly ordered two men to come and help her. It was several moments before either Robbie or Ian was conscious enough to sit up, but her concern over how badly they were hurt quickly faded. Sir Brett had judged the matter right. The injuries done the two men were just enough to allow the thieves to escape.

"Them bastards took our flock," grumbled Ian as he looked around, all the while patting Dun, and then he glanced at Triona and blushed. "Pardon, m'lady."

She waved aside his apology. "They deserve whate'er one wishes to call them. Weel, mayhap 'tis fair to say that their laird, Sir John, deserves it. Did ye e'en see who it was, Ian?"

"I didnae see anything. Just felt me head break all of a sudden."

"I saw them, m'lady," said Robbie, rubbing his hand over his bruised jaw. "They were Sir John's men. Nay doubt about it. I saw Duncan, a mon I have kenned for years and who was wooing me cousin Meg e'er this trouble started. Nay sure about the one what hit me, but he did say he was sorry. And isnae that a strange thing, aye?"

"Aye, but it strengthens a feeling I have had recently," said Triona. "I have begun to wonder if the men simply do Sir John's bidding, and do so verra reluctantly. I just couldnae believe his men could be as incompetent as they appear to be." She stood up and brushed off her skirts. "Let us get ye both back to the manor now."

"Och, nay, m'lady," said Ian. "We need to wait and see if any of the flock is returned. E'en if it is, we may still have to go asearching for some. We will be fine. We were nay hurt bad."

"Then I shall leave some of these men with you. Sir Brett, Sir Brian, and their men may have some need of all of ye when they return. Sir Brett believed the thieves couldnae have gotten far."

"Hope the mon proves to be right."

So did Triona. She briefly thought about staying, waiting for Sir Brett herself, and then shook that thought aside. He knew what was needed, as did the MacFingals. There was no need of her staying here any longer. She mounted her horse and, with three men to guard her, made her way back to the manor.

Brian sat on his horse next to Brett and shook his head as they watched the thieves struggle to move the sheep along. "Idiots."

"Nay, just nay shepherds. Sir John sent the wrong men after the flock."

"Weel, that may be true, but I was thinking more on how they are nay paying any mind to anything but those cursed sheep. Our men have them completely encircled and they havenae e'en noticed. So, do we kill the fools, or nay?"

"Nay. Most of the people at Banuilt dinnae seem to really blame Sir John's men. And it appears there has always been a lot of mingling amongst the two clans. I would just as soon catch them alive, too, for one ne'er kens when one of them may have had enough of this and will be willing to tell us—and anyone else—just what his laird has been doing."

"Alive it is, then."

Brian signaled the men surrounding the thieves by bellowing out a war cry that left Brett's ears ringing. Laughing softly, he rode toward Sir John's men. The capture of the six thieves was so quick and easy that Brett was a little disappointed. The hunt and preparing for the capture had fired his blood for a fight, but Sir John's men, after a fruitless scramble to run away, offered none.

He ordered the captives to herd the sheep back to where they had found them, as he, Brian, and the others rode guard on them. It was a slow journey, for none of Sir John's men appeared to know anything about how to handle sheep. The MacFingals proved more skilled at it, and Brett suspected that skill harked back to a past that included a lot of raids. After turning the flock over to Ian and Robbie, they then herded the captives back to the manor.

"A shame they didnae fight," said Brian as he dismounted and stood next to Brett to watch the prisoners taken away. "I was hoping for just a wee battle."

"Still nay back in your wife's favor?" Brett grinned when Brian glared at him.

"She is being stubborn. I told her what ye said I should, and she has ceased to glare and bellow at me, but she says she needs to consider what to do next. I have no idea what she means by that. Told her that her considering better nay include leaving me. She rolled her eyes at me and walked away."

Brett laughed. "She is just making ye suffer for a wee while."

"I thought that may be it. Weel, at least there is work to do here. That lass of yours needs help, and it does me good to offer some."

"She isnae really my lass, Brian."

"Why not? I see the way she looks at ye when ye are nay looking at her, which is rare. She could be your lass, and she would be a good one to choose."

"Because of all this?" Brett asked, spreading his arms to indicate Banuilt.

"That doesnae hurt, but nay. Just something in the way she looks at ye. 'Tis nay just a lusting. Nay a look like some of the other lassies here are giving the men. There is more, and it is the more that does a mon good."

"I ken it. I am just nay sure it would be right of me to act upon it."

"Weel, think on it then. I need some ale to wash the dust from my throat and clear the stink of sheep from my head."

Brian strode toward the manor and Brett followed him. He liked the idea that there was more in the looks Triona gave him than a mere lusting. He had had his share of women who gave him the simple lust he had looked for but had quickly tired of them. It had not been anywhere near as fulfilling as what he had shared with Brenda, and he knew that was because what they had shared had been that *more* Brian spoke of. He wanted that again, but he was not sure his own guilt and ghosts would allow it.

Triona and her women had drink and some light fare ready for them, and Brett sat down to enjoy it. He smiled at her when she sat down across the table from him and smiled a little wider when she blushed faintly. There was more there than lust between them, and it tempted him to try for it more and more each day.

"So the sheep have been returned to their field?" she asked.

"They have," he replied. "Ian said a few were missing but that Dun would soon collect them. Sir John sent out men who had nay idea of how to move a flock of sheep, and were easily followed and caught. I assume ye will want to talk to them."

"Aye, although I doubt they will give up their laird. Bad as he is, he is their laird, and the Gormfeurach men are verra loyal. They truly do see the laird as almost part of the land they have been born in and love."

"And thus far he hasnae asked them to kill anyone."

"There is that. Although—" She hesitated to speak of her doubts about what had really happened to her men.

"Although what?"

"Weel, I have begun to wonder about my men again," she confessed, and began to think on how to explain her worries and suspicions without sounding foolish.

"The ones who left ye in a keep with nay a decent guard, just so they could go and fight for someone else?" asked Brian.

Triona sighed. "I ken it was bad of them, but, weel, ye would have had to have been here. We had all suffered from the fever. Most everyone had a loved one die. Naught got done as we fought to save those we could and bury the far too many we couldnae save. So the harvest was going to be poor, the weaving nay done, many of the skilled workers were gone and would need to be replaced, and what money we had here was going to have to be used to fill the larder. Then some man comes along and tells them of a way to get some money doing something they have been doing all their lives, using their skill with a sword. It was too tempting and, mayhap, they just needed to get away from this place for a wee while."

Brian slowly nodded. "Aye, I can see that. But ye now wonder if they actually did that?"

"Aye, for there has been no word from them. I ken

few of them could write, but there must be priests and monks in France, men who would write a letter that could be sent. And, aye, I ken it would take a long time to get here, but it has been almost two years. We havenae e'en had a dead or wounded mon returned here for burying or tending to. That isnae usual, is it?"

"Nay, it isnae," said Brett. "My men and I thought the same, but we havenae been able to find out much."

"I trailed them to the far edge of Gormfeurach land, but havenae been able to get any farther than that. Lost the trail and havenae been able to get back there and try to find it," said Harcourt.

"Why would they ride west?" asked Brian. "Ye need to ride east if ye are going to find a port and sail off to France."

Everyone stared at Brian, who just shrugged. Then Triona looked at Brett, who was scowling in thought. "He is right. Why would the trail go west, unless they followed an established road and planned to turn east later?"

"I think we need to have a talk with Sir John's men," said Brett as he stood up.

Triona hurried to follow him as he strode off, and noticed that Sir Brian and a few others came along, as well. "I cannae believe that Sir John's men would help him do harm to mine."

"That may be true, but that doesnae mean they dinnae ken anything at all."

When she saw the men in the dungeon, Triona tried not to feel bad for them. They might be reluctant to follow the orders of their laird, but they were still doing so. A few days in the dungeon was the least they deserved.

"M'lady," said one of the men she suddenly recognized as the Duncan whom Ian had mentioned. He stood up with the others and bowed to her.

"We have come to ask ye a few questions," said Brian. "I was wondering what ye might ken about the near thirty men who left here to go to France."

Duncan frowned. "Just that they left. Heard they decided to try to recoup some of the coin lost when the fever struck and because the harvests were bad."

"Ever hear of a mon called Birk?" asked Triona.

"Weel, he has been round at the keep once or twice but nay for many months now. The laird brought him back from some trip he had taken to a neighboring laird. We didnae have much to do with the mon." He glanced back at the other men, who shook their heads to indicate that they had had nothing to do with the man, either.

"Who was Birk?" asked Brett.

"The mon Joan says convinced my men to go to France to fight," she replied.

Triona nodded when everyone stared at her. She could see by the scowls forming on the faces of Brett and the others that the implications of Sir John knowing such a man were clear to them as well. It was hard to see how he could have arranged the disappearance of thirty strong men, but she was even more convinced that Sir John had done just that. She could only pray that he had not had them all killed.

"Ye think our laird took your men?" asked Duncan.

"They were convinced to go to France by a mon named Birk, and your laird had a mon named Birk visiting him at about the same time. Aye, I begin to think Sir John had a lot to do with the loss of all of my garrison."

"But why would he . . ." Duncan stuttered to a halt and then cursed softly. "Left ye undefended, didnae it."

"Exactly. I dinnae suppose ye ken where the mon Birk came from."

"Nay, m'lady. As I said, the laird went off as he often does, returned with the mon, and then, after one or two more visits, there has nay been any sight of him."

"Ye cannae think our laird killed your men, can ye?" said a tall, thin youth.

Triona looked at the young man and nearly winced. The youth was attempting to look insulted, even disbelieving, but he could not hide all his doubt. Sir John had lost the faith of his men. They did as they were told, doing their best to lessen the severity of the results of the laird's orders, but they no longer trusted him. Deny it though they wanted to, every single man in her dungeon now feared that their laird had had a hand in the disappearance of her garrison.

"Nay, I dinnae think he had them killed," she said, and prayed she was right to think so. "But I think he had a part in their disappearance."

"Ye mean in their sudden need to go to France," said Duncan.

"Nay, I begin to think they ne'er went there. There has been nary a word, Duncan. None of the wives, or betrotheds, or mothers, or children have heard a word. Nothing. There hasnae even been the return of the dead or wounded, and ye ken as weel as I do that any one of my men would wish to be buried here, nay in France."

"And the trail led to the far edge of Gormfeurach," said Brett. "I dinnae think a mon can reach a port and a ship to France that way." He nodded when Duncan paled.

"If he had a hand in the loss of your men, I cannae think what he has done with them, m'lady," Duncan said after a moment of heavy silence. "I truly cannae. I wish I could help."

She believed him and nodded. Brett and Brian asked the men a few more questions, but she paid little mind, all of her thoughts on where her men might be. Triona did her best to push aside the fear that they were all dead. She loathed Sir John, but even she found it difficult to believe he would kill all those men. If nothing else, they would be of use when he got what he wanted and sat his arrogant arse in the laird's chair at Banuilt.

By the time they all returned to the great hall and she had had food and drink sent down to the prisoners, Triona had gone from being afraid to angry to afraid and back to angry. She tried very hard to cling to the anger. If nothing else, she could not bear to think that Joan may have lost her beloved Aiden.

"We need to look harder for those men," said Brett as he sat down and poured himself a tankard of ale. "Mayhap they did go to France, but I begin to think something else has befallen them. The question is, where could a mon keep near thirty men?"

"It would have to be on some land he owned or kenned was abandoned, and it would have to be in a verra secure place. Ye cannae just chain up that many men, I would think," said Brian.

"Guards and supplies would be needed," said Callum. "That may be where to begin the search for answers."

"Aye, he has the right of it," agreed Brian. "E'en if ye were nay feeding them weel, ye would still need a lot of food and need it regularly. Somewhere there is a merchant who has gained himself a verra good customer. And anyone near where the men are being held would have to ken something about it all. Many wouldnae question whate'er some laird is doing, but they would see and they would remember."

"Then we need to go back to where Harcourt lost the trail," said Brett. "Ye cannae move that many men without someone seeing something."

"He wouldnae have killed them, would he?" Triona asked, needing some reassurance from men who knew more about such things than she did.

"It wouldnae have been wise," replied Brett. "Murder isnae something that can be hidden weel, and he wouldnae be able to have his friends save him if it was discovered. It would also have been verra difficult to keep such a thing a secret. He would need enough men to do the killing and the burying and then, if he truly wished to keep it secret, he would have needed to silence those men, too. Nay, killing so many men and hiding the fact would be too difficult. He has either sent them all to France to some fate there, or he has them somewhere in this country."

"And I would wager it isnae all that far away," said Brian. "He may nay have much to do with holding them, but he would need to send coin or supplies, and he would want to be able to bring them back as quickly as possible if he got ye to the altar."

"I hope we find them, for I cannae think that wherever they are, they are being treated verra weel," she said. "And I think we should nay say much about this to my people. I dinnae wish to get their hopes up, for we cannae be sure now exactly what has happened to the men."

"Agreed," said Brett, and the other men nodded. "We will find them, lass. Ye have some of the best hunters in the land sitting right here swilling your ale. If they are out there, we will find them."

"Thank ye for that," she said and then stood up, all the men hastily scrambling to their feet. "I really cannae thank ye enough for all ye have done already, and now there is this. I pray we find them, but I will always ken how ye helped and be grateful for it, nay matter what unfolds. And now I believe I will retire. It has been a verra long day."

Brett watched her leave as he sat back down. She had looked so sad, yet held herself straight and showed no sign of weakness. He knew how deeply she cared for all the people at Banuilt, and this had to be breaking her heart.

"Weel, I hope we do find them," said Brian. "I hate

to e'en think of so many men riding off thinking they were about to have an adventure, see new places, and get some coin, only to be cut down by some hired swine."

"If we find them alive, we will be dealing with men who have been imprisoned for almost two years. I am nay sure that is all that much better a fate," said Brett.

"Nay. E'en though I can see why they would think it a good idea to go to France, I dinnae like that they all rode away leaving this place mostly unguarded, but near two years in prison is more than they should have had to suffer for that idiocy," said Brian.

"If they are out there, we will find them," said Harcourt, and Callum nodded.

"I pray ye do. I will leave the hunt in your hands, then. If ye find anything, I wish to ken it, for ye will probably need many of us to free them," said Brett.

"I will start in the morning," said Harcourt, and left to seek out his bed.

"There is something else to consider," said Brian.

"And what would that be?" asked Brett.

"Any mon who would take away and imprison his own allies for near to two years probably isnae quite sane."

"I have begun to fear that myself, old friend."

Chapter Eight

The sky was so bright with stars that Triona was lost in the wonder of it. She leaned against the wall and sighed. She had come up on the walls of Banuilt to think, but the beauty of the night had quickly distracted her. Such sights had been a great comfort to her during her marriage. The wonder had already begun to fade, however, and her mind was slowly turning back to all the troubles she suffered from and just how she might be able to put an end to them. Troubles that not only did not end but seemed to multiply like rabbits.

The men they had captured yestereve were now loosely confined, no one concerned that they would escape or prove a danger to Banuilt. She had seen how troubled, even hurt, Sir John's men were by how quickly their laird had denied them. Sir John had callously tossed six of his men to the wolves, knowing that those men could be hanged for what they had done.

Unfortunately, that still left her without the hard proof of Sir John's guilt, which she had believed she

had gained, for one happy moment. No one would
heed accusations made by men guilty of stealing
sheep over Sir John's claims of innocence. The same
poor men now also had to consider the possibility that
their laird had done something to the entire garrison
of Banuilt, a garrison whose men many of them had
known for years. Some were even related. The people
of Gormfeurach and Banuilt were intertwined in so
many ways that something like this could never sit easy
with any of them.

At the very best, she had just gained a fortnight or
more of peace. Sir John was cunning enough to know
that if he continued his harassment of her too soon after
his men had been caught stealing, it would be enough
to add some weight to her accusations against him. She
now needed to decide how to make the best use of the
short time of peace this latest trouble would give her.

Her mind refused to settle to the task of planning
anything for Banuilt. The thoughts of what her garrison might be suffering preyed on her mind. She still
shied away from even thinking of the possibility that
they were dead, refusing to believe that even Sir John
could heartlessly slaughter so many. Yet, nearly two
long years of imprisonment would leave its scars on her
men as well. If they were being held somewhere, she
could not be certain they would be cared for properly.
Prisons of any sort were harsh places and full of disease.
The fact that all she could do was pray for their safe
return frustrated her. It also took all of her strength not
to give in to the urge to confront Sir John and demand
he tell her what he had done with her garrison.

In an attempt to stop thinking of her men, she tried to think of what to do to make sure the promise of a good harvest was not stolen away, but thoughts of Sir Brett Murray kept intruding, turning her mind to images of a pair of fine, dark green eyes and memories of a heated kiss. Scolding herself for behaving like some witless love-struck maid did not stop it, either. Triona prayed that no one at Banuilt noticed her distraction or guessed at the reason for it. She knew she looked at him a lot but hoped she had succeeded in hiding just how deep her interest in him went.

She was going to have to decide what to do about Sir Brett Murray of the fine green eyes. It was tempting to simply thank the man for his help and send him on his way. Arianna had her husband with her now, even if the couple were still at odds, so Sir Brett and his friends were no longer needed as her cousin's protectors. There was no good reason for telling the man to go, however, nor could she ever deliver such an insult to a man who had been nothing but helpful to her and her people. In truth, her people readily turned to Sir Brett for advice, treating him as a part of Banuilt. And there was no denying that she also really needed his and the other men's help in finding out the fate of her garrison.

It was all rapidly becoming more than she could bear. Triona stared up at the sky again and sighed. Sometimes just looking at the vastness of the night sky was enough to make her see her troubles as small in comparison, but it was not working this time. She could see no way to end the trouble with Sir John that did not include giving in to his demands, if only to aid her garrison. Yet every day that passed, she became more and more drawn to Sir Brett Murray. Memories of how it felt to be held in Sir Brett's arms, to kiss him, turned into dreams in the night that left her starving for more kisses. Ignoring that growing hunger was making it more and more difficult to think clearly about the trouble with the laird of Gormfeurach. The needs of the people of Banuilt had to take precedence over the needs of her body, but she was having a great deal of trouble abiding by that very honorable tenet.

"A fine, clear night, m'lady," said Sir Brett as he stepped up beside her.

Triona was startled by his sudden appearance but struggled not to reveal it. It was humiliating to think she had been so lost in her thoughts that she never heard his approach. A woman in her position could not afford to be so oblivious to what was happening around her.

"That it is," she replied, pleased to hear no hint of nervousness in her voice. "And nay so cold that ye cannae enjoy it for a wee bit."

Brett looked up at the sky. "And there is a sight certain to humble any mon."

"Aye. Did ye come out to see the stars then, or is the fighting between Arianna and her husband still raging?" Triona smiled, thinking of how her cousin and her husband still occasionally had a loud exchange, but the anger and hurt behind the words had definitely lessened.

He laughed. "It is still raging yet not as loudly. I

dinnae think she is as angry as she was before. Now I
believe she is just making him suffer for his crimes by
being less than loving, irritating him when she can,
and keeping him at a distance, which is driving the
poor fool half mad and thus the occasional descent
into a shouting match."

"I can understand her upset. There were things in
her past, heart-deep injuries that were all stirred up by
her finding out about Mavis, by thinking her husband
had lied to her. And, truly, how can a mon forget his
wife?" she asked, fighting the urge to laugh with him,
for she knew she would feel like a traitor to Arianna if
she did.

"I dinnae think it was that he truly forgot Mavis as
much as it was that he just didnae think it was important to speak of her." Brett grimaced when Triona gave
him a fleeting look of womanly disgust. "I dinnae believe he thought of her much at all once he returned
home to Scarglas. It was o'er five years ago and the marriage didnae last verra long. Aye, he wanted her
enough to run off with her e'en though she was chosen
to wed his brother, but that caused no trouble for him.
Her father was happy and his brother didnae want the
lass anyway. Brian didnae gain anything from the marriage either, so no land or coin to explain. He simply returned to Scarglas and fell right back into the life he
had always lived, save that this time he did so with plans
to get what he craved—his own lands, through his own
hard work. As he told me, that work filled his mind and
heart, and near all his time, for five years."

"I think I begin to understand. 'Twas such a short
time in his life that poor Mavis became little more

than just some lass he kenned in the past. She wasnae there long enough to leave her mark on him, poor lass. I suspicion there was no great heartbreak in it all for him, either."

"Nay, I think not. He cared for her, liked her, and lusted after her. Said so himself. He would have been a good husband to her and given her bairns, tended her lands, and all that."

"And his brother clearly didnae woo her verra weel."

"Weel, he wasnae there. He had been to see her and her father, agreed to the match, but was taken for ransoming on his journey back to Scarglas. 'Tis where Gregor met his Alanna. Mavis wondered what had happened when Gregor didnae return as promised, and she and her father came to Scarglas looking for him. That was when Mavis met Brian. When Gregor returned to find Mavis there, weel, it didnae go weel, for he had Alanna with him, and soon enough Mavis had run off with Brian."

"Ah, I see."

Brett leaned closer to look into her eyes. "What do ye see?"

"Mavis kenned that Gregor didnae truly want her, and so she chose her own mon. 'Tis a shame she had so little time to enjoy her choice."

Unable to resist the allure of her moonlit skin, he lightly stroked her cheek with the backs of his fingers. He knew he was going to do his best to seduce her into his bed. It had been too long since he had enjoyed the heat and hunger of a clean lust, one born not only of the body but of the heart and mind as well.

He liked and respected Triona, something that only heightened the need that gripped him more tightly with every passing day. The fact that Brenda's spirit did not trouble him each time he kissed Triona only made him more eager to have her.

Smiling faintly, he put his arm around her shoulders and pulled her close. Brett had the passing thought that she fit perfectly in his arms, her face coming to rest against his chest and her soft hair brushing against his throat. She was small enough to make him feel big and strong, yet not so small that he feared he could hurt her. She was also very stiff, he mused.

"What are ye doing?" she asked, and then decided that was a very foolish question.

"Holding ye," he replied, and could not keep all of his amusement out of his voice.

"Ye ken weel what I am asking, ye rogue."

Triona knew she should be pushing him away, should even display a righteous outrage over his forward behavior. Just because she had already allowed him two kisses did not mean he had the right to accost her whenever he felt like it. Instead, she slowly began to relax into his embrace, because she had to admit she rather liked being accosted by him. He was warm and he made her feel that warmth inside as well as outside of her body. She knew she was experiencing the desire so many women spoke of, the heat that she had never discovered in her marriage.

What few twinges of desire she had felt for Boyd had died on her wedding night. The fragile hope she had clung to that the act had been cold and passionless because Boyd had been as nervous as she was, that now that she was no longer a virgin it would get better, had also died a swift death. Triona knew that even if Brett was not a greatly skilled lover, he could show her more about true desire than Boyd had ever done. She also knew that if she were not the laird of Banuilt, not a woman who needed to hold tightly to the full respect of her people, she would be dragging the man straight to her bedchamber to find out if he could give her all the passion his kisses promised her.

"I am preparing to kiss you," he said, slipping his hand beneath her chin and tilting her face up to his.

"Are ye actually asking permission to do so this time?"

"Aye, I suppose I am."

"Oh, I am nay sure that is wise, nay if ye really wish to kiss me. Asking gives me time to think about it. Then I start to consider the possibility that someone might see us, that it could hurt my standing here if I am caught in a mon's arms, or e'en that every priest I have e'er listened to has spoken of such stolen moments as the first step on the path to sin."

He kissed her, smiling against her lips when she laughed. It pleased him to make her smile, as she had been sunk deep in sadness and worry since finding out that her men might really be in danger and not just traveling around France trying to make money to bring home to their kin. And then Brett stopped thinking of anything but the sweet taste of her.

Triona wrapped her arms around his neck and clung to him and he kissed with all the passion and need any woman could want. She was astonished at just how quickly a kiss could make her ache for so much more. Brett's kiss twisted her innards with an aching want and had her blood running hot. She had never experienced anything like it before. By the time he moved his mouth from hers and began to kiss her neck, she was panting as if she had run miles.

"Anyone who is out can probably see us up here," Triona whispered, but her concern was not strong enough to move her out of his arms.

"Aye, Mama, they can. I did. 'Tis how I found ye."

Brett caught hold of Triona when she jerked out of his arms so fiercely that she put herself in danger of tumbling off the walls. Lightly holding her arm, he turned with her to look at Ella. The little girl was dressed in a lace-trimmed nightdress and was smiling at them. Brett suspected the panting Triona was doing now had very little to do with passion and much more to do with a parent's fear at seeing her small child up on the high walls, alone.

"Ella Mary Margaret McKee!" Triona gasped and tugged free of Brett in order to reach out and grab her child.

"Uh-oh. Ye just said all my names. Am I in trouble?"

"Aye, ye most certainly are. What are ye doing up here? These walls are nay a safe place for a wee lass to be, and I think ye ken that weel. And yet here ye are with naught but your nightdress on, nay e'en wearing shoes. And where is Peggy?"

"Sleeping." Ella lowered her head a little and gazed up at her mother through her lashes. "I had a bad dream, Mama, and I needed ye."

Brett looked up at the stars, fighting a smile. The child was beguiling, and that look would be enough to soften the anger of any adult. He doubted it was going to work on Triona at the moment. The risk of a fall for such a small child, making her way up onto the walls, was far too great for a loving mother to allow big blue eyes, a sweet face, and a coaxing voice to stem the anger born of fear.

"Ye should have awakened Peggy then and had her come and find me. Ye never, never should have climbed up on these walls alone."

"But, Mama . . ."

"Nay. I said never, and I meant never."

A quick look revealed the child's full lips quivering and two big, fat tears slowly slipped down her cheeks. Brett noticed that although her body softened in its tense stance, Triona's stern expression never changed. Ella was a beautiful little girl and bright, but he suspected she was also one of those children who would always be in some sort of trouble.

"Am I going to be punished?" Ella asked in a small, shaking voice.

"Ye are. I will tell ye what that punishment will be on the morrow. For now we will get ye down off these walls and back to bed."

"But I didnae tell ye what my bad dream was."

Triona looked at her child and nearly shook her head. One had to be firm with Ella. She was a sharp-witted little girl, and her curiosity constantly got her into trouble. When Triona had seen her standing there on the walls, alone, her heart had leapt into her throat, and it was not really back where it belonged yet. For a moment she felt a horrible guilt over the fact that her child had walked into danger while she had been kissing Brett, but she quickly shook it off. The other times Ella had put herself in some danger, Triona had been doing nothing that could be called neglectful or selfish. The child had a knack for putting herself in some kind of trouble, even if one stood next to her holding her little hand.

"Ye can tell me what it was as I take ye down from these walls and back to Peggy."

"Let me carry her down, lass," Brett said as he stepped closer. "Ye have those skirts to watch out for."

For just one moment, Triona hesitated, finding herself reluctant to release her hold on Ella after seeing her in such danger, but then she nodded and handed Ella to Brett. The way the man settled Ella in his arms and told her to hold on to his neck made her certain he was no stranger to children. Ella revealed no fear of him, either, but clung tightly as he started to climb down the ladder that led to the bailey. Triona hurried to follow.

"Mama, I saw a ghostie," Ella said.

"In your room?" Triona asked. "A bad ghostie or a good ghostie?"

"A good ghostie, but I was still afraid. It was a lady and she smiled at me. I thought she was wanting to eat me up."

"Nay, ye didnae. Weel, unless she had some verra big teeth."

"They were nay that big, but I didnae like a ghostie

in my room when I was supposed to be sleeping. I think that was rude."

"So ye climbed out of bed and came looking for me, wandering all over the place in your nightdress with nothing on your feet and, when ye saw me, decided ye would just climb all the way up onto the high, high walls to tell me that ye had a rude ghostie smiling at ye. Have I got that right?" Triona asked as she hopped down the last step to the ground and faced Ella, who still sat comfortably in Brett's arms.

"Aye," Ella replied a little warily. "I thought ye would want to ken all about it."

"Ye could have called to me from down here. Ye could have woken up Peggy and had her bring ye to me. Ye could have asked any of the people I believe ye snuck around to bring ye here. Ye didnae have to come here all alone in the night."

"Aye, I could have. I am going to have to do a really big punishment, arenae I."

"I think it might be a verra big one." She reached out to take Ella from Brett's arms, ignoring the sharp amusement in his eyes. "I think ye ken it was a verra bad thing to do."

"Aye." Ella stared at the lace-trimmed front of her gown and idly toyed with the brooch pinned at her shoulder. "I willnae have to wash anything, will I? I dinnae like washing things."

"I will think on it. Now say good night to Sir Brett, who so kindly carried ye down."

"Good night, Sir Brett. I promise I willnae climb up the walls again when ye are busy kissing my mama."

Brett bit the inside of his mouth to keep from laughing when Triona blushed so brightly he could see it in the dim light in the bailey. As she hurried back into the manor he saw the little girl looking at him over her mother's shoulder, smiling at him in a way that told him she was a handful and probably always would be. Shaking his head, he turned around to find Brian standing behind him, his arms crossed over his chest.

"Kissing the lass who isnae your lass on the walls in the moonlight, were ye?" Brian asked, putting on a face so mournful it nearly made Brett laugh. "And seen by a poor, wee innocent lass, too. I am nay sure what to say about it."

"Nothing would be good," drawled Brett. "And that child may be wee, but I begin to think one should nay call her innocent, nay as ye mean it. She is and probably always will be a wee bit of a devil."

Brian laughed. "Aye. I saw her tiptoe by, but didnae catch her ere she started up the walls. Decided it was safest to just be quiet and be there to catch her if she fell."

"Aye, startling her would have been a mistake."

"Nay fear in the wee lass."

"Nay sure that is a thing a mother would like to hear."

"True, a brave heart and daring when they are so small is a worry, but it will serve her weel when she is grown."

"True. And I must assume that ye are out here walking about because your wife still hasnae welcomed ye back into her arms."

"Soon. I understand now that I scratched at some old wounds, and I can be patient. She needs to see that my being a bit of a heartless bastard concerning Mavis doesnae make me the same sort of heartless bastard she was wed to in France." He grinned when Brett laughed. "I will give her a few more days. I fell in love with a wounded lass, and I kenned it would be a while before all the wounds healed."

"Sad. I wish we had kenned what was happening. We would have been off to France on the next boat, and that bastard would have been dead and buried ere she e'en realized we had arrived." Brett nodded toward the manor. "This lass doesnae have such wounds, but I think her husband and all that has happened with Sir John has left her skittish."

"Nay doubt. Harcourt and Callum are off looking for the trail of her men. Now that they ken a few things about it, I am thinking we will soon ken what has happened to them."

"They are good at tracking people down."

"Best I have e'er seen, and coming from the kin I do, 'tis a verra high compliment I just gave them. Just dinnae tell Harcourt. Your brother doesnae need anything else to feed his arrogance."

"Callum often says the same."

"So what are ye going to do about the lass?"

Brett looked around the bailey, easily seeing all that was good about Banuilt. He felt comfortable here, welcomed and needed. It was a good feeling. Although he would never marry a woman for her land or coin, he could see himself settling in here with ease. Triona's people already came to him for advice on occasion, accepting him as one who could and would help them. He liked the land that surrounded the manor, liked the people, and liked the fact that it was a peaceful place. The longer he stayed, the more reluctant he was to leave.

The problem was that, if he decided he wished to stay with Triona, he was going to have to make sure she understood it was for her and not for Banuilt. Both her husband and Sir John were more concerned and more interested in Banuilt than her. Something like that could easily leave a woman doubtful of any man who expressed the desire to have her for his own. Since he himself had no lands and only a modest purse, he did not know how he would convince her that he was not after her properties. Brett knew she trusted him in most things, but also understood that old wounds could make her reluctant to trust in him when it came to the matter of marriage.

A simple solution to the problem would be if he had an equal fortune, in both land and coin. He did not see that coming his way anytime soon, however. There were ways he might gain such things, but they could take a very long time, and it would be unfair to just leave her to find such wealth when he could not even tell her when he might return. At the moment he had no real plans to ask her to marry him, but he also knew he needed to think on the possibility that he might want to do so.

Before he succeeded in seducing her, Brett knew he had to make a firm decision as to whether or not he truly wanted to stay with her. Triona was not a woman one seduced and then left. She was too tenderhearted and too innocent in so many ways. Despite how much he wanted her in his bed, he did not want to hurt Triona in any way, and he was certain that a woman like Triona would never be able to separate the needs of her heart from the needs of her body.

"I need to be certain that I wish to stay with her ere I take the next step," Brett said.

"Seducing her into your bed, ye mean."

"Aye, that. I think that she is a woman that one cannae really take as a lover, enjoy, and then walk away from."

"Ye think she will fall in love with ye if ye bed her, is that it, ye coxcomb?"

"Nay, Brian. I do think she is a woman who cannae keep desire separated from emotion, and I cannae allow myself to just ignore that. Triona is a woman who tries verra hard to hide all that passion I ken she has inside her, just as she tries to hide her soft heart because she wishes to be a strong, competent laird."

"That soft heart that tries to be understanding about her entire garrison deserting her and riding off to France?"

"Aye, that soft heart."

"Ah, so ye are afraid ye might break her heart."

"What I am afraid of is that *I* will fall in love with *her* once I have looked too closely into that soft heart and tasted that passion she tries to hide."

Chapter Nine

Triona straightened up from scrubbing the threshold stone of the cottage she was cleaning and rubbed her lower back. Now that they had so many extra men at Banuilt, she had decided it would be a good idea to clean and mend a few of the cottages. There were a few repairs that she and her women could not manage, but the places would certainly be livable again when they were done. The skilled warriors could remain within Banuilt while a few of the men in training could move into the cottages for a while, giving them all a little more room. At the moment her back and knees were complaining loudly about that plan.

A part of her prayed that she would soon have her own garrison needing to be housed. There had been no word from Sirs Harcourt and Callum yet, but she had finally allowed a small piece of hope to embed itself into her heart. Both Brett and Sir Brian were confident that if anyone could find something out about where her men had gone, those two men could. She badly wanted the garrison back, and not just for the protection of Banuilt; she had come to know all the men in the garrison very well during her years of marriage and hated to think they were suffering somewhere.

The heated embrace she had shared with Brett last night had almost made her change her mind as to who should move into the village. The depth of what he had made her feel frightened her a little. A woman's simple desire for a man was something she had felt she could deal with, perhaps even find some way to satisfy it, and her own curiosity about it, without everyone at Banuilt knowing what she had done. Brett made her feel so much more than that, however. He stirred far more than just her body's needs; he set hope in her heart and dreams of a future in her mind. That was dangerous.

That was when Triona had briefly considered moving him and his men to the village. It would have put a nice safe distance between them, but she finally had to admit that it would have been cowardly of her. It could also have been seen as an insult to men who had freely offered their aid to Banuilt. And it would have been useless, she thought, as it was but a short walk from the manor to the village, and she and Brett would be coming face-to-face every day as he worked to help her, trained her men, and dined with her. He would still be a strong temptation to her. In fact, she thought with an inner grimace over her own weakness for the man, she would probably have to send him to France to have any hope of easing the temptation he presented.

Joan stepped out of the cooper's cottage with a bucket of water that was blackened from the cleaning of the hearth, and moved to toss it on the ground a short distance away. "I am nay sure why we are bothering to clean these places," she said as she looked at the threshold stone Triona had just cleaned. "'Tis men ye are meaning to put in here, and they willnae notice all the work we have done. Struth, they will be quick to dirty it all up again and then look about for us to come and clean it again."

Laughing as she stood up and brushed off her skirts, Triona nodded. "Verra true. 'Tis needed, though. The manor is too full of men. E'en the peel tower that houses the garrison is getting crowded. Our untrained but eager garrison plus twelve more? Far too many. And I think it was needed anyway. We have left the cottages empty and uncared for, for far too long."

"Aye, ye are right about that." Joan glanced at the other cottages already cleaned or being cleaned by the other women. "It was looking sad here. I grew weary of looking at them some days. 'Tis as if each empty cottage was whispering that we have lost the fight and it would break my heart each time."

"I got that feeling myself from time to time. It all began to carry that air of defeat. I dinnae think I could have abided it for verra much longer anyway."

"And now that there will be some men in the village at night, I suspicion some of the women will go back to their own homes. Alone as we were, we felt much safer crowded together. Aye, there were still a few men about, but e'en they kenned they were little protection—being mostly old, infirm, or nay more than beardless lads. At least the ones returning here will ken which end of the sword ye should stick in a mon."

Triona had to bite the inside of her cheek to keep from telling Joan all she feared about their real garrison. Joan was so worried about Aiden, and yet she never complained. Until Triona had some word of what had happened to the men, however, telling Joan her fears would only worry her even more. Waiting, unable to do anything and not knowing the fate of the men, was a hell she did not wish to inflict upon her friend.

"And they will continue to be trained," Triona assured her. "Every day. I am nay certain how long my cousin, her husband, and his men will stay, but Sir Brett and his men have all vowed to stay until the troubles we suffer are ended."

"Aye, so I heard from Angus. That Sir Brett is a verra fine-looking mon, and I be thinking he likes the look of ye, m'lady." Joan laughed when Triona blushed.

"He certainly is a verra fine-looking mon," Triona agreed, "as they all are. And mayhap he does gaze at me warmly, but he isnae staying here. He and his men will help us because they see a need and are honorable men who see the injustice in what we are suffering. They will do as they have promised, but then they will leave, as they all have homes and kin to return to. And I will admit to ye that I feel most warmly toward him, but ye dinnae need to fear that I will act upon that."

"And why should it trouble me if ye did?"

"Weel, I am the laird, and I should behave respect-fully, with all honor and virtue."

Joan rolled her eyes. "Ye sound just like your hus-band, God rest his soul, when ye talk like that. So righteous the mon was. Aye, he was old enough to be my father, but I did ken him far longer than ye did. So did my mother and father, God rest their souls. Sir Boyd always talked of honor and virtue and all of that, but wed his first wife for coin and this land, and then wed ye for the coin needed to pay for things for this land and, mostly, that manor. And he didnae do much more than train the warriors, try to breed a son, and act virtuous and honorable."

"Ye didnae like him at all, did ye?"

"He was my laird and I respected that. E'en my parents did little more than that. We didnae dislike the mon, but he ne'er really gave anyone a reason to like him. My mother once said that she had ne'er met a more passionless or humorless mon in her life, that the mon was nay much like the ones who had come before him. Ye are the one who gave us a good life here, returned this place to what it was—and more—before Sir Boyd's first wife's grandfather died. I was pleased that my mother lived long enough to see the promise of ye, for she had oft bemoaned how neither the father nor the daughter's husband had a true love of Banuilt. They just liked to sit in the laird's chair and wave their swords about."

Triona grimaced. "I fear I had that thought myself now and then, and then would feel so disloyal and ungrateful. Yet, I could ne'er fully shake the feeling. He didnae e'en like to talk about what needed to be done about plantings, or harvestings, or livestock. He always told me to speak to the steward or one of you, for ye would all ken what to do."

"And so we do, but we need the laird to be certain we have what is needed to do it. Until ye came, all we had was that steward, and he was useless. But 'tis nay the laird's failings we need to speak of, and one ne'er wishes to speak ill of the dead if one can avoid it. Nay, we need to speak of how ye have a verra fine mon smiling at ye and ye are nay smiling back like any lass with blood in her veins would do."

For a moment Triona could only stare at Joan in shock. They had become friends within a fortnight of her arrival at Banuilt as Boyd's new wife. Boyd had frowned upon her being so friendly with a mere weaver, but for once Triona had ignored him and his wishes. Only a few years older, Joan had become her confidante and her adviser. That the woman would now advise her to give in to her passion for a man who was not her lawful husband and would soon walk away from Banuilt, shocked her a little. She was pleased to hear, however, that Joan did not think she was smiling back at Sir Brett, so she had clearly kept her growing desire for the man hidden from most eyes.

"He is trying to seduce me, Joan, nay woo me. He looks for a lover, nay a wife. I am certain of that."

"Mayhap that is what he looks for now, but that could change in time." Joan shrugged. "And if it doesnae, then ye go on alone, just as ye did after Sir

Boyd died, but this time ye will do so with a few verra sweet memories to ponder now and again."

"Nessa said the same. She told me to work on that."

"Good advice."

Triona was about to express her concerns about losing the respect of her people when the hairs on the back of her neck stood up. Looking around to find out what had alarmed her so abruptly, she saw only the women working and the children playing. She frowned, for despite the peaceful scene she watched, the wariness that had gripped her so tightly did not fade away. A part of her thought to just shrug it aside, but she had always had a sense of danger and she had begun to learn how to trust in it. Looking down the road that ran through the village, she finally found the reason for her sudden unease. There were men rapidly approaching, slipping from shadow to shadow but close enough that even the shadows could no longer hide them completely from sight.

"Joan, ye and the women grab the children and run for the manor," she said, never taking her eyes off the men still sneaking up on them, although she did her best not to be too obvious about it.

"What is happening?"

"Some men are trying to creep up on us. I cannae see how many there are, but they are nay ours. Of that much I am certain."

"Then we had best run."

"Nay, I will stand firm. Ye run and gather all the others to run with ye. Do your best to hide your fear until ye can play that game no longer, and then run as fast as ye can the short distance to the manor and tell the men what has happened."

"Aye, and I mean it when I say 'tis best *we* get started then."

"Nay. Ye get started. I will stay here to hold their attention, just as we always planned. It is the only way to give all the rest of ye a chance to get to the manor and let the men ken what has happened. We both ken that Grant is after me, so if these are his men, they will be here to try to catch me."

"Ye cannae fight them all off by yourself."

"I dinnae plan to even try. I but need to delay them so that the rest of ye can get out of here and sound the alarum. The children need to be gotten away, Joan. Go. Now!"

Despite how pale she had become, Joan walked away from Triona in a calm, steady manner. A quick glance was all Triona needed to tell her that Joan was warning everyone she passed as she walked away. All the women began to move, subtly pulling the children from their games and herding them in front of them. It was something they had practiced from time to time, always expecting Sir John to actually, and finally, openly attack Banuilt. Triona was pleased to see how well everyone had learned the trick. It was almost enough to make her feel like a true warrior who did what needed doing to protect her people.

Knowing that the women and children would start running soon, alerting the men that they had been seen, Triona kept one eye on the men and looked around for something she could use as a weapon. All that was at hand were a broom and a bucket. The bucket was solid and heavy, with a rope handle, so it would be easy to swing. If it struck a man it could hurt him badly enough to make him back off. The broom would, however, allow her to keep the man from getting too close. Because she realized she had very little chance of getting away from the men, she chose the bucket. At least she would leave them with some serious bruises when they took her.

She knew exactly when the women began to run, for one of the men cursed loud enough for her to hear. The men then rushed toward her as she stood her ground. Triona knew she was but a small, easily defeated obstacle, but she only had to make them pause long enough for the women and children to get to safety. As the first man came within reach, she swung the bucket and caught him on the shoulder, tumbling him to the ground, cursing and clutching at his arm. Maybe not such a small obstacle after all, she mused, and swung the bucket at the next man.

Brett was just walking out of the manor when a cry went up from the men on the walls. Instead of the gates being immediately shut, however, several men raced to them, standing and looking toward the village. He moved quickly to join them, thinking to order them to get the gates closed, and then he saw what they were watching. Women and children, some running on their own and some being carried by the women, were making their way to the manor as swiftly as they could. He realized the men were waiting to defend them if needed and shut the gates right behind them.

It was not until the women and children were nearly all inside that he understood what had happened. He could not see Triona. Brett began to push his way through the women, looking carefully for some sign of her. His hope—that she was just hidden in the crowd—was soon dashed. He could not find her anywhere.

Joan pushed her way through the crowd, a wide-eyed bairn in her arms, and after taking a moment to catch her breath, said, "M'lady stayed to hold them back so that we could all get here safely."

"She thought to hold back the men attacking ye?" he asked, caught between astonishment and fear for Triona.

"Aye. 'Tis how we have practiced it for months now. She kens that Grant wants her and feared that if he actually attacked Banuilt, he would hurt us to get to her. So we practiced escaping while she drew all attention to her. I ne'er liked it and tried to get her to come with me, but she wouldnae." Joan kissed the top of the bairn's head. "I couldnae wait any longer and risk a child being left there."

Brett saw Uven and Tamhas and waved them over to him. "Some men, probably Sir John's, are in the village and Lady Triona is still there."

He did not even wait to see if they would join him but started to run toward the village. The sound of booted feet on the ground told him he was not alone, though he was not sure how many men were following him. With every step he took, he feared he would find her gone, and was not surprised to find no one in the village. It had been Grant, of that he had no doubt, but the attack had come much sooner than they had anticipated. Triona had believed the man would be cautious for a while after having his men caught stealing, but it had been only three days.

Brian arrived with horses as Brett searched the ground. He found where a struggle had taken place. There was a bucket with blood on it and some blood on the ground. He told himself that it was a man's, that Triona had attempted to defend herself, but fear was a hard knot in his belly.

"So he finally just took the lass, aye?" said Brian.

"It appears so." He watched Brian look over the ground and study the bucket for a moment. "I think that is from her attempt to hold them back."

"So do I. The bucket is probably the one she used to clean the threshold stone. I would wager a few of those men are now wearing some bruises. But such a small lass couldnae hold them back for long, nay even long enough for us to get here. And we got here verra quickly."

Brett was so startled that Brian would notice something like the fact that someone had been cleaning the threshold stone, he just stared at the man for a moment and then shook his head clear of the distraction. "So they cannae be far away."

"I wouldnae think so, nay. So we go and fetch her back, do we?"

"Aye. Let us hope he is fool enough to think we will be slow to do so. This time we may just catch him doing something e'en his friends cannae excuse. She is, after all, considered the laird here, and one doesnae just grab a laird whenever one wishes to."

"Unless that laird is an unwed lass and every mon hereabout believes she needs a mon to rule this place as it should be ruled."

That was an ugly truth Brett did not want to think about at the moment, even though he was sure that the men of Banuilt did not think like that. He swung up into the saddle of the horse Brian had brought him and, with his gaze fixed upon the ground, began to follow the trail left by the men who had taken Triona. Just outside the village he saw that they had had horses waiting, and he cursed. They could follow that trail as well, but not move as swiftly as the men with Triona could while they did so, as they would be tracking them and would have to stop at times to check for signs. Even the arrival of Callum and Harcourt did not lift his spirits much.

"The mon has to be a bit mad," said Brian as they cautiously rode along, keeping an eye on the trail left by Triona's kidnappers.

"I suspect he has ne'er been verra sane as concerns Banuilt and the land he feels was stolen from his clan," Brett said. "Mayhap trying to defeat a wee lass for nearly two years has finally pushed him deeper into that dark place."

"If some of his kin were traitors to the king, as I heard they were, then the loss of a wee strip of land was merciful punishment. Most people would do their best to hide that dark part of their kin's past, nay push to get back the penalty the fools had to pay and stir up everyone's memories all over again."

"Who kens how such a mon thinks? There doesnae need to be sound reasoning behind this, just his greed and sense of injustice done him and his family."

"True. I also wondered if he was so ashamed of the cause of the loss of the land, the tale that there were traitors dangling from the family tree, that he sees getting the land back as a way to clean away that stain. A fool's idea, but, then again, how can one e'er understand why a mon would do this."

"'Tis surely a mad fool who treats such good allies this way."

"Callum says this is really all Triona's now. That cannae be disputed, e'en if too many men dinnae like a lass holding land. It is all in the way the deeds and such are written. He thinks it was done so because there was a sad lack of sons born to the McKees, and they didnae want the land passing out of their hands simply because all they had were daughters."

"Yet the name lingers."

"Made the men marrying one of their lasses take the name. Sir Boyd did so. Nay every family can produce sons like a MacFingal," he drawled.

Brian grinned. "Weel, we have to be good at something in life, aye?"

Brett grinned and shook his head, but the brief respite from his fear for Triona was already fading. Sir John Grant wanted her and was obviously tired of waiting for her to come to him. He did not want to think about what might be happening to her in the man's hands, but his mind was all too ready to show him.

"She will be weel and we will get her back," said Brian.

"She had better be."

"Have a fondness for the lass, do ye?"

"I like her and respect her. She cares for this land and her people. She doesnae deserve this." He grimaced when Brian just grunted. "I am nay looking for a wife, so ye can just dim that glint in your eyes."

"Ye are five and thirty. Do ye mean to die unwed and childless?"

"My clan willnae suffer if I dinnae have children. I had my chance once and it ended badly. I willnae do it again. I dinnae need another ghost to haunt me," he muttered.

"We have all lost ones we loved, although I have been fortunate to nay lose many. Death comes when it chooses to and cares nay what we want."

"Brenda, the lass I wanted to wed, found hers whilst coming to meet me. I will always carry the guilt for that."

"Why? Did ye force her? Didnae she ken more about why it may nay be a good idea to slip out to meet ye and just how far someone in her family might go to stop her?"

"Nay, I didnae force her to meet me, just tempted her, and it wasnae her family who killed her but her family's enemies. Some of them caught her out alone and beat her to death. She managed to live long enough to crawl to our meeting place, but then she died in my arms. She and my child that she was carrying."

Brian sighed. "A sad ending, but I see nay reason for ye to be feeling guilty."

"She was coming to meet me."

"As hundreds of lassies have done for hundreds of years, and I suspicion some have died in the doing of it. She could have said nay, refused to slip around and lie to her kin in the doing of it. She could have even stood up and demanded she be able to choose her own mon instead of wedding the one her family chose for her. She also kenned more about the land, what was happening on it, and what dangers were there, than ye, I suspect. Nay, I still cannae see why ye continue to feel guilty about what happened. Sad, aye. Your fault? Nay, I dinnae see it."

Brett wanted to ask why then did Brenda's ghost still appear to him? He was afraid that Brian would begin to question his sanity, however. He often did himself. The fact that Brenda's spirit appeared when he was abed with a woman, satisfying a man's lusts, would probably make the man laugh, but Brett was all too aware of how chilling it was to a man's passion. It was why he had been almost completely celibate for so long, the occasional attempt enough to reveal that the haunting had not stopped.

Seeing years of celibacy stretching out before him, Brett decided it might be time to talk to one of his kin. There were a few who claimed to be able to see the spirits of the dead. They might also be able to make those spirits go away. It was not just his ability to bed a woman that was suffering, but each time he saw the ghost, all his guilt returned in force. He might not agree with Brian's opinion that he shared no guilt in what had happened to Brenda, but he did think seven years of suffering for it should be enough.

He looked toward Harcourt and Callum, who were following the trail left by the ones who had taken Triona. They had to be tired, as they had only just returned from yet another hunt, but they did not hesitate to help. Instead of resting after a long search for the garrison of Banuilt, they were here trying to find Triona. They had all gotten pulled into the need to solve her troubles, but it did not really surprise him: Banuilt was a place of mostly women and children, youths and old men, and it stirred a man to want to help. The fact that the troubles they suffered were inflicted by a man who was supposed to be their ally only added to that need.

"Someone needs to kill that mon," muttered Brian.

"Aye, but sad and annoying as it is, one has to consider the trouble that would come of a nice, quick end to all this. The mon does have a lot of powerful friends."

"So do the Murrays."

"Verra true, and I have thought that, if this isnae ended soon, I would reach out to a few of them. All that allows this conflict to continue is that the ones Triona can turn to willnae accept the word of a woman o'er that of a mon they have claimed as a friend and ally. If naught else, that would so annoy the

women in my clan they would push the men to get
this ended."

Brian laughed. "Aye, they would indeed. And it
could be a good step to take if this cannae be stopped
soon."

"I had begun to think that *soon* would be after
another theft or another field burned. Now, weel, we
will see how Triona fares after this to determine
whether I need to make use of all those powerful
connections my family has made o'er the years."

Chapter Ten

The arrogance of the man so stunned Triona that she could only gape at him, the words she wanted to say stuck in her throat. She then feared he was mad, that he had caught the fever that had so devastated their lands and had been left with some disorder of the mind. He had to know he could not get away with kidnapping her, that he was giving her the proof she needed to gain justice for Banuilt and put an end to his destructive games.

Or had he? she wondered, glancing around at the men who had dragged her to Sir John and dumped her on the ground at his feet. She did not recognize any of them as Gormfeurach men, although she could not really claim to know every one of those men by sight. Instinct, however, told her that these were not Sir John Grant's clansmen. That meant that he had gotten himself some hirelings who would fade away once paid and dismissed.

"If ye think ye and your hired swords"—she noticed the fleeting look of surprise on Sir John's face and knew she had guessed right—"can steal me from my land, force me afore a priest, and nay suffer some consequence for this madness, then ye have truly lost your wits, Sir John."

Triona fought the urge to scramble backward when he glared at her and clenched his fists. She refused to cower before this man. It would only give him even more power over her. Her father had taught her how to deal with a man who tried to beat obedience into a child, and Boyd had taught her how to deal with a man who used aloof condescension to keep a woman under his boot. She had managed to do just as she pleased most of the time while under the rule of those men. What she wanted to do now was to get as far away from Sir John Grant as possible. All she needed was a small chance, a short moment of distraction on his part.

"Ye will wed me, lass," he snapped. "'Tis the easiest, surest, and quickest way to get back the land your late husband's first wife's family stole from mine."

"They didnae steal anything. The land was given to them by the king himself, a reward for saving him from some foolish plot your ancestors had devised. And they also saved most of your kin from dying for that foolishness. Wheesht, ye probably wouldnae be here if it were nay for the McKees."

"All lies! Lies told by the McKees to get their greedy hands on the best part of Grant land! They used false accusations to fatten their own purses."

"So it wasnae your kinsmon found standing o'er the king's bed, sword in hand, and all ready to plunge it into the king's heart?"

"'Twas nay but a madmon acting alone. The whole clan shouldnae have been made to suffer for what he tried to do."

"Nay e'en the ones caught thieving from the king whilst that kinsmon went in to kill him? Or the one caught still working on the speech that would declare the king's murderer the new king? Or the ones who slipped into the queen's bedchamber, thinking to dishonor her and all the lasses serving her? Or . . ."

"Be quiet!"

Triona was not surprised when Sir John's bellowed command echoed through the wood. The way his men glared at him or grimaced and shook their heads in disgust told her they shared her thought: Sir John had just sent out a clarion call to anyone out there looking for her. She prayed someone had been close enough to hear it.

"It will nay be easy to drag me before a priest, Sir John," she said. "'Tis best if ye give this up right now. I said nay when ye first told me to marry ye, and I still say nay."

"I dinnae have to drag ye anywhere. I brought a priest with me."

She watched as he signaled to one of his men, who quickly ducked into a small tent and came back pulling along a tall, thin man with gray hair, a priest she recognized because he occasionally came to Banuilt when they desperately needed one. "Father Mollison!" She glared at Sir John. "Ye are forcing a poor village priest to commit this crime? Our own liege laird's cousin?"

"I commit no crime," said Sir John. "I but take a reluctant bride. It has been done before. E'en our liege laird thinks it wrong that ye, a lone woman, play at being a laird as if ye ken what needs doing. That will end today. Once wed and bedded, there will be no changing it, nay matter how loudly ye protest. I will become the laird of both Banuilt and Gormfeurach. Most men will congratulate me for doing what is both right and wise."

There was too much truth in that statement to argue with it. The moment the vows were exchanged and a blessing given, even that could be enough to leave her bound to Sir John for the rest of her life. Bedding her would only affirm her fate. She would also find few if any allies when she tried to have the marriage ended simply because she had said no.

Her only hope was to delay the marriage for as long as possible. There had to be someone hunting for her, and she needed to still be unwed when they arrived. Fighting and perhaps killing a kidnapper could be explained and excused, especially with so many witnesses to the event. Killing a new husband could rouse a lot more questions and doubts, especially as that would leave Gormfeurach needing a new laird, as Sir John had no heirs. One look at the pale, trembling Father Mollison told her that she was on her own. The priest did not have the courage to protest this travesty. Triona braced herself for a good long fight and prayed that a rescue was on its way.

* * *

Brett waited tensely as Harcourt searched the ground for the trail they needed to follow, while Callum disappeared into the trees. It slowed them down each time they had to hesitate like this, but he knew it was necessary. There was nothing to gain in racing about the countryside bellowing Triona's name as a nearly uncontrollable part of him wanted to. He had had to wrestle hard with himself to keep his hunting skills keen, trying to keep diverted by talking to Brian or thinking of ways to end the troubles with Sir John.

The thought of how humiliated he would be if he gave in to the blind panic gnawing at his insides helped as well. He took a nearly sinful pride in his ability to remain calm in battle, in his hunting and fighting skills, and he refused to lose them now, even if he had good reason. Brett also knew he had to find the time to think on how fierce his fear and concern were for Triona, and why.

"Found them," said Callum as he rode up beside Brett.

"Then why have I spent all this time looking for a trail when ye obviously could just wander up to them?" asked Harcourt as he joined them.

"Wasnae sure if the birds were acting strangely because of a predator or because of men. Needed to look first. It was men." Callum looked at Brett. "The lady is hale, so hale she is shredding Sir John with a sharp tongue, but he is about to try to force her to say vows afore a terrified priest. That poor mon will do naught to stop the marriage."

"I cannae believe his men would stand beside him in this," said Brett. "Everything we have seen and learned has revealed that Sir John's people dinnae like what he has been asking of them."

"I dinnae think these are his people, nay all of them. I think the mon has gone and hired himself a few swords, paying strangers to do this dirty work for him."

"And dragged a terrified priest along as weel. Let us go and end this before he finds a way to force Triona to say those vows." Brett frowned when a cry echoed through the wood. "What was that?"

"A bellow of rage, I believe. The lass is doing a verra good job of making Sir John verra, verra angry."

"Then we best get there before she drives him to the point of hurting her."

It was slow work slipping through the trees, trying to stay in the shadows and move as silently as possible. Their horses were well trained for such work, as they themselves were, but it took only one snapped twig to alert someone with keen ears. Or a guard watching for them, Brett thought as he heard someone crashing through the woods. A moment later there was a bellow of warning. Brett looked at Callum.

Callum shrugged. "Missed him," he said and then, unsheathing his sword, he let go a battle cry that sent every bird in the woods flying up in panic.

Brett cursed as Callum charged toward the sounds of men attempting to run for their lives. He unsheathed his own sword, kicked his horse into a gallop, and followed his cousin. The other eight men with them did the same. A stealthy approach might have been a better strategy, but Brett had to admit that this way appeased some of the fear and anger knotting his insides.

Sir John and what was left of his band of men came into view just as Triona punched Sir John in the face, forcing him to release her. The man had been dragging her to his horse, she fighting and cursing him every step of the way. Brett felt his anger flare hot again over the way the man was so roughly handling her. Sir John was mounted and fleeing before Brett got close enough to make him pay for mistreating her, however. He paused in the chase only long enough to look Triona over and assure himself that she was unharmed.

Triona stood up and brushed herself off. She looked up as Sir Brian walked up to her. The man was grinning, and she had to admit that he was a handsome man with a smile that undoubtedly had led to Arianna's falling in love with him. She was not sure what he was grinning at, though.

"A weel-delivered punch, m'lady," he said and then turned to the priest. "They didnae hurt ye, did they?"

"Nay, sir," said the priest. "I was but roughly dragged along to this place to perform a wedding between Sir John Grant and Lady Triona McKee."

"A *forced* wedding," Triona said. "Ye should have been protesting that as heartily as I was. Ye should have been doing something, anything, to help me."

"I was in fear for my life and wasnae about to lose it

just because some lass doesnae wish to be wed to a mon, a laird no less, and one with his own lands."

Triona had not realized that she had curled her hand into a fist, until Sir Brian leaned closer and said, "I am nay sure ye should show the priest how weel ye deliver a punch. It might be a sin, ye ken, and one with a high penance cost. Although I wouldnae mind watching ye do so." He winked at her when she looked at him.

She laughed and shook her head. It was evident that in the time she had been the laird of Banuilt, she had lost all tolerance of men who thought they knew what was best for a woman. Being laird and not doing too badly at the job, all without a man's assistance, gave one a great deal of confidence. Ignoring the priest, she waited for the other men to return. It disappointed but did not surprise her when they came back without Sir John. Triona did not know how the man was doing it, especially since she was confident in the skills of Sir Brett and the others, but he was proving to be very good at disappearing and staying out of reach.

Without a word, Sir Brett held out his hand, and she let him pull her up into the saddle behind him. Triona wrapped her arms around his waist and rested her cheek against his broad back. Slowly all her anger and fear melted away. It seemed weak to find such comfort in a man, but she did, and it was too good a feeling to push aside just because she feared it, perhaps even resented it just a little.

In fact, she mused, there were a great many good feelings Sir Brett Murray caused her to experience, which she was weary of running from or trying to ignore. She had just been faced with a forced marriage to Sir John Grant, a man who left her cold—if she ignored the anger he stirred in her heart. She knew he would have consummated that marriage as quickly as possible to make it even more difficult to protest it. The very thought of that man taking her to his bed made her shudder with revulsion. She also knew that until he was caught, she could face that threat again, and yet she had turned aside the passion Sir Brett stirred inside her, again and again. Triona decided it might be time to reconsider protecting her virtue from a man she wanted. It did seem rather foolish, when there was another man she hated, trying so hard to steal it away.

"Now we may seek justice for ye," said Brett.

Triona sighed. It was not time to seek justice, for Sir John had been trying to make her do what nearly every man of power in the area, including their liege laird, had advised her to do—get a husband. Brett was not going to understand her reluctance to bring any attention to herself for her continued refusal of Sir John, not without hard proof of crimes other than his attempt to marry her. She knew she was about to enter into an argument that could last a very long time.

* * *

"Nay, we cannae. 'Tis still Sir John's word against mine."

"And the word of every mon who went to get ye back from Sir John, a mon forcing ye to marry him."

"What Sir John did was nay more than what every mon of any power and influence in this area believes ought to be done."

"He kidnapped ye."

Triona turned to face Brett, ready to continue the argument they had started on the way back from where Sir John had taken her and continued over the evening meal. He wanted her to send word to her liege laird, and she would not do it. It would be the surest way to starkly remind her liege laird that she had yet to take his advice to find a husband, but Brett was not heeding her fears about the trouble that could bring down on her head. Then she suddenly realized that they were in her bedchamber, that Brett had followed her right into her room. She opened her mouth to tell him to leave, only to watch him shut the door, lean against it, and cross his arms over his chest.

The argument she had been so determined to continue fled her mind, and all she could think of was that she had just come far too close to having to accept into her body another man who would give her no more than soreness and seed. Yet now, right in her bedchamber, was a man whose kisses promised her a great deal more. She had spent six long years with a man who had used her as no more than a breeder, and almost two years working her fingers to the bone to keep her people fed and safe. Now she fought to stay out of the grip of a man who wished to force her into marriage so that he could claim her lands. Ella had been the only true bright spot in her life. Maybe it was past time she did something just to please herself.

Brett tensed and studied Triona. There was a glint in her eyes that he was certain was caused by a growing desire. He knew men could have their lusts stirred by a battle or a heated argument, but he had not considered the possibility that women could as well. He was not sure he ought to trust in his own judgment on the matter.

"Are we done arguing?" he asked as he watched her eyes change to a deep, rich blue, a color he had seen each time he kissed her.

"Aye, I believe we are. I think I would like to do something else right now."

"What?"

"I would like ye to kiss me."

He had her in his arms so quickly she gasped. For one brief moment she wondered if she was about to make a very big mistake. Then he kissed her and she no longer cared. She wanted this, needed it. For once in her life she was going to be bold and daring, was going to reach out and take what she wanted without a thought to the consequences.

There was something different in her kiss, Brett realized, a fierce lack of hesitation that had his heart pounding. "Triona, I believe we are past the stealing of a few kisses and naught else."

"Och, aye, I do hope so," she murmured, and kissed him.

Brett decided to see that as acceptance. He lifted her up in his arms just enough to get her feet off the floor, and started toward the bed, still kissing her. The sound of her shoes hitting the floor explained the odd little wriggle she made in his arms. It was, in his mind, yet another invitation.

He gently laid her down on the bed. Watching carefully for any hint that she was about to change her mind, he shed his clothes. The way her eyes widened as he did so was rather flattering, especially when he saw no sign of unease. Climbing onto the bed beside her, he kissed her again and began to unlace her gown. He tightly grasped hold of all his control so that he could go slowly, for even though Triona was no virgin, he was certain she had not gained any true experience or confidence in the art of lovemaking from her husband.

Triona closed her eyes and fell into his kiss, letting every stroke of his tongue in her mouth and faint nip of his teeth on her lips stir up the fire in her veins. The image of Brett naked was now seared into her mind. He was lean and taut with muscle. A small patch of black curls was centered on his broad chest, his long legs were well shaped and muscular, and he had only a few scars. He was all that was beautiful in a man. It both inflamed and intimidated her.

The touch of his hand against her skin made her tremble with pleasure until she realized she was naked. She had never been naked with a man before, as her husband had left her night shift on her, simply pushing it out of the way. Then she suddenly thought of her birthing scars, but an attempt to cover them with her hands was swiftly thwarted by Brett when he grabbed her hands and lightly pinned them to the bed. Then he kissed each mark bracketing her womb. She stared at him, both shocked and moved, as he lifted his head and smiled at her.

"Ye shouldnae think ye need to hide these marks," he said, releasing one of her hands to trace each mark with the tip of his finger. "They are the scars of a woman giving life to a child, scars as hard-won and honorable as any a noble warrior wears."

There was such sincerity in his voice that she could think of nothing to say. She murmured her pleasure when he kissed her again, a pleasure born of the way he ravished her mouth, the way the heat of his skin touching hers fired her blood, and the way his calloused hands sweetly caressed her body. It was not until he slid one of those beautifully skilled hands between her thighs that any hesitation occurred in her rapidly soaring passion.

He was touching her *there*, she thought wildly. Her husband had never caressed her there, barely touched her there at all, even when he was preparing to join their bodies. Since Brett was not indulging in any fumbling attempt to join with her like Boyd had, she had to assume that he liked touching her there. The way her body was reacting to his stroking fingers alarmed her even as it pleased her so much that she could not make herself pull away from the shocking intimacy of his caress. Before she could make any sense out of her emotions and confused thoughts, Brett turned his attention to her breasts, fondling and kissing them, even suckling her, and every thought in her head was burned away by the fire raging in her blood.

When he finally began to ease inside of her, her head cleared of desire's fog just enough to remind her what she was supposed to do. She went still, as still as she possibly could, despite the aching need to touch him, to rub her body against his and to kiss him. When he also stopped, thrusting no deeper within her, she frowned and fought the fierce need to grab him by the hips and make him move.

"Do ye ken, if your eyes were nay squeezed so tightly shut, nor your hands clenched so tightly at your sides, and your body nay weeping in welcome, I would think that ye had just swooned," he said.

"My body is weeping?" Triona gasped when she realized she was wet down there. "Och, nay. Ye . . . I . . ."

He kissed her. "That is how it should be, love. Och, poor wee Triona, your husband was a cold bastard, wasnae he."

She knew she ought to defend Boyd, but she could not. Then Brett grabbed hold of her legs, spread them wide, and eased inside of her. Triona heard herself begin to pant, the heat and fullness of his possession robbing her of breath.

"Put your legs around me, love," he said. "Aye, wrap your whole sweet self round me if ye wish."

Triona did. She clung to him, quickly catching the rhythm of his movements, welcoming his every thrust with her whole body. The rub of skin against skin, the feverish little kisses they exchanged, all delighted her. The only shadow over it all was the growing tightness low in her belly, an increasingly frantic demand her body began to make that she did not understand. It should have been distracting her from the desire she felt, or even dimming it, but instead it was making her more frantic in her need.

"Let go," Brett whispered, and nipped at her earlobe. "Just let go and come with me. Give it to me."

Brett knew the moment Triona stopped fighting her release. He held on to his own control just long enough to watch how her lithe body arched into his as she cried out his name. Then the way her body squeezed him inside and out, even the way she drummed her heels against the back of his thighs, pulled him along with her.

Only faintly aware of Brett calling her name, Triona clung tightly to him as her body convulsed with the release of all the tension that had been building. That hot, blinding pleasure tore through her whole body, from head to toe, leaving her gasping from the force of it and tingling from the strength of the desire heating her blood. The feel of him thrusting deep and spilling his seed only heightened those feelings. By the time she began to calm her breathing,

Brett had separated their bodies but was still sprawled on top of her, watching her.

Brett idly stroked her breasts as he watched her, waiting to see if she would suddenly reveal regret over what they had shared. He hoped not, for he wanted more, a lot more. His body still thrummed with the residue of the passion he had shared with her. Although he knew memory could play tricks on anyone, he could not say for certain that it had been as good with Brenda. For a moment he waited for that admission to cool his blood and raise the specter of his guilt, but nothing happened.

"Oh," she whispered, desperately searching her mind for something to say that did not sound ridiculous. "That wasnae quite what I suspected it would be."

Brett laughed. "Nay quite what I expected, either. Nay, 'twas far, far more," he murmured, and brushed a kiss over her forehead, all the while looking around the bedchamber but seeing no sign of Brenda's ghost, despite the fact that he had, for the very first time, compared what he had shared with her with what he had just shared with another woman. "I believe your husband was an idiot. He ne'er bothered to give ye pleasure, did he?"

"Weel, nay, but he sought only to make a son."

"As I just said, he was an idiot, for he nay only robbed ye of pleasure, but himself also."

"It didnae hurt," she whispered, a little embarrassed to speak of what they had just done, even though they were naked and in a bed. "With you, it didnae hurt."

"And it ne'er should hurt, for a mon should make verra certain the lass welcomes him, that her body welcomes him."

"The weeping?" He nodded and smiled. "Weel, I thank ye most kindly for showing me how it should be done."

"Nay, dinnae thank me yet, for I am nay done showing ye, lass." For the first time in too long he was not haunted by his dead lover's spirit when he bedded down with a woman, a woman he truly liked and respected as well, and Brett intended to take full advantage of that.

"Nay?"

"Nay. I am thinking we willnae get much sleep this night," he said, and kissed her before setting out to show her that his words had not been just words, but a promise.

Chapter Eleven

Opening one eye, Triona found a grinning Nessa standing next to her bed. She did not know what the woman found so amusing but was too tired to ask. Nessa patted Triona's cheek, chuckled, and then hurriedly put out heated water for washing and some clean clothes. It was not until a still-chuckling Nessa left, quietly shutting the door behind her, that Triona began to guess what had so amused her maid.

She looked down and saw a strong male arm draped around her waist. Then the memories of all that had happened last night washed over her, heating her blood. Triona groaned and pulled the sheet over her head as embarrassment overtook that lingering desire. Nessa had caught her in bed with Brett. Everyone at Banuilt would soon know about it. No wonder the woman had been chuckling so merrily. Nessa had never before had such news to spread, and

Triona had no doubt that the woman would be spreading it far and wide and to anyone she met.

Fear over what she would soon face upon confronting her people crept into her heart and mind. She fought it, if only because she knew she needed to appear confident when she walked out of her bedchamber, needed to reveal not one tiny hint of guilt or shame. Searching her heart, she found that she actually felt none, and that troubled her a little, for she had bedded down with a man who was not her husband. That was a sin, and if the village priest had not died from the fever and never been replaced, reducing them to occasionally borrowing a priest from another village, she should be headed straight to him to make her confession and do a penance.

A little smile curled her lips when she realized she would not have felt any real inclination to do that, either. The old priest might have tried to shame her into doing so, but he would have been wasting his breath. After facing Father Mollison, a man so willing to force her into marriage just to keep himself safe and unharmed, she doubted she would be running to him, either. No matter how hard she tried, she could not bestir even the smallest spark of shame in her heart.

Triona did not believe that it was just the fullness of the passion she and Brett had shared that left her so untroubled. She was lying there, shamelessly happy, because what she had shared with Brett felt right to her, in both her heart and in her mind. It felt right because she had foolishly fallen in love with the man. That realization robbed her of all her good humor.

This was not going to end well, she mused as she watched his strong, long-fingered hand slide up her body and cover her breast. She was not plain, but she was no beauty. Sir Brett Murray was one of the finest-looking men she had ever seen, and the way the women of Banuilt looked at him told her that they thought so, too. She was a wren and he was a king-fisher. He was her lover, had never even hinted that he wanted to be any more than that, and he would leave once Banuilt's troubles ended. It hurt to think on that, but she knew she would be a fool to ever forget it.

Warm lips touched the back of her neck and she shivered with pleasure. "We have been discovered," she murmured, tilting her head a little so that he could warm the side of her neck with his kisses.

"I heard Nessa cackling to herself." Brett shifted and tugged her onto her back. "Are ye upset?"

She decided it was somehow wrong for a man to look so good in the morning. His dark green eyes were still a little clouded with sleep, but it only made them look more seductive. His thick black hair was tousled, and he had a hearty crop of beard stubble. Even the crease mark from the bed linen, which ran over his left cheek, did not dim his beauty. Triona was sure she looked as if she had been dragged through a hedgerow backwards, yet the way he looked at her made her feel beautiful.

"Aye, Nessa was here and, aye, I was upset. For just a moment." Unable to resist, she lightly stroked his strong chest, idly toying with the small patch of hair in the middle.

"Only for a moment?"

"Aye, only a moment. Then I thought of a few things. I am laird here. I am a widow, a mother, and five and twenty. For almost eight years I have been doing all I could to make life here good for these people, and ne'er veered from the path of virtue. So, nay, I decided I willnae act as if I have committed some great sin." She grinned. "Of course, it helps immensely that we have nay priest here to remind me that I have done exactly that."

Brett grinned back at her. She looked beautifully mischievous. It was not a part of her she revealed often, and he liked it. He realized he wanted to be the one to give her the freedom and ease to reveal that side of her nature much more often.

That could be a problem, he thought. He was not sure he could stay with her. The fact that Brenda's ghost had not appeared last night to chill the heated passion he was sharing with Triona was as close to miraculous as he suspected he would ever see. It told him he could be Triona's lover, but his heart refused to offer more than that. Brenda's ghost might not have appeared, but her specter obviously still had a tight grasp on him. Brett preferred to call his reluctance to allow himself to care deeply for any woman again merely a wise man's caution, not fear.

Deciding his thoughts were growing too deep for the morning hour, especially a morning when he woke in the bed of a woman he desired, he kissed her.

That her kiss aroused him as strongly as it had before, despite how thoroughly he had satisfied his lust last night, pleased him even as it disturbed him. It could be part of the reason he had not been haunted last night.

"'Tis morning, Brett," Triona protested halfheartedly as he kissed his way down her body until he began to lavish attention on her breasts. "We shouldnae do this now." His kiss had already stirred her desire for him strongly enough that she hoped he had a good argument as to why they should indulge their passion again, no matter what time of the day it was.

Brett was pleased with the challenge of proving her wrong. His desire for her was running hot, but his own thoughts were scattered. Now he could set those thoughts on one very clear path, showing a faintly blushing Triona that they could and would make love in the morning. Soon her gasps of pleasure, the movement of her soft skin against his, and the way the heat of her desire wrapped itself around him, drove every thought from his head.

Triona was still panting when her mind finally cleared of passion's haze. She could feel the faintly damp heat of Brett's breath against her neck and knew he was also recovering, his breathing slowing back to normal. The fact that she, little Triona McKee, could make such a man weak enough to collapse in her arms, unable to do more than struggle to breathe for several minutes, was enough to make her heart swell with pride.

With the fading of her desire, however, came the realization that she had a very large man sprawled on top of her. They were also both a little sweaty. Then her stomach rumbled in an embarrassingly loud reminder that she had not yet broken her fast. She blushed when he laughed, pushed himself up on his forearms, and grinned at her.

"Aye, 'tis time to eat." He gave her a quick, hard kiss and then got up and began to tug on his clothes. "I will try to nay march boldly from your bedchamber like some conquering hero," he assured her and then left, still lacing up his shirt.

Triona stared at the door for a moment before sitting up. "Conquering hero?" she muttered as she got up and went to wash off with the now tepid water Nessie had brought to her earlier.

By the time she reached the great hall to break her fast, only Arianna remained. Triona frowned as she sat down and chose food from the sadly depleted platters and bowls. The men were often gone, leaving early to hunt for Sir John and returning late and empty-handed. Yet in the last few days, the long absences had only gotten worse, and she even wondered if Sir John was really what they were now hunting for. She also sensed that there was something they were not telling her.

"Ye are looking a bit irritated for a woman who spent such a wonderful night," drawled Arianna.

Triona cursed. "Nessa."

"Aye, she was most talkative."

It was impossible not to blush, but Triona knew it was not shame that heated her cheeks, for she still felt none, only embarrassment over someone knowing something so deeply personal about her. "I am sorry if I have disappointed you, Cousin."

Arianna waved her hand in a dismissive motion. "I am nay disappointed. Ye are a widow and nay some young virgin. Ye have earned the right to do as ye please." She bit her lip and then sighed. "I but hope ye—weel, that ye are nay thinking ye have just found a husband. Nay that he might ne'er decide to be just that for you, but—"

"I ken it," Triona said, interrupting her cousin's stumbling words. "That is nay what I seek, and I willnae allow myself to hope for it. I but wanted, just once, to choose for myself who climbed into my bed."

"Och, aye, I can understand that. I had some choice with my first husband, in that my family truly desired the match and I was fooled by Claud's charms. Yet I didnae really choose, did I? I acquiesced. I chose Brian and, to be honest, I also chose him, in heart and mind, as a lover before there was talk of his being a husband. Nay only that, but then I had to make him see sense, or he would have sent me away because of some fool's idea of nay being good enough for me. His pride, too, in a way."

"And how fares the trouble between the two of ye?"

"'Tis settled. I am still puzzled o'er how he could forget a wife, but he has explained himself and I finally calmed enough to try to see it all through his eyes." She grinned. "Through the eyes of a MacFingal male. Instead, I actually feel bad for poor Mavis. She died young and left so little mark. But Brian and I are fully reconciled now, and we will be staying here until the troubles plaguing ye are done."

"That is verra kind of ye."

"'Tis nay just because ye are kin, either. What is happening here is wrong. Verra wrong. If that liege laird of yours would just come and look at Banuilt, come and talk with ye and your people, he would see that ye need no mon if ye choose to have none. And, as Brian says, the fact that it is the verra ones who swore to be your allies, hurting ye and your people, makes it all the more wrong."

"I ken it could help if my liege laird came here just once, but I would prefer he just forget about me. He is of the ilk that believes no woman can fare weel without a mon at her side." Triona began to cut up an apple. "So Brian is off hunting with the others?"

"He is, but I am wondering if it is really Sir John they search for at the moment."

"I was just wondering the same thing." Triona tensed and looked at Arianna. "Do ye think they may have found some hint of what has happened to my garrison?"

"Mayhap. If they have, we best pray it is good news." Triona sighed and nodded.

As the day wore on and she suffered no trouble or unkindness from her people, only the occasional laughter-filled teasing from some of the women, she realized she would not lose their respect for having a lover, and relaxed. The only thing that continued to trouble her was that Brett might not be telling her exactly what he and the others were now looking for. When he returned that evening, she briefly considered confronting him and demanding to know what was going on, but discarded the idea as they tumbled into bed. She would do her best to just leave him to the search, certain he would tell her anything she had to know if necessary, and also keep praying that it all turned out well.

"Are ye certain about this, Harcourt?" asked Brett as he stared through the trees at the ruin of a peel tower where a few rough-looking men stood guard. "How could Sir John keep near thirty men in there?" This was the third place they had come to in as many days, this one chosen by Harcourt and Callum, and even though he had the greatest confidence in their abilities, he feared they were about to be disappointed again.

"Note the bars and the heavy doors. They are new. I spoke with the mon who put them there. The only openings are ones to put food in and to take waste out. There are also chains, shackles, and rings set in the wall to hold a mon with rope or chains. He said he guessed it must be a prison the laird wanted, something far from his own keep so that he didnae have to worry about kinsmen trying to free someone."

"Jesu," Brian whispered. "Near two years held in there? If ye are right, how many could still be alive?"

"I couldnae get close enough to have a look," said Callum. "Nay sure I would have seen much if I had, as there is no way to look inside of the place, every opening covered in bars and heavy iron-banded doors. Couldnae get any idea from the people in the village of how many prisoners might be held there, either. They take food there from time to time, but it didnae sound like much. I also watched the guards help themselves to a lot that came to this place, picking o'er what was in the carts and setting it aside. A few people in the village are suddenly living verra weel."

"The guards are from the village?"

"Aye. I was told they are rough men, too, nay weel liked or trusted."

"Hired swords," said Brett. "So, since we cannae be certain the Banuilt men are being held in there, I am nay sure what to do next. My doubt is stirred mostly by how close this is to Gormfeurach. Sir John has to ken that, if we found the men here, it would implicate him."

"I feel certain it is the Banuilt men in there," said Harcourt. "I had the old mon who cares for the stable at Banuilt describe some of the horses that the men rode when they left to go to France. I have seen horses matching his descriptions in the village, at the homes of the men guarding this place. Nay all of the horses— some I suspect may be found at Gormfeurach—but a few."

"I think that proof enough to go down there and demand a look," said Brian.

Brett studied the place, counting only six guards.

There were twelve in their own group, so the odds were definitely in their favor. It would also mean that they could subdue the guards without bloodshed, which would be wise if it turned out that the prisoners being held were not the garrison of Banuilt.

"We shall just ride down there," Brett decided. "Eight of us shall ride up and four of us shall slip up behind the guards once their attention is fully on us. That way any one of them who takes it into his head to fight can be quickly subdued."

"Verra cautious," murmured Brian.

"It may be that the men in there are nay the ones we search for, and I dinnae wish to be killing guards if it can be avoided, at least nay until I see who *is* being held there."

Brian nodded and directed four of his men to start slipping up behind the guards. Brett approved the choice, for he knew well just how skilled MacFingals were in such matters. He then signaled the rest of the men to remount and they headed down the hillside to the peel tower. Instinct told him they had found Triona's men, but he wanted to be sure before any punishment of the guards was dealt out.

All the guards turned to them as they rode up, and Brett inwardly shook his head at their stupidity. They had now left their backs—and even, to some extent, their flank—wide-open to attack. Sir John did not choose his hirelings for skill, he decided. Either that, or after almost two years of no trouble coming their way, the guards had grown lax.

"What do ye want?" the biggest of the six demanded,

drawing his sword as he stepped closer and glared up at Brett. "This is nay some inn. Best ye ride on to the village."

"What do ye have locked up in there?" Brett asked.

"'Tis none of your concern. 'Tis just where a laird keeps those deserving of some punishment."

Since most lairds delivered punishment by their own hand or with a rope, Brett just stared at the man. "I believe I should like to see what ye hold in there."

"Weel, ye can just—"

Brett smiled when the man's words were cut off by the sharp point of a sword in his back. Three of the other guards were on the ground, and the other two also had swords at their backs. Brett decided he was very glad that the MacFingals were his allies, and after the big guard had tossed aside his sword, he dismounted and held out his hand.

"Keys," he ordered.

The moment he had them in hand, Brett walked to the door, Harcourt, Uven, Callum, and Tamhas right behind him, along with a scowling Brian. When he opened the door, the stench was so overpowering he took a step back. Once the fresh air from the outside lessened the power of the smell a little, he cautiously stepped inside, but it was too dark to see clearly. He could hear movement and the rattle of chains, but could see only shadows.

Light flared and he glanced back to see Harcourt with a torch, and nodded his thanks. Then he looked around and began to curse. Men were crowded into the room, and he could glimpse a few peering down at him from the upper level. They were filthy, dressed in rags, and looked as if they had not had a meal for far too long. The smell of the place told him that they had been left to rot in their own filth as well.

Before Brett could ask who they were, one tall, bone-thin man stood up, although he had to lean against the damp stone to stay upright. He was shackled hand and foot to the wall, and Brett could see the sores the shackles had caused. If these were the men of Banuilt, it was going to be difficult getting them all back home, he thought.

"Who are ye?" asked the man. "New guards?"

"Nay, we have come searching for some men who went missing nearly two years ago," replied Brett. "We search for the garrison of Banuilt."

"We are the garrison of Banuilt. I am Aiden McKee and was the leader of that garrison."

"Then we have come to take ye home."

To Brett's astonishment, the man looked down at himself and then gave Brett a crooked smile. "That may nay be so easy to do."

It was not easy just getting the men unchained and out into the fresh air. The way every one of them winced at the light of the sun was all the indication Brett needed to know that they had been caged in the dark for too long. He and Callum were just bringing out the sickest of the men when three of the guards attempted to escape. Before he could move to stop them, Brian and his men struck them down, and the other three guards, watching how quickly their fellow hirelings had died, made no move to try an escape themselves.

They did not have enough water or clothing to clean away all the filth the men of Banuilt carried, but they did what they could. Brett was just handing Aiden some water and an oatcake, suspecting the men would need to eat with caution for a while, when Callum walked up and crouched in front of Aidan. The last he had seen of Callum, he had been talking to one of the guards.

"Ye have been here for almost two years," Callum said. "Do ye have any idea who caused ye to be imprisoned?"

"It was Sir John Grant," said Aiden.

"Ye saw him?"

"Only once, a wee sighting, as he didnae come close, but 'twas enough. They must have thought every one of us asleep, or too dull witted to see him. He and some men collected our horses and weapons as we were chained up for the journey here. I didnae recognize any of the men with him, though. I dinnae think they were from Gormfeurach."

"Probably not." Callum looked at Brett. "It appears that Sir John has been planning on taking hold of Banuilt for a verra long time, as this takes work and careful scheming. So does convincing an entire garrison to ride off so that ye can get your hands on that land."

"Ye didnae fight?" asked Brett.

"Nay, for we were asleep, or near to," Aiden replied. "Something was in the ale, I think, and we were thinking we were amongst compatriots who would soon be fighting with us in France." He frowned at Brett. "What made ye come looking for us? All who kenned us believed us to have sailed for France."

"It began to trouble Lady Triona that there had been no word from any of ye, nor bodies returned to be buried at home, nor even wounded come home to be cared for. Nothing. When she mentioned how that puzzled her, made her increasingly uneasy, we got to thinking on how, with all her trained fighting men gone, it made it all so much easier for Sir John to cause her trouble."

"Aye." Aiden shook his head. "All we saw was glory and riches. 'Twas nay a good thing to do, and mayhap we deserved some punishment for it." He looked at the peel tower. "But, I think, nay this."

"Nay, this was undeserved. But, in a way, ye will be serving your lady weel. This is something she can use against Sir John. This is something that e'en her liege laird cannae accept and excuse."

"How many have ye lost?" asked Callum.

"Four men. They just couldnae abide it anymore, I am thinking. Hunger and thirst also make it hard to fight disease. They are buried close to here—they would take a few of us out to do the burying when one died." He glanced toward several of the Banuilt men who were carefully being set on hastily made litters. "We may yet lose a few more." He looked back at Brett. "Ye say it has been nearly two years?" When Brett nodded, Aiden cursed. "Then I am surprised we have lost so few. There is nay a curse strong enough to fling at Sir John Grant for this."

"Nay, I agree, but this may nay have been his plan. I think the guards began to enrich themselves with what was meant to keep ye and the others alive. I dinnae excuse the mon, nay at all, but it would make no sense to let ye all rot, when he plans to wed Lady Triona and rule over Banuilt. Trained men are nay so easy to come by."

"Aye, but he didnae pay heed to what was happening with us, either, or the guards couldnae have stolen anything. He set us in this hole and then forgot about us, or near to."

"Verra true. But now we must think of how to get ye all back to Banuilt."

"I could walk if it came to it, although I would need to rest many a time along the way."

"There will be nay walking. A few carts are all that is needed." He looked at Callum. "I have the feeling ye would ken where to find some."

"Aye, and the horses to pull them," Callum replied as he stood up and, briefly grinning at Aiden, hurried off to get what was needed to take the garrison home.

"Do ye ken a woman named Joan at Banuilt?" asked Aiden.

"Aye, I have met her. She is weel," replied Brett.

"And still weaves the finest cloth in Scotland?"

"So Lady Triona claims."

Aiden looked down at his bone-thin, weakened body. "Well, I willnae be coming home to her in the best of looks, but 'twill be good to be back with her."

"She will be pleased that ye are alive and home. The rest can be mended."

"I pray ye are right, Sir Brett."

Brett prayed he was right, as well. The men were badly weakened, and the ones being put on the litters the MacFingals had hastily made looked too close to death for his liking. It was a sad end for men who had ridden off thinking they could sell their skill for coin to help their families. It was also difficult to understand how any man could do such a thing to so many men innocent of any crime save that they protected something he wanted. About all he could say in Sir John's favor was that the man had not simply slaughtered them all, but his neglect and disinterest in how they fared had nearly done the deed anyway.

The only good thing about this whole tragedy was that it provided the rope to hang Sir John with. Brett was certain that when Triona and Sir John's liege laird heard about this, he would end all protection for Sir John Grant. Triona finally had the hard proof she had been seeking to condemn the man.

Chapter Twelve

"M'lady! They have returned!"

Triona stared at Angus, who was so agitated that he was nearly hopping from foot to foot as he stood before her, and struggled to understand just what he was telling her. "Who have returned, Angus? Sir Brett and his men?"

"Ye must come and see, m'lady. Your mon and the rest are in the bailey now. Come! Follow me!"

Your mon, she thought as she stood up to follow Angus out to the bailey. She and Brett had been lovers for only three nights, and yet all of her people now called him her man. Brett had to know that, but he did not seem bothered by it. Then again, he had not been around much during the day. He had actually become very secretive, and all of her questions about what he was doing had received very vague replies. She knew she had decided to leave him alone about it, trusting him to tell her what she had to know when he could, but curiosity had nearly made her change her mind half a dozen times.

A small part of her was a little upset, even a tiny bit hurt, at how quickly her people had accepted Brett. Even though they had never insisted she get a man, had never even shown any dislike of her sitting in the laird's seat, the speed with which they had joined Brett's name to hers made her wonder if they had all actually wanted her married but had just been being kind. They looked to him for direction now as often as they did her. She sighed and told herself she was being foolish, but it still stung just a little.

I need to remind him that I am laird here, she thought crossly, as she forced her thoughts away from such petty concerns and back to what the man was hiding from her. Triona had no fear that he had any regrets that they were now lovers. His passion for her still burned hot, something that continued to astonish her. Yet he was keeping something secret, and she badly needed to know exactly what. She was no longer certain she had guessed right about the cause.

She stepped outside, took one look at what was happening in the bailey, and had her answers. Brett had been hunting for her men. He had said he would, had even sent Harcourt and Callum out to find out what they could, but she had not thought much about how that hunt was going, since she could do nothing to help with it, only pray it would go well. Now she knew he had been successful. Her man had brought home her garrison.

And if her men had actually gone to France, they had fared very badly, she thought as she slowly went down the steps. They all looked ragged, dirty, and hungry, a few of them so weak that they had to be brought home on litters. There was also no sign of the horses and weapons they had taken with them when they left. That was a costly loss and one she would not be able to replace for a very long time. They had the garrison back, however sad and weakened they looked, she thought, and that was really all that mattered. She would worry about all the rest later.

It was difficult, but Triona finally shook off the shock and confusion that had kept her from doing little more than standing and staring. Chaos ruled in the bailey as family members crowded around looking for their sons, fathers, and brothers. The men also needed to be attended to as quickly as possible. Straightening her shoulders, she walked into the crowd and began to snap out orders. There would be time later for all her questions to be answered.

Brett dismounted and handed his mount over to a wide-eyed young boy. As his companions came to stand by him, he watched Triona bring order to chaos with but a few sharp words. She even made time to comfort the people who had found out that the men they looked for would never come home. It was a miracle that the number of men lost was so small, only four, although several of the men brought in on litters might yet die.

When Triona hastened to the side of one man standing surrounded by others, and paid him particular attention, Brett experienced a sharp stab of jealousy. Despite the rags, dirt, and harsh marks of hunger, the tall man appeared to be a handsome devil. He was just realizing that the handsome devil was Aiden when Triona turned, jumping up and down and waving at her friend Joan, who was just rushing through the gates. Brett's jealousy faded rapidly when he saw the looks exchanged by Joan and the man before they embraced. His relief that Triona's care and concern had been for her friend's man, that there was no lurking romance, told Brett that a large part of him wanted to be far more than Triona's lover.

"Sir John needs to die," said Harcourt, his voice hard and cold.

"Aye," agreed Brett. "Slowly, just as he left all of these men to slowly rot."

"Would have been more merciful just to kill them all the day he lured them away. I cannae imagine what it must have been like to sit in the dark for so long, your belly cramped with hunger, and smelling your own stench."

"I doubt Sir John has given them another thought since he got them away from here," said Callum. "He had them chained up and ne'er looked back. He had accomplished what he wanted to, leaving Banuilt with no trained guard, and so he didnae care much what else happened concerning the men he betrayed."

Brett had to agree. The guards watching Triona's garrison had been hired men who had clearly helped themselves to most of the supplies that might have been sent to feed and clothe the prisoners, had even confessed to it at sword point. Sir John had helped himself to most of the horses and weapons and simply ridden away, giving little thought to the Banuilt men after that. The guards they had brought back as prisoners would attest to that. Finding the missing horses and weapons at Gormfeurach would be even more proof of a crime dire enough to get the man hanged. Watching as the last of the men were helped into the manor, he thought that a far better punishment for Sir John would be to be imprisoned and forgotten in the same manner as he had forgotten these men.

He watched a pale Triona walk toward him. There was a glitter in her eyes that told him she was fighting the urge to cry. The moment she was in reach, he put his arms around her shoulders and pulled her close. It did not surprise him when she began to weep quietly. Triona cared deeply for the people of Banuilt, even ones she had occasionally been angry with for deserting Banuilt to seek personal glory, as she had believed.

"Why didnae he just let them all sail to France?" she finally asked as she stepped back and wiped the tears from her cheeks with her sleeve.

"Mayhap because they would have discovered his trick once there and come back home," said Uven, and then he frowned. "It would have been difficult to hold fast to the lie if they had arrived in France and all was nay as they were told it would be."

"And mayhap he feared they might actually get hired, get some coin, and come back here to help strengthen Banuilt," added Harcourt.

"But to just let them slowly starve?" she whispered.

"I am nay certain one can say that was actually his plan," said Brett, hating how he was actually defending the man. "What he did was hire some guards, send them supplies or the coin to buy some—or told someone else to see to it—and then ne'er looked to see if they were doing what they had been hired to do. So, kenning that they were nay being watched, had no one to answer to, the guards helped themselves to what was sent to care for the prisoners. Any fool could have told him it was a verra bad arrangement."

"Those three bound men ye had taken aside were the guards?"

"Aye. I thought ye might wish to talk to someone with a tale to tell, someone who can help ye get your liege laird to finally heed your accusations against Sir John."

"Och, aye, and I shall write to the mon right now. I can send the missive off with a few men and those guards, within the hour." She started toward the manor and then stopped, slowly turning back to Brett. "Sir John stole all the horses and weapons, didnae he?"

"I suspicion he did, save for the few Banuilt horses we found to pull the carts, ones taken by the guards themselves. So, as soon as we have something to eat and drink, we will saddle some fresh horses and go have a wee look for them."

"Do ye think Sir John will be at Gormfeurach?"

"Nay, I dinnae, but I do think he will ken that we have gone there. He watches all that happens here verra closely, and will soon ken we have discovered the garrison. He has also proven verra elusive since the day he grabbed ye and tried to force ye to marry him."

"So he is weel into the wind."

"We will find him."

"I have nay doubt of that. Just be verra careful. For my sake. And dinnae do anything too harsh to the mon if ye catch him soon, nay until I have an answer from my liege laird. I cannae believe the mon will stand by Sir John after this is kenned, but I think it would be best if we have some firm decision from the mon on what we can do ere we act."

"Agreed."

Triona hurried off to write her letter and Brett looked at his companions. "It will be hard to nay just kill the bastard if we find him, but she is right. 'Twill be best to get the nod from their liege laird first so there is nay question, nay doubt, and nary one wee concern about retribution from any friends Sir John may have."

"Aye," agreed Brian. "We are nay from here, nay part of either clan, and need that mon's word that we can do as must be done. Now, I mean to go and make certain my wife doesnae get near any of these men until it is certain that they dinnae carry any illness."

"I am eager to go to Gormfeurach to see if the horses and weapons are there, have even just told Triona I would do that," said Brett, "but I am also weary of riding about this land." He smiled at the murmurs of hearty agreement he heard. "I believe it can wait a wee bit longer."

"On the morrow?" asked Callum. "Do ye think she will hear from her laird by then?"

"Cannae say. The mon has defended Sir John far longer than I think reasonable, but I do believe he will nay be able to accept this or e'en try to excuse it. Nay sure we need his acceptance of Sir John's crimes to go and inquire about some missing horses and weapons, either. I will think on it. It may, in the end, serve us best if we wait for some word from her liege laird, for it will make it easier for us to get into Gormfeurach. Mayhap we will just go ahunting for Sir John again come the morning." He had to smile at the way the others groaned.

Brett soon found himself standing alone in the bailey. He wandered into the manor and was confronted with what appeared to be chaos, but he suspected it was far more organized and controlled than it looked. Men were crowded into the great hall and others were rushing in and out with tubs and buckets of water. Women with cheeks still wet with tears were hurrying back and forth with clothing and rags for washing and tending wounds.

As soon as he found a path to take, Brett slipped into the great hall and looked for Triona, knowing she would not have been able to walk past such disorder. She was standing by a table covered in clothing and rags, quietly directing all the women and youths who worked to clean and bandage the men of the garrison. If her liege laird could see her now, Brett mused, he would not doubt that she was doing perfectly well without some man to lead her.

"I dinnae believe I have e'er seen so many naked men in one place before," he drawled as he stepped up beside her.

Tired and upset as she was, Triona had to smile. "That is true. 'Tis also odd how modesty disappears completely when 'tis such a crowd, all your companions are also naked, and all of you are desperate to get clean. He left them to rot in their own filth," she said, the anger she tried to control hardening her voice.

"I ken it. I also suspect ye will now have a garrison that is going to be verra particular about how clean they are. It can happen like that. Many people arenae so quick to bathe, as it can be a laborious process or they believe it unhealthy, as some do, but once denied the ability to wash the filth away, to have to suffer your own stench day after day, such a thing becomes verra important."

"Weel, that would be nice, I think, although it may mean I need to have something readied for them to use as they wish to. A large washing cottage or something. I worry right now that this filth has aggravated their wounds, e'en poisoned them. The marks of their chains are particularly worrisome. Many have broken the skin and done so more than once."

"There will be scars. I have seen such before."

"Ah, how sad. They will be forced to remember this each time they see them." She nodded to where the prisoners from Gormfeurach helped with the bathing of the men. "Sir John's men are appalled. Ye can see the pain in their eyes. This has shamed them all and was done by a mon they swore allegiance to."

"It will make it easier for them when he is gone then." He looked at her. "Have ye already written that letter?"

"I was about to go and do so. I but needed to make certain all is being done that can be done for the men. I will send it straight to my liege laird. Sir Mollison cannae ignore this. I mean to send several men so that those guards ye captured may go along as weel. If naught else, I dinnae want the responsibility for punishing them, and sending them to Sir Mollison means he will have to do it." She turned to wash her hands in a small basin. "Then I can return to help see to the wounded."

When she began to go to her ledger room, Brett fell into step beside her. "Ye nay longer fear that another complaint will have the mon demanding ye wed?"

"He can try. I will then be quick to remind him of the one he favored as my choice."

Brett laughed but quickly grew serious again. "I can ride with them if ye wish, but it might be best for ye if this is kept to only your own men."

"Do ye think they are ready for such a thing? Sir John could be watching for them."

"Then send a few MacFingals along, as they ken how to avoid being seen. Then your men can ride alone once they are near your laird's land."

She agreed, and he left her so that he could go to his bedchamber and wash. The smell of the prison was probably no longer clinging to him, but he could still smell it. Brett doubted it was a smell he would easily forget, but getting clean and changing his clothing would help.

Triona sighed and watched the men ride away to deliver her letter to Sir Mollison. The bound guards went with them, as did three of Sir Brian's men. Or rather, three of the man's brothers, and she idly wondered just how many brothers the man had. She shook aside the thought and said a quick prayer that this time her liege laird would not disappoint her.

"Ye have done good, m'lady," said Nessa as she stepped up next to Triona. "Ye brought our laddies home."

"Nay all of them, and I wouldnae have been able to do it without the help of Sir Brett and Sir Brian's men."

"True, but 'twas ye who thought on how odd it was that we had heard naught from our lads. The rest of us just accepted it, didnae e'en think on it much except to wonder when the fools would tire of France and come home. Ye have a keen wit, m'lady, as does your wee lass. She will be as quick as ye, once she ceases leaping into trouble."

"My wee Ella is an angel," drawled Triona, and smiled faintly when Nessa laughed.

"I am sure she is, and I would probably be able to see her bonnie angel wings if she wasnae covered head to toe in mud."

Wondering what Nessa meant, Triona looked in the direction the woman was staring and gasped when she saw her daughter rolling around in a shallow mud pit. "Ella Mary Margaret McKee!" she cried as she hurried over to the child.

"Uh-oh." Ella stood up to face her mother.

"What are ye doing wallowing in the mud like the swine?"

"I wanted to see why they like to do that."

After seeing that there really was no place to grab hold of the girl without getting mud on herself, Triona grasped the little girl's hand and started toward the manor. "They do it because it cools them down and eases itches. Wee lassies dinnae need to wallow in mud to do that."

"Am I going to have to do a punishment?"

"Aye. And ye are also going to have to be scrubbed from head to toe."

Realizing she could not take a child dripping with mud up to the bedchambers, and idly wondering where Peggy was, Triona sighed and started to walk through the great hall. She would have to scrub the child down in the kitchens. When she caught sight of Peggy helping to tend to the men of the garrison, she decided she would not scold the young woman for taking her eyes off Ella.

Then she noticed how many of the men were looking at Ella and the trail of mud she was leaving behind. To her amazement, many of them smiled, a couple even laughed softly. The fact that every little wave Ella sent to the men splattered more mud around only added to their amusement. Her daughter would still have to be punished, but seeing how she had restored some light into the men's lives, Triona decided it would not be too harsh a one.

At the doorway to the kitchen she met Brett, who was doing a very poor job of hiding his amusement when he asked, "Is that wee Ella under there?"

"Aye, sir," Ella replied, and tried to wipe a bit of mud off her face, only to scowl at how much mud was on the sleeve of the gown she wore. "I was wallowing. Had to see why the pigs do it. It wasnae as much fun as I thought, since I will have to do a punishment now."

"Aye, ye will. Best to leave that sort of thing to the pigs, sweet girl." He looked at Triona. "Need help?"

She opened her mouth to say no and then realized all the women in the keep were tending to the men in the great hall. "I thought ye were going to go to Gormfeurach to look for my missing horses and weapons."

"I am thinking it might be best if we wait for word from your laird. I want nothing to steal the power of the accusation ye send your liege laird this time." He smiled again as he heard another lump of mud fall loudly onto the floor. "So, do ye want some help?"

"I think I may, but ye dinnae have to aid me in scrubbing mud off a child."

"I have done it before," he said as he stepped aside so she could go into the kitchen, and then followed her. "I come from a verra, verra large family."

He proved to be surprisingly skillful in the chore of cleaning up a muddy child. An apologetic Peggy hurried in with clean clothes for Ella, but Triona waved away her offer to take over, telling her the men needed her help more. Once Ella was clean, her hair braided, Triona sent her off to help the other girls tear up cloth to be used as bandages for the men and to do anything else that might be asked of her. She stood in the doorway watching how the men who had the strength to do so greeted the little girl, teasing her about how pretty she was, now that they could actually see her.

"Nay such a harsh punishment," murmured Brett as he stood next to her.

"I watched them smile, even laugh, as I walked Ella through the hall, and I just couldnae punish her too harshly. She gave them a touch of lightness, if only for a moment."

"Aye, she did. She reminded them that they are home now, home where wee lassies get covered in mud and mothers have to scrub them. A simple thing, an innocent childish bit of mischief, but a needed reminder that they are indeed home."

"Yet I just realized that some of the men are still unclothed. Mayhap I shouldnae let a wee lass wander about the hall so freely at the moment."

"I dinnae think she has e'en noticed, and the women are doing their best to hide the men's bodies from the sight of Ella and the other young lassies helping."

"Weel, good enough then. I have sent the men off with the captured guards and the letter to my liege laird. I but pray that the mon doesnae take too long to send word back. And now I best go and help in the tending of the men. Some will probably be able to go home with their wives or mothers, but it may be a while ere all of them are out of the great hall."

"We can eat in the kitchens, if needed."

Her smile warmed him, and he watched her hurry off to help with cleaning and bandaging the men. Brett then saw that one man, now clean and bandaged, was being helped by two small boys and was walking toward the doors of the great hall. Realizing some of the men would be more than ready to get back to their cottages, he moved to help. It was going to be a long day, he mused, as he relieved the two grunting little boys of the man's weight and began to help him get outside, where a cart waited to take him home.

Triona yawned as she shed her clothes and washed up. Most of the men had been taken home by their families. Others who were just in need of rest, food, and the occasional check on their small wounds, had been moved to the peel tower, which the unwed members of the garrison had always called home. Eight very weak men remained in the great hall, where it would be warmer and easier to immediately render any aid. She was hopeful that they would recover now that they were free, with ample food and water, and many willing hands to help nurse their wounds.

Just as she tugged on her night shift, Brett walked in. She blushed and then silently cursed. It was foolish to blush, after all they had done together, but she did seem prone to doing so. Triona wanted to be mature, calm, and ladylike before her lover, but she began to think that was never going to happen. The man entered her bedchamber and she was immediately reminded of the passion they had shared, and then she blushed again.

"A long day," he murmured, and brushed a kiss over her forehead. "I went to see the men in the peel tower, to make certain it didnae trouble them to be in one again."

Triona groaned and rested her head against his chest. "They were held prisoner in a tower. I should have thought of that."

"The one they were in was a dark ruin, with chains, no light, little food and water, and no women dashing in and out to make certain they were weel. I but wanted to make certain they could see that difference. They were more than content for, to them, it is home. They are in their own beds and nay chained to a wall. Dinnae fret."

"If ye are sure they willnae suffer for being in there . . ."

"I am verra sure. As one told me, it is nay the same. They can see out the wee arrow slots that are now windows, e'en open them, and most important, if they do begin to be troubled, they can step outside." He picked her up in his arms and took her to the bed. "They will be fine. And I think the ones we feared might die, will be fine as weel."

She watched him shed his clothes, and idly thought that she would never tire of the sight. "I began to think the same thing as they gained a wee bit of strength simply from being clean and seeing their families, their friends." She opened her arms in welcome when he joined her on the bed. "Thank ye for bringing them home. Thank ye for helping them."

"No need to thank me. Although"—he plucked at her night shift—"ye could promise to nay put this on again."

She laughed. "'Tis habit. Boyd was verra precise about how I should always wear it." Suddenly feeling very daring, she sat up and tugged it off. The way his gaze grew heated as she did so made her own desire stir. "Better?"

"Much, although I find I actually like to take it off myself from time to time," he said as he pulled her into his arms and kissed her.

Triona fully gave herself over to his lovemaking, losing herself in the passion they shared. She needed the heat of it to burn away the sadness of seeing how abused the men of Banuilt had been, how they had suffered. She also needed to fill herself up with the memory of his touch, his kiss, the way he filled her, for she knew he was only a lover, that he offered no words of love or any promises of a future. No matter what her heart cried out for, he would leave when her troubles ended. Triona wanted her heart, mind, and body so crowded with memories that the pain she knew she would feel when he rode away could be eased by them.

Chapter Thirteen

Triona stared at the letter her liege laird's man had just given her, reading it again in disbelief. She had not been surprised when the laird had sent one of his own men back with hers, for this was a grave matter. But she had been puzzled as to why the man carried two letters for her. He had met with only a few of her slowly recovering men, listening closely to their tales, and then he had very carefully ripped up one of those letters and handed her the one she now held. With a curt bow and wishes for a good hunt, his face tight with anger, he had then silently left.

"I hope that missive doesnae say that we have to show Sir John any mercy," said Brett as he stepped up beside her and lightly stroked her back, concerned about how pale she had become.

The warmth of Brett's hand on her back slowly pushed away the chill that had seized Triona as she read the words in the letter. She wondered if he realized he was acting with her in a rather intimate, even affectionate way, in front of everyone gathered there.

It would probably be wise to step away from that soothing caress, but she could not find the strength to do so, and she could see that no one was paying any particular attention to what he was doing. Turning her head, she saw that he had his saddlebag over his shoulder, obviously prepared to set out after Sir John as soon as possible.

"Nay, it doesnae, although I suspicion the one that mon tore up may have said something of the like," she replied. "He was sent here by the laird to confirm what the prisoners we sent him had said, and did so by speaking to my men. Aye, and by looking at them. It has been only three days since the men came home, and what they suffered can still be clearly seen in their gaunt faces. Struth, I was a wee bit surprised at how quickly Sir Mollison replied."

"I would wager the laird's mon heard much more than just the tale of their imprisonment. I watched him as he spoke to a few of the women as weel."

"And ye. He spoke with ye, too."

"He did. He wished to ken who we were and why we were here. I told him. It appears he also kens a few of my kinsmen from the king's court, meeting them from time to time when he goes there on the laird's business." He grinned. "And he has heard a lot about the Camerons and the MacFingals." He quickly grew serious again, before Triona could ask what the man may have heard. "So, he may have wondered if your men would lie for your sake; but with the word of men who have no true bond to Banuilt and its people, and have naught to gain with any lie, he was satisfied."

"I think he was also appalled by how my men had been treated by a mon who claims to be our ally. Over the years, the fighting men of Banuilt have served our liege laird verra weel."

"So what does your liege say we must do about Sir John Grant?"

"Whate'er we deem necessary to end his crimes against Banuilt. He has removed all protection from Sir John and has given us full rights to the meting out of justice in any way we deem fitting."

"Good. As of this moment, Sir John Grant is naught but a walking dead mon."

Startled by the cold fury behind his words, Triona began to protest, "But—"

"Nay, lass," said Sir Brian MacFingal as he stepped up to them. "The people of Banuilt ne'er harmed that mon, were always allies—and verra good, trustworthy ones—ready to aid the people of Gormfeurach whene'er it was needed. In return the mon near starved to death all of your fighting men, imprisoning them as if they were the lowest of reivers, tried his best to make certain ye and your people were also left hungry by burning your fields and stealing livestock, and he even tried to force ye to wed with him. Aye, and he did all of these things when, by his own trickery, he left Banuilt undefended and with mostly just bairns and women here. Nay, he dies." He looked at Brett. "I will fetch my lads."

Triona watched her cousin's husband walk away. "Weel, when put that way . . ."

Brett chuckled and kissed her cheek. "Brian joined

this fight because of how the mon was making women and bairns suffer when he should have been helping them. What was done to your men enraged him, as it has every mon here, those belonging to Banuilt and those just visiting. Aye, and those Gormfeurach men we had so lightly imprisoned. Triona, Sir John's own people are so horrified and humiliated by their laird's actions, they would probably hand him o'er for punishment themselves."

"So what happens now?"

"First we go to Gormfeurach and leave some men to secure it against Sir John. I hesitated to go and look for the weapons and horses as planned, because I had hoped Sir Mollison would give me more power to do so, and he did. Now Sir John has been cast out by his own liege laird, so his people can act against him by nay denying me. I dinnae think he will try to return there, as he must ken how his people feel. Yet, he has taken to hiring swords, so one cannae be certain. I continue to think the mon isnae right in the head."

"Nay. He appears to have let the return of the land he believes stolen from his clan rule his mind. And if he does hire men to get back into his keep, I cannae feel certain he would care verra much how many of his own people got hurt in the doing of it."

"Something I believe his people are now weel aware of."

"So ye dinnae believe the people at Gormfeurach will fight ye when ye set men there to hold it against their laird?"

"Nay. And I shall be able to tell them that Sir John's

liege laird himself has condemned him, called him outlaw, in a way, and given us full right to hunt the mon down. I am also taking Duncan and the others back so they can speak for me."

Triona handed him the letter. "Take this. E'en those who are willing to accept your word will feel better acting upon it if they see this. 'Tis nay easy for a mon to take up arms against his own laird, but the words of their liege laird giving them the right to do so, removing all protection from the mon, will settle any unease they feel. 'Tis bad enough that they are now a people without a laird. I cannae help but fear what may become of them."

"Since there appears to be no heir, Sir Mollison will probably find them a new laird."

"Then I pray the new one will be better than the one they have just lost."

Brett nodded and tucked the letter into his bag. He brushed a kiss over her lips and turned to leave, only to stop at the sight of Joan and Aiden. A few days of his wife's tender care had done a lot of good for the man, but Aiden still looked gaunt and weak.

"I ken I am in nay condition to ride at your side, but if one of ye will let me share a mount with ye, I would like to go to Gormfeurach with ye," said Aiden.

"Why?" asked Brett, ignoring Triona's soft murmur of protest.

"Because I ken many of the men there, am e'en kin to a few, and seeing me will set the truth of the tales they have heard firm in their minds."

"Joan," Triona began, and pressed her lips together when Joan shook her head.

"I dinnae like it, lass, but he has the right of it," said Joan. "Our men have fought side by side with the men from Gormfeurach from time to time. The people need to see with their own eyes how that món has treated the best, truest allies Gormfeurach e'er had. Duncan and the others can only tell what they have seen, and there may be ones who willnae heed what they say. Aiden will be the proof they can look at with their own eyes. And, if I guess right, I suspicion some of them have found life under the son a fair lot harder than it e'er was under the father. They will need but a wee nudge to turn against Sir John, and mayhap my Aiden can do the nudging."

"Are ye certain ye have the strength for it, Aiden?" Triona asked.

"I ken I still look more dead than alive, but, aye, I can do this."

"Then go, and I will pray that ye are right." She walked up to him and patted him on the arm, saddened by how thin it was. "Just be sure to rest ere ye return, e'en if it means ye must stay a night away."

"Already done promised my Joan that, m'lady," he answered, and grinned.

"Then let us go," said Brett as he strode out of the great hall.

Triona walked beside Joan as they followed the men. She watched Aiden walk to Harcourt's mount and swing up into the saddle behind the man with much of the same grace and strength he had had before his capture.

"What are ye feeding Aiden?" she asked Joan. "His step is nearly as sure and steady as it used to be."

"I think some of that may be show before all these other men," said Joan, "but I have been giving him a hearty ale with a lot of herbs mixed in, twice each day. It appears to help. Either that or my Aiden is one of those blessed with a strong heart and body."

"That could be, but I believe we shall start giving your potion to all the men."

Triona hooked her arm through Joan's and walked them back into the manor, where Arianna waited. Her cousin had been wanting to help tend the men brought home to Banuilt, but her husband had been right to tell her to stay away from them until one could be certain they carried no disease. Now she had something she could let Arianna help with, for mixing up herbs in ale would aid in the healing of the men while keeping Arianna away from them. And, she thought, it would also keep her too busy to worry about what Brett and Brian would find at Gormfeurach.

The men of Gormfeurach looked as if someone had killed their favorite mount, thought Brett. They also looked embarrassed and ashamed. Realizing where their new weapons and horses had come from only added to that.

"Ne'er seen a people look so defeated when one

hasnae e'en unsheathed a sword against them," muttered Brian.

"Weel, how would ye feel if ye were told that your laird had done to your allies what Sir John has done?" asked Brett.

"I'd want to kill him."

Brett shook his head and laughed softly. "Aye, ye would, wouldnae ye. Ye have led a harsher life than these people, Brian. I havenae been here verra long, but I begin to think all the fighting men's training and skill is only occasionally used by Sir Mollison. Here, in this land, they do verra little fighting, face verra little danger. I dinnae think I have e'er kenned two clans to be so intertwined as these two are, so at peace with each other and with many who are nay of either clan."

"Aye, ye have the right of it. They are nay in the way of most trouble here, are they? Nay too close to the border, nay too close to the heart of the Lowlands or the heart of the Highlands. Nay close to any of the king's courts and all that intrigue, either. Nay truly e'en a clan, neither of them, yet I dinnae ken what else to call them. I wouldnae be surprised to find out that this whole place started because some knight found it a good place to rest on his way home from a battle, and the drovers who pass by stopped here. 'Tis indeed a peaceful place, verra sheltered from the world." Brian shook his head. "They have been dealt a hard lesson now, though." He looked at Brett. "Are ye certain ye could be happy in such a place?"

"And who says I e'er thought of staying here?"

Brett ignored Brian's snort of disdain as he walked toward the man Aiden was speaking with. "Sit down, Aiden," he told the pale man, and nodded when Aiden eased himself down onto the steps of the keep. "I believe we will rest here for the night."

"This is Gunn, Sir John's steward," Aiden said. "He says he hasnae seen Sir John in days."

"Nay, sir," Gunn said, and ran a hand through his graying brown hair. "I think it has been near to a sennight, almost a week, actually. And before that, the mon would slip in and out like a ghost. I grew weary of chasing him down to speak on the work that must be done here. Now I ken why." He sighed. "Now I ken that we have no laird."

"Do ye think everyone will feel the same?" asked Brett.

"Aye, sir. Sir John wasnae a verra good laird and he could be harsh, so I think there wasnae much affection for him from the people here. Yet, he was our laird." He looked at the letter from Sir Mollison that he still held in his hand. "This means he is nay longer laird, may e'en be dead soon, aye?"

"Aye. E'en if all we do is capture him and send him to Sir Mollison, I believe he will still be killed for what he has done. Ye do ken it was more than just what he did to the garrison of Banuilt, do ye not?"

"I do, sir. We all do. There were some men who thought the lady of Banuilt should indeed have a husband, but e'en they didnae like the way Sir John was trying to bring her to heel. She and her people have always been good allies, always willing to help when help was needed."

"We also kenned there were little more than bairns and women there, and it didnae seem right to give them trouble," said a burly, dark-haired man as he stepped up behind the steward.

"My son Ailbert," Gunn said. "He leads Sir John's garrison."

"What happens to us now, Sir Brett Murray?" asked Ailbert. "We have no laird and no heir to step into his place."

"I suspect Sir Mollison will see to that. For now, I wish to set a couple of my men here to watch for Sir John."

"To keep the gates barred against him, aye?"

"Aye. Do ye have any objections? Or think someone else might?"

"None. And ye will have no complaint from any here. Sir John was ne'er a good laird, but in the last two years, since his father died and he sat in the laird's chair, he has been a poor laird indeed. And hard. He has a temper, and it could spill o'er for no reason, at the oddest times, and he was harsh when it did."

Brett had no doubt the man spoke the truth, and he went to find which men he would leave behind. He could see signs of neglect about Gormfeurach as he moved around, speaking to a few of Sir John's people and watching over the collection of the weapons and horses that belonged to Banuilt. Sir John had not kept up his own keep very well as he had worked to take Triona's lands.

He paused as a woman approached him leading six little girls, and frowned when she stopped in front of him. "May I help ye?" he asked.

"I am Meg, the nurse, and these be the children of Sir John," she said. "I ken that they are just wee bastards, but I would like to be kenning what ye mean to do with them now that their father willnae be coming back here."

"They live here, Meg?"

She nodded and revealed her nerves with a hasty brushing back of a strand of black hair. "Their mothers left them here, thinking they would be better cared for." She leaned closer to Brett. "Nay the sort of lassies who would make verra good mothers, if ye ken what I mean." She straightened up. "The laird put them in my care, and Gunn made sure I had all I needed to bring them up as the daughters of the laird, bastard born or nay."

"Then they will stay, and all will continue as it has," he said. "I dinnae ken who will be put here in Sir John's place, however. I will swear to make certain Sir Mollison kens that there are matters that should be allowed to remain as they are."

"Thank ye, sir. I was afeard of what may be done with them. They have nay e'en a tiny claim to this place, but some would still see them as a threat."

"If that proves true, I will see that ye and the lassies are taken care of."

He shook his head after she nodded and herded the little girls away. It was not going to be easy to see that the children did not suffer for the sins of their father. Brett also suspected the ones truly responsible for the girls' care were Gunn and Meg. It was probably something he should speak to Triona about.

Thinking about how he would be spending the night without her made him curse softly. Now that Sir John was marked as an outlaw by his own liege laird, it would not be long before the troubles that had been plaguing Banuilt ended. Then he would leave. Brett was no longer surprised at how the thought of leaving Banuilt made his heart clench.

He needed to decide what he would do about Triona. It was easy to ignore the need for such a decision as he pursued an enemy for her, but he could not keep doing that. Yet he was not sure he could stay, either. Sir Boyd McKee had wed her for her dower and Sir John pursued her for her lands. Since he had nothing of great value to bring to her if he stayed, he feared she could see him as just another man after what she had.

For a moment Brett considered riding right back to Banuilt, even though he had no real urge to get back on his horse. He decided he was being foolish. It would be nice to curl up in bed with Triona, something he was becoming dangerously accustomed to, but he had no news to tell her immediately, and he had made no firm decision to change how matters stood between them. Suddenly appearing at the gates of Banuilt when it was expected that he would be gone for the night would require one or the other.

Instead, with Gunn at his side, he went inside the keep. It quickly became apparent that Sir John had spent a lot of money on finery—or his father had. The great hall had furniture and tapestries to rival any Brett had seen before. The man's bedchamber was equally opulent. Yet, as he walked through the place, he realized that much of the rest of it had been left to wear down, age, and break. He had to wonder why, when Sir John was so clearly incapable of caring for his property, he would think to add to it.

"I believe this place has been in need of a new laird for quite a while," he said to Gunn as he settled in a chair in the great hall and the man poured them each a tankard of ale.

"I fear ye may be right, sir," Gunn admitted. "My father was steward before me, and he often bemoaned the ways of Sir John's father. Then the father died, and mine lived just long enough to shake his head and say he thought it was all about to grow worse. I was saddened on the day I realized he was right. What do ye think will happen to us now? Sir Mollison will choose someone, I ken it, but what if he brings all of his own men, other people for the village?"

"I dinnae ken, Gunn," Brett answered honestly. "I have ne'er kenned of a place where such a thing has happened. There must be clans who find themselves without an heir to the laird's seat, but this isnae a clan as I ken it, and I pray ye take no offense at that."

"Nay. We think of ourselves as such, but many of us are nay e'en related by blood. We have no long lineage to speak of. This place was begun by a knight who decided he liked the look of it and claimed it, bringing his men with him and later gathering some women. He didnae care where they came from. Then it somehow fell into the hands of a Grant, through a marriage, and that lasted for the past four generations. I believe Banuilt has a similar story."

"I wondered if it was that, and 'tis rare such a thing happens. So, nay, I cannae tell ye what will happen. But Sir Mollison has been a good liege laird, so one must hope he chooses a good laird for you." He grimaced. "And that was verra little comfort, I am fair certain."

"Weel, 'tis better than none," said Gunn, and he smiled but quickly grew serious again. "Find Sir John, sir. For a long while I have worried that he has a sickness in his mind. There is nay telling what he may try to do when he kens he has been cast aside by Mollison. And worse, ye willnae be able to decide where to look or what to look for, as there is nay sense in what a madmon does. Nay one we can see."

That was exactly what Brett feared. The man had to know, or would very soon, that he had lost everything. When one considered all Sir John had done to try to gain something he wanted, Brett did not like to think what the man would do in retribution, or even in some mad attempt to return to what he had lost. He knew who Sir John would blame, however, and he suddenly regretted not giving in to the urge to ride to Banuilt and spend the night in Triona's arms.

"The men have obviously decided to stay at Gormfeurach for the night," said Arianna as she stood up and stretched. "I believe I had best go to bed. The bairn makes me tire e'en though he is still so small."

Triona turned from where she had been blindly staring into the fire and smiled at her cousin. They had settled down in her bedchamber because there were still men in the great hall, but she had been so lost in her thoughts, she knew she had been little company for Arianna. She knew that, aside from simply worrying over where Sir John was and what he would do next, she simply did not wish to crawl into her empty bed. Trying to make Arianna stay so she could avoid worrying would be unkind, but it was a tempting thought.

"I have been poor company for ye," she said.

"Nay, ye just have a great deal on your mind."

"And ye just said *he*, so are ye now thinking ye carry a son for Brian?"

Arianna laughed and rubbed her stomach. "Nay, I dinnae ken what I carry. I but say *he* on one day and *she* on the next. It grew tiring saying *the bairn* all the time." She patted Triona on the shoulder. "Get some rest, Tri. Ye have done so much these last few days that ye could do with a good night's sleep."

"I was but trying to think of what Sir John will do next."

"Ye cannae guess what a madmon will do. Ye will only make your head ache. The men will return on the morrow, and then ye may have some better idea of what to worry about. It will be over soon. I am certain of it."

"Do ye have a touch of the sight then?" she teased.

"Nay, I just have confidence in my cousins and husband. And now I shall go and sleep alone. I find I hate that now," she murmured as she left the room.

Triona sighed. So did she, and she had had the pleasure of Brett's company in her bed for only a short time. Just looking at the bed made her think of him, and her blood warmed a little with sweet memory. There would be no big, warm body to curl up with this night, however.

Knowing Arianna was right, that she needed some rest, she finally stood up and shed her clothes. After a quick wash in the tepid water that had been left for her, she donned her night shift and crawled into bed. She had never shared the bed with anyone but Brett, having left her husband's bedchamber when he was ill and never returned, making this room her own. Now she was all too aware of how alone she was. Curling up beneath the heavy covers did not truly ease the chill, either.

Brett had made her all too aware of what a man and woman could share. Climbing into bed beside her husband had always been a chore; the nights he did no more than sleep were a relief. Now she looked forward to getting into bed knowing that Brett would join her and make her body burn with passion. It was difficult not to think about it as she settled in to sleep without him. She did not think there would be too many more nights when she would be able to savor the joy of bedding down with him, either. Sir John was, as Arianna's husband so bluntly put it, a dead man. He just needed to be found and put in the ground, and Brett and Brian, as well as all the men with them, would soon see to that, after which she would be standing at the gates waving farewell to them all. Then life at Banuilt would return to what it had been before she met Brett. Work and an empty bed.

"Get used to it, Tri," she told herself, and smiled fleetingly over the name Arianna had always called her when they were young.

He was leaving soon, she told herself firmly, and refused to let her heart break over that. She had taken him into her bed as a lover and he had never offered her anything else. If her heart now rested in his hands, it was her own fault, not his, and he should not be made to pay for that. Nevertheless, she did wish she could think of some way to make Brett want to stay with her, to return the love she had for him. It was a foolish young girl's hope, for if he did not love her now, he would not stay. She had given him everything she had to give, and when he left she would just have to accept the sad fact that it had not been enough for him.

Chapter Fourteen

"Has anyone seen Ella?"

Triona told herself the fear that was threatening to choke her was unwarranted, but it continued to build. She looked all around but could find no sign of her daughter. Ella had been happily skipping around the hedgerows with half a dozen other little girls, each one taking turns hiding and then leaping out to make the others squeal with laughter. Now Triona saw only the other little girls, and despite watching for her daughter to leap out of the hedgerow for several minutes, nothing happened.

A deep breath and then another did nothing to ease that throat-tightening fear, either. Nor did reminding herself that her daughter had an unmatched skill for finding trouble but had managed to avoid any true danger to herself. Something was wrong. Every motherly instinct she had was screaming that at her.

"She was o'er there playing with the other lassies," said Joan as she stopped weeding and looked around.

"Must be her turn to be the scary beastie leaping out of the hedgerow."

"I thought that, too, but it has been several minutes and she hasnae appeared," Triona said as she stood up and started to walk toward the hedgerow.

"Mayhap she found a bug or a worm," said Joan as she hurried to catch up to Triona. "Ne'er kenned a lass who was so interested in such things."

Joan's attempts to ease her fear did not work. With every step Triona took, her alarm grew. She had begun the day with such confidence and hope that it would be a good day, especially since she had found the perfect way to keep her thoughts off Brett, who had yet to return from Gormfeurach, only sending a message to say they would look for Sir John close to his keep for a day or two before riding back. The sky was clear, it was warm, and all the women and older girls had gathered quickly to work in the fields. Ella had been delighted to come along to play in the sunshine with the other girls too young to be of much help in the fields. Sir John had not been sighted for a week, and since the day they had found her men, there had been no more fires or thefts. Triona feared her good fortune had just ended and prayed she was wrong.

The other women joined her in searching for her daughter. Triona fought her panic as all her calls went unanswered and no one found any sign of little Ella. It took every bit of control she could grasp hold of not to start racing over the countryside screaming her child's name.

"How could she just disappear like that?" she asked Joan, wrapping her arms around herself as she began to shake, her fear for her child hard to control. "We are surrounded by open fields, yet none of us saw anything." Guilt over not watching her child closely enough swamped Triona, but she fought it down, knowing it was not only unwarranted but useless at the moment.

"They may be open, but they are nay empty," said Joan. "Our crops have grown enough to give some clever mon something to hide in if he had a mind to, and there are hedgerows and trees to shelter behind. And there are certainly enough places for a wee lass to be hidden."

"Do ye think she has been taken?"

"Ah, lass, I dinnae ken. I do ken that there is naught about here where she could just disappear, nary a hole or burn or cliff or the like. We have always made certain of that before allowing the wee ones to play near us while we work. Yet, why would anyone want to take the wee lass?"

"To get to me."

"Och, weel, aye, but the only mon who would do it is fleeing for his life. The wisest thing he could be doing is getting as far away from here as he can and ne'er turning back. He would have to be utterly mad to return here where e'en his own clan has turned against him."

"I believe we have already decided that Sir John might be a wee bit mad. I am nay sure if it is because he has become so obsessed with getting that land back, or if he sees getting it back as part of taking the stain of traitor from the family, which was why the land was lost to begin with. But, aye, I do believe he has become nay quite right in the head. And now he may ken that he has lost Gormfeurach as weel. That news would only unsettle his mind even more."

Joan cursed and then grabbed Triona by the arm, pointing at the riders headed their way. "Look, there be our men finally come home. Mayhap they have some news or can help."

Triona realized that even Joan now referred to Brett as her man. It was something she really ought to put a stop to, she thought a little wildly, and wondered if fear for her daughter was making her wits slide into the mire of madness. What did it matter if the whole of Banuilt called Sir Brett her man? Whatever they wanted to call him would stand, as long as he hurried over to her and then went and found her little girl.

Brett noticed Joan waving wildly at them and looked at Aiden. "Your wife appears to want your attention."

"She gets a lot of it," he drawled, and then frowned. "But, nay, I am thinking she wants us to ride o'er there. Nay sure why she needs to welcome me home here in the midst of the fields, but what else could she be wanting?"

"Whate'er the reason for her waving at us to come,

I doubt she wants us to trample everything in the fields."

Aiden laughed. "Nay, we can pass near the hedgerow. I wonder what the women are searching for. Mayhap that is what she wishes to speak to us about."

Even as Aiden spoke, Brett heard the name all the women were calling, and his blood ran cold. The women were all searching for little Ella. When Aiden cursed viciously, he knew the man had just heard what he had. He then saw that all the other children had been gathered up together and a woman was standing guard over them. Brett signaled the other men to wait and started to ride over to Joan and Triona, Aiden following on his own mount, as he no longer needed to ride with another man to stay in the saddle.

Brett's mind filled with images of the little girl waving farewell to him every time he left Banuilt, giggling while they played with the kittens in the stable, and listening to his stories with wide blue eyes. He could also see her covered in mud, standing on the high walls of Banuilt and trying to look so innocent, and sticking her tongue out at a laughing Brian. Brett realized that it was not just Triona who had burrowed deep into his heart. The mere thought that someone might have hurt or even just frightened that happy, mischievous child made him blind with fury. He took several deep breaths to push that rage aside. Triona would need him to be calm and clear-headed.

He and Aiden had just reached the women when a cry came from one of the women searching the area outside the hedgerow. Brett and Aiden dismounted to follow Joan and Triona as they raced toward the woman, who stood by a small, wind-contorted tree and pointed to the far side of it, the one facing away from the field. A dagger pinned a piece of parchment to the bark. Brett moved to stand next to Triona as she read what was written there, her hands pressed to her mouth.

"He took my bairn," Triona whispered. "I didnae want to think it possible, but he took my wee Ella."

When Brett put his arm around her, she leaned against him. She struggled to draw strength from him. Her whole body shook with a stomach-churning mixture of fear and fury. Despite the calm strength she gained from Brett, she could sense his own anger and she used it to feed her rage. Fear clouded her mind and weakened her. She needed to get a firm grip on her cold rage if she was going to be able to help her daughter.

"He wants me to come to him willingly, and then he will release my Ella," she said, pleased to hear that the tremor of fear had left her voice.

"Ye cannae give him what he wants," said Brett.

"He says he will hurt, e'en kill my Ella if I dinnae." She held up her hand when Brett tried to argue with her. "Ye have nay seen the way he looks at my little girl, e'en after he must have kenned that she might nay be Boyd's heir. He sees her as less than nothing. I cannae say he loathes her, but something about the way he would look at her always chilled me to the bone. There is certainly none of the softness most people feel for a child in him."

"Why, if she may nay be the heir to all he wants to steal?"

"I wondered if it was because he was enraged that I gave Boyd a child, but I think it is more than that. I heard once that he had bred a few bastards and they were all lassies. Ne'er a son." She shrugged. "Who can say? Mayhap e'en he doesnae ken the why of it all, nay clearly. The why of it doesnae really matter, does it? All that matters is that I ken he willnae hesitate to do as he threatens."

"Ye still cannae go to him." He pointed at the message. "He doesnae e'en tell ye where to go to meet with him."

"I suspicion I will be told soon enough. He will let the fact that he holds my child eat at my innards for a wee while, thinking that it will make me much more compliant."

"Aye," agreed Aiden. "He wants ye so twisted with fear and worry for your bairn that ye will do whate'er he asks."

Brett cursed, yanked the knife from the tree, and grabbed the message as it fell. "Then we have time to find him ourselves."

"Ye could put my child's life in danger if ye try to hunt him down," Triona said.

"Nay, love. It shames me that he did this e'en as we have been hunting him, that he got so close to ye and Ella, but we can hunt him now with a stealth that few can match. Trust me in this. Before we didnae much care if he kenned we were hunting him, for at first just keeping him busy hiding helped ye some. Then we were searching for your men, and then Grant was aware that he had been as good as outlawed, so there was no need to be secretive. He also had few places to turn to back then, since he was trying to hide what he was doing—and now he has none at all. And, aye, I will confess that it took us a wee while to understand that the mon had a true skill at hiding, that we suffered from our own arrogance in thinking him less of a challenge than he proved to be. But, between me and mine and those MacFingals who can, as their father liked to say, steal the coins from a dead mon's eyes e'en as his kin pray o'er him, we will be the shadows on his trail that he ne'er sees coming."

Triona nodded slowly. She did trust in him, and she had heard enough about the MacFingals from Arianna to believe in their ability to slip around like ghosts. The very fact that he would admit to arrogance only added to her trust in him. He had seen their error in judgment and they would now act accordingly. She would leave the hunt in his hands and do as he asked. If they had not found her daughter by the time the man sent her word of where to meet him, however, she would not promise not to go to Sir John. She just hoped Brett did not press her for that promise. If he did, she might just discover that she could look a man she loved in the eye and lie through her teeth.

"Best get the women and children out of here," Brett said. "I dinnae think there is any danger to them, but the mon has come too close."

He watched as she moved to get the women and children out of the fields. Brett could see how hard she was fighting her fear for her child in the way she moved, a lot of her easy grace missing from her step. He turned to look at Aiden.

"I want ye and the men of Banuilt to keep a verra close watch on all of the women and bairns," he said. "I want Banuilt shut up tight. If the mon sends word to her as to where to meet him, I want his messenger found. I also want to be certain that Lady Triona doesnae go to him."

"Ye think she would go, dinnae ye." Aiden frowned in the direction of his wife and Triona. "I think ye may be verra right about that."

"I am. She has nay doubt that he would hurt Ella if she doesnae do as he demands, and I think she may be right to think so. He kept his bastard daughters at the keep, but he didnae have anything to do with them. They did weel only because of Meg and Gunn."

"They kept the lasses out of his way. Gunn told me that when I asked where they had gone because I had nay seen them but the one time Meg confronted ye. Gunn said they felt it safer for the girls if they didnae trouble Sir John at all."

"And thus remind him that he had bred no son. Go with the women and we shall go and start hunting that bastard as we should have been hunting him before, as the rabid beastie he is."

"He took wee Ella?" Arianna rushed forward to hug Triona. "The mon is more than just a wee bit mad.

Have the men already returned? They can hunt him down." She tugged Triona over to a seat at the table and poured her some cider. "Drink."

Triona drank and was a little surprised when the simple act helped her regain some calm. She sipped the cider and glanced around the great hall, pleased to see that it was empty save for her and Arianna. Not sure how long that would last, she pulled the small note from a pocket in her gown and looked at it.

As she had walked through the wood on her way back to the manor, a man had slipped it to her and disappeared back into the trees before she could utter a word. She had tried to follow him but had given up quickly, finding no sign of him and not skilled enough at following a trail to know what to look for. Sir John had wasted no time in telling her where to meet him. She suspected he knew any men at Banuilt would ride out to try to hunt him down, and used that to slip her the information as to where she should meet him to trade herself for Ella.

"What is that?" asked Arianna as she sat down next to Triona.

"'Tis the instructions as to where to meet Sir John and trade myself for my daughter," Triona replied as she read it again.

"Ye cannae go and meet that mon alone."

"Nay alone. He allows me to bring three women with me to handle the child and get her back home safely. I am nay sure why he specifies three women for one child, but mayhap 'tis but monly ignorance about what is needed. He says again that he will hurt her, that I risk her verra life if I try any tricks and dinnae do exactly as he says. He had this weel planned. I expected there to be some time between his taking my bairn and getting this message, but his mon caught me and gave me this on my way back from the field where Ella was taken."

"Ye cannae go, Triona. Ye cannae trust the mon."

"Och, I dinnae trust him at all. Nay as far as I can spit. But I will go. He has my child, Arianna. He has my wee Ella. A mon who isnae quite right in the head and who has always looked at her as if she offends him by merely breathing has my child. Aye, I will go."

"Oh, Tri, this cannae end weel," Arianna murmured and grasped Triona by the hand. "I do understand, though. But, wouldnae it be better to wait until the men return?"

"Ye think they will return here? They are out hunting Sir John to try to rescue Ella. Why would they return here?"

"Fresh horses if naught else. They are still riding the ones they rode from Gormfeurach. Or one of them could realize that they are doing just what Sir John wants them to, riding off to search and leaving ye alone to get that message. It would but take one of them to let his thoughts veer for a moment from the need to find Ella, and every one of them is clever enough to realize this could all be a trick to get ye alone so ye can go to Sir John without a guard at your heels."

Triona had to agree that that was a real possibility.

"Nay matter when they return, I will be gone by then. I can only hope that the men can follow my trail."

"He means for ye to meet him that quickly? Does he nay fear he will be found by our men? Ye would think he would hide and wait a wee while just to be safe."

"Ye would think so, but I believe he will again have a priest with him, and he means to get the marriage done as quickly as possible. That was what he did last time he grabbed me, and I believe he has the same idea in mind this time. Mayhap he is mad enough to think that will mend everything or shield him in some way from our men when they do find him. I dinnae ken why he would think he would be safer if he were wed to me, but he could think it would help him with Sir Mollison."

"Where are ye to meet with him then?"

"I cannae tell ye, and please dinnae press me to do so. That, too, is written here. And I truly believe the mon would ken if I told someone. I dinnae ken how it is, but he does seem to learn far too much about what is happening round here. I think there may be someone telling him things, and I shall find out who when this is done. It could be a traitor or it could be just some foolish lass telling things to a lover, who then runs back to Sir John. For now, I just need to find a way to slip out of here, collect three women from the village, and go to meet him." She frowned. "Although I doubt he himself will be waiting for me at this place. He will let some hirelings make the exchange, in case our men are near or following me.

Better those hirelings suffer than he does. That would be his way."

Arianna cursed softly and rubbed her hands over her face. "Can ye slip out? All the Banuilt men are here and preparing to keep a verra close eye on ye. They intend to shut this place up verra tightly."

"I ken it and, aye, I can slip out. I found ways when I first came here." She shrugged when Arianna frowned at her. "My father was a mon who was quick with his fists if ye angered him, and I learned ways to ne'er be easily found. The moment I came here with Boyd I looked for ways to ne'er be found here, to get away and hide if I needed to. I ne'er really needed to, as Boyd wasnae a mon who got angry or used his fists on a woman." She grimaced. "He wasnae so kind with his words, however, though the criticisms were always spoken in a gentle, almost fatherly voice."

"I ken weel how words can destroy. So ye can get out, but can ye get a few women to slip away with ye without anyone kenning it?"

"I believe so. The men are all here right now, preparing to make sure I dinnae leave and that all is readied to protect all of us if the need arises. There will be few men in the village, and I ken how to slip into Joan's house. Boyd didnae approve of my friendship with her, so I made certain he didnae ken just how often I visited her. There are ponies there as weel that we can use. It willnae be easy, but it can be done, especially if I do it now while everyone is busy readying themselves for trouble."

"Then go, and quickly. Aye, go before I think too

much on how angry Brett will be when he finds out ye have gone to meet that mon."

"I am sorry ye will have to face him, but I suspicion it willnae be too bad. Brian willnae let it be."

"Go now, Tri, and be verra careful. Ye are dealing with a madmon."

Triona nodded and left the great hall. It was going to be difficult to get out of Banuilt, but she had to try. The men were very busy trying to lock her in, and might not think she would even consider leaving. She only hoped that, for once, luck would be with her. She did not want her child left in Sir John's hands any longer than was absolutely necessary.

Brett stared down at the ground, wondering why he was finding it so difficult to fix his mind on the hunt. Something was gnawing at him, making his thoughts veer from what he needed to do. Then his confused thoughts began to clear and he cursed, the swirl of ideas, suspicions, and worries settling into one clear revelation. Fear for both Triona and Ella crowded his heart and mind and he fought it back. If what he now believed was true, he was going to need a clear head, and fear did not allow for such a thing.

"We need to go back to Banuilt," he told Brian, who rode beside him, reining in when Brett suddenly did.

"Why? The trail leads this way," Brian said.

"I ken it, although I begin to think Sir John has learned how to lay a false trail. It would explain why we have hunted for him for so long and nay caught him. We are too good to be failing this badly. Fell victim to our own arrogance, probably. We just didnae expect him to be as good as he is at eluding us. But that isnae what troubles me now. Nay, I think we need to go back because this is just what he wanted us to do."

As the others noticed that they had stopped and began to gather around, Brian shook his head. "I am nay understanding ye. Of course the mon has to ken that we would hunt him down. We have been doing that for most of the time we have been here, save when we were looking for the Banuilt men. And this time he has stolen a child."

"Aye, we are hunting him, which means Triona is nay being watched by us. Aye, I ken the Banuilt men have gone to watch for any trouble and keep the women and children safe, but they will need a wee bit of time to get ready to do that—to gather together at Banuilt, arm themselves, and secure it against anyone who might try to get in. This isnae what was expected, and some of them are still nay at full strength and willnae be for a while. Unless someone thought to put a guard on Triona from the moment we rode off, I suspicion she will be alone a time or two ere the true watch on her and the others begins. Aye, she may even have been alone during the time she was returning from the fields."

"And they may nay ken just what a woman is capable of when her bairn is in danger." Brian cursed. "Ye think he planned this. Planned for us to ride out to hunt him and has already sent her word as to where to meet him."

"I do. The mon probably wrote the letter even before Ella was taken, telling Triona where to meet him, and put it in the hand of some hireling who was ready to slip it to her at any moment that was provided to him. One mon with the right skills would nay be seen amongst the confusion that the loss of Ella caused. He kenned that for just a brief time the men of Banuilt would be busy preparing to protect the women and bairns, and she could slip away if told where to meet him."

"So we return to Banuilt and do what? Shut the lass up in the dungeons?"

"'Tis a thought," Brett muttered, even as he turned his mount to begin the ride back to Banuilt. "She is terrified for the safety of wee Ella. She willnae think of anything but doing what must be done to get that child out of that mon's hands." He looked at his men. "Harcourt, Callum, I want ye to go to the village."

"To see if we can catch the lass?" asked Harcourt.

"If I am right, she is already gone, but if ye happen to see her, make verra certain she cannae slip away from ye. Nay, I am sending ye there because I think we may be able to pick up the mon's trail near the village. If nay his, then Triona's. She cannae just walk out of the manor, so she will have to slip into the village, out of sight of the guard at the manor, and then head to the meeting place."

"And there will be signs that she has done so even

if the men havenae noticed yet," said Callum. "We will find a trail for ye."

Harcourt nodded and rode off toward the village, Callum close at his heels. Brett prayed they would be lucky enough to catch Triona before she went to meet Sir John, but he did not hold out much hope for that. He now felt certain that the word about where and when to meet with Sir John had been given to Triona at some time during her journey in from the fields. If Sir John had carefully planned all of this, the man would make certain that she had to act quickly. And she would. Even as he spurred his mount toward Banuilt, Brett was certain he would not find her there.

Chapter Fifteen

"She did what?"

Arianna fought down the urge to step back from all the fury Brett did nothing to hide. Out of the corner of her eye she saw her husband move to stand beside her and glare at Brett. The rage her cousin revealed interested her even as it made her uneasy. It confirmed her opinion that Brett felt far more than lust for Triona. No man could be so angry or afraid if the woman concerned was no more than a lover he could easily walk away from. She hoped he would be smart enough to understand what he could have with the woman if he would just find the courage to reach for it.

"She got word about where to meet Sir John and when," Arianna replied. "She then went to meet him just as he asked."

"I told her nay to give him what he wanted."

"Aye, and ye should nay be so surprised that she didnae heed your command. The mon has her bairn, Cousin, and she cannae e'en fool herself into thinking he wouldnae hurt that wee lass if her mother ignores his orders. Considering all else the mon has done, the way he cared nothing for how his prisoners fared or how what he did here could have starved women and children, I didnae think he would hesitate to kill that bonnie child, either."

"This will give him all he wanted, all of Banuilt in his grasp." *And Triona in his bed*, his mind whispered, but Brett pushed that thought away, knowing it could easily drive him to do something rash.

"And just how long do ye think he would hold it? E'en if Triona or one of his people didnae end his miserable life, his own liege laird has condemned him. The mon just isnae thinking clearly if he feels his scheme will work. E'en if he gets her married to him before ye find him, that will nay change his liege laird's mind, nay after all he has done."

Brett tilted his head back, staring up at the ceiling of the great hall as he took several deep breaths to calm himself. He knew some of his fury came from his inability to find Sir John and kill him. The hunt for the man had become a tedious, enraging, and futile waste of time. It was maddening that the man contin-ued to be so successful at hiding. Brett had to believe that there was some cunning criminal past in the man's life that explained Sir John's uncommon skill. If he had not been so eager to kill the man, he would take the time to find out what that past was.

Although it was tenuous, Brett decided his grip on calm was strong enough to allow him to speak to Arianna again. "Did she tell ye where she was to go to meet him?"

"Nay. She dared nay. She feared it would put Ella in danger." Arianna sighed. "I didnae press her because she asked me nay to and I kenned she wouldnae give me e'en the smallest of hints. She also reminded me that the mon has shown an uncanny ability to ken everything that is going on here. Something she intends to look into later. And she said it wouldnae matter anyway, as she verra much doubted it would be any more than a place to trade her for Ella, a trade that will be made by hirelings."

"Just in case we are actually close enough to stop it, the mon would want to be as far out of our reach as possible. It would have given us a place to start, a place where we might find a trail to follow, however."

"Then ye can ask the women she took with her when they return to Banuilt with Ella."

"She took others with her?"

"Aye, three. They are to collect wee Ella and get her safely back home. The mon obviously had enough sense to realize such consideration for the child's safe return would work to get Triona to do as he asked. She did wonder why he thought it needed three women to do that but decided it just revealed his ignorance about how one cares for a child."

"True, they could help, but as we wait for the women to return, Sir John has time to get Triona far away from here," he snapped. "I suspicion he had the sense to ken that, too."

"Brett," Brian warned, putting his arm around Arianna.

Brett held up his hands and then dragged them

through his hair. "Pardon, Arianna. 'Tis just that the hunt for this mon has near to driven me mad. E'en Harcourt, who is as skilled a tracker as ye could e'er find, cannae sniff out a clear trail. Now Sir John has Triona, who has always been the prize he sought. And, aye, he cannae hold what he gains, as he is a condemned mon, nay better than the meanest of outlaws, but to take it back from him will cost blood, and Triona will be right in the middle of that danger."

And the man would waste no time in consummating the forced marriage, Brett thought, and gritted his teeth against the urge to bellow out his fury. Triona was a lot stronger than even she realized, but no woman could survive that sort of violation without scars. He knew he had to push the thought of his Triona being hurt in such a way out of his mind, and keep it out of there, or he would be useless to her.

"We will find her, Brett," Arianna said. "And if he hurts her or that child, every mon, woman, and child at Banuilt will be his sworn enemy. I have seen that, despite their liege laird's doubts, everyone here sees Triona as their laird, and she has their loyalty and love. As does that wee lass. And since Sir John has already turned near all of his own people against him, and his liege laird as weel, there is nowhere he can rest easy. Nay, nor can he hire enough swords to guard his back, for he is already a condemned mon. 'Tis little help, I ken it, but 'tis something to keep in mind, aye?"

"Aye, it is." Brett kissed her cheek. "It may mean a lot of people are at the ready to kill him but, e'en more important, it means there will be a lot of people ready to aid Triona." He sighed. "Now we can only wait until the women return with Ella."

"We can do that in the village," said Brian. "Harcourt and Callum may have found something by now."

"Aye. It would be nice if luck was on our side for once."

"This is madness," muttered Joan as she rode her pony up next to Triona's.

"This is for my bairn," Triona said. "I have no other choice in this and I think ye ken it."

"Och, I ken it weel enough. I would do the same." Joan lightly brushed her hand over her belly. "I am thinking I will soon have a fuller knowledge of what ye are suffering now."

"Joan? Ye are with child? Wheesht, how can ye tell so soon? Aiden hasnae been home all that long."

"True, but weak as he was, he was capable of celebrating his freedom," she drawled. "I am nay sure I am with child just yet, but everything within me says it is true. 'Tis a feeling in my heart and mind, one I truly believe my body will confirm within a fortnight."

"Then ye shouldnae have come with me. This could be dangerous."

"Nay, this is where I must be. And I dinnae think it will be dangerous for any of us. The mon doesnae want Ella. He doesnae want we women, either. He wants ye. He will think himself weel rid of the burden of the child when he hands her over to us. I have but one fear."

"Oh, aye? What is it?" Triona could think of far too many things to fear at the moment, including the chance that she was leading three women straight into the heart of danger.

"How does the mon think to keep us women from telling anyone where we left ye?"

Fear surged through Triona's body and she needed a few minutes to beat it down. "There are many ways. I doubt he means to stay in the place where this trade is going to be made. And I think he would have told me to come alone if he feared ye would be any threat to him. Nay, I believe he means to hand over Ella, grab me, and flee. He only told me to bring women to collect Ella because he kenned I would need that assurance of her safety, and he thinks us all too dim-witted and useless, save to serve men. Probably why he thinks it needs three of ye to take one wee lass home. He only sees a mon as a threat."

Joan slowly nodded. "I suspicion ye said most of that to convince yourself, but I think ye are right all the same. The mon simply willnae worry that we poor foolish women could e'er be a threat to him." She pointed to a small cairn that had marked the far northern edge of Banuilt land for more years than any knew. "And there is where we will discover if ye are right."

They did not have to wait long. Triona suspected the five men who rode up to them had been watching for them. She saw no sign of her daughter or Sir John, but before she could demand to know where Ella was, four of the men rode up beside her and each of her women and thrust strips of dark cloth at them.

"Put them on and then we will go and fetch your whelp," said the big, black-bearded man watching the others.

Silently cursing, Triona tied the cloth over her eyes, knowing her women were doing the same. Rough hands tugged at it as the man beside her made certain that she was truly blinded. She did not like this but could see no way to avoid it. The simple trade she had expected had suddenly become more complicated and dangerous. As a jerk on the reins started her pony moving, she prayed that she had not brought her women to their deaths.

It was no surprise to her that Sir John was not the first one she would meet, although she had hoped otherwise. The man would stay safely out of reach to be certain there was no one behind her ready to attack him. There was still a chance he would be where the trade would actually be made, but she was beginning to doubt that as well. He had revealed a marked preference for his own people and his hirelings to do most of the work and take most of the risks.

The ride was rough, and she was forced to cling tightly to her pony's mane to stay in the saddle. It was mercifully short, however. Just about the time she thought she would cry out if her bottom bounced on the saddle one more time, the journey ended. When the horses stopped and the cloth was taken from her eyes, she had to blink several times before she could see clearly. Her heart sank when she did not recognize the place. Nor did she see Sir John, only two more men as rough as the ones leading the ponies.

"Mama!"

Ignoring the curses of the man holding her pony's reins, Triona dismounted and ran to catch her daughter up in her arms when the child darted out from behind one of the men. She then kneeled down and looked the child all over, and much of her fear eased when she found no wounds. There was a red mark on Ella's cheek, which told her someone had slapped the little girl, however. It took Triona a moment to quell her anger over that, knowing it would serve no purpose to let it show. She kissed Ella's bruised cheek.

"Have ye come to take me home?" asked Ella, glancing warily at the five men guarding them. "I didnae like being taken away. It was my turn to be the scary monster."

"I ken it, love. Ye can play the game the next time we go to the fields."

"Give her over to the women now," ordered the bearded man. "We cannae sit here any longer."

Those words made Triona determined to eke out every minute she could, even as she doubted it would be much more than a few. If the men feared pursuit, she wished to give those hunting for her as much of an advantage as she could. Standing up, she picked Ella up and walked over to Joan.

"I didnae like the mon who came before ye did, Mama," said Ella as Triona settled her in the saddle

in front of Joan. "It was Sir John Grant, and he gave
me that mean look again. I told him ye were going to
come and cut him into wee pieces and feed him to the
ravens, and he slapped me."

"I will remember that, loving," Triona said, and idly
wondered where her little girl had learned such
bloodthirsty talk. "Have nay fear."

"Ye havenae got on your pony so I can ride with ye."
She glanced over her shoulder at Joan. "I love ye,
Joan, but I want to ride with my mother now."

"Joan is going to take ye home, love," Triona said.
"I must go and speak to the mon who slapped ye. He
needs to be told to ne'er do it again."

"And then ye will come home?"

"Aye, love." Triona turned to face the men, noticing how nervously the other six watched the area all
around them while the bearded man glared at her.
"Ye need to tell my women how to get back on the
path to Banuilt."

"They can find their own way," the bearded man
snapped and pointed at her pony. Get back on the
pony. We must leave now!"

"It could be verra dangerous if they got lost."

"If they get lost I am certain someone will be able
to set them on the right path. Get on the pony."

She was tempted to run but then saw how the other
men moved closer to the three women and Ella, their
hands on their swords. "Such brave men to be afraid
of women," she grumbled as she mounted the pony.
"'Tis nay as if they are any threat to ye."

"Go," the bearded man ordered Joan and the others.

Triona saw the women hesitate and nodded. "Go on, Joan. Get wee Ella home."

"M'lady—" began Joan.

"Nay. This is how it must be. Take Ella to safety."

She was watching the women ride off when the bearded man yanked on her reins and they were riding hard in the opposite direction. Triona suspected she was on Gormfeurach land, but she could not be sure. She rode the boundaries of Banuilt every year but never ventured inside the Gormfeurach land on her western border. If she was gifted with some miracle and got away from these men, she would be thoroughly lost within a very short time. She had to wonder if that was Sir John's intent.

Fear tried to rear up and tie knots in her belly, but she fought it down. Her child was safe now, and that was all that mattered. Sir John did not intend to kill her, just marry her. He would have to keep her alive for a while after that, as well, if only to prove he did have a wife who gave him rights to Banuilt. There was time for her to try to escape. She just prayed it would be before Sir John forced her to consummate their marriage.

The thought of such a thing made her stomach roil. It would be rape, for she would never willingly accept that man into her body. Triona was not sure how well she would survive such an assault. Worse, she feared what it would do to her memories of her time with Brett. She doubted that, if he rescued her, she would be falling back into bed with him anytime soon, not even for one more night before he left Banuilt. Her husband had been cold, giving her no pleasure at all, but she had accepted it as her wifely duty; but she knew she would never be able to accept Sir John if he dragged her to his bed.

Forcing all thoughts of that aside, Triona tried to convince herself that there was a chance she would be rescued before a marriage could happen. She refused to allow herself to recall all the times Brett and the others had not been able to catch Sir John; rather she chose to remember the time they had rescued her before and had rescued her garrison. It gave her the small thread of hope she needed as they rode into a small camp and she saw Sir John standing there.

When he strode over and pulled her out of the saddle, she struggled to keep on her feet. That struggle ended after he dragged her before a tall, gaunt man and shoved her down onto the ground. When she attempted to rise he held her there so that she could only get up on her knees.

"Lady Triona, meet Father Mure," said Sir John. "He is about to marry us."

Triona took one look into the priest's eyes and knew she would find no ally there.

"I cannae believe no one saw four women ride out on ponies," said Brett as he and the others followed the trail Harcourt had found.

"Women can be verra stealthy when they have good

reason to be," said Brian. "Saving her child would be seen as a good reason."

Brett cursed, for Brian was right. From what little Triona had told him of her father and her husband, he also suspected she had learned young how to be stealthy. A child who has a parent with a heavy fist either crumbles beneath the weight of it or learns ways to escape it until old enough to walk away. She had walked away into a cold marriage, but he suspected most days she found that preferable. And she had called Ella her bright light in that marriage. Sir John had threatened that bright light, and Brett knew Triona would do anything to retrieve Ella and get the child to safety.

"And there are the women," said Callum pointing off into the distance in front of them.

"Jesu, the mon has eyes like a hawk," grumbled Brian.

It took a moment before Brett could see what Callum did, and he had to agree with Brian. Riding toward them were three women on little sturdy ponies. In front of one of the women was a small child with hair bright enough to be seen from such a distance. He nudged his mount into a trot along with the others, and they quickly closed the distance between them and the women.

"Och, thank ye, God," said Joan. "I feared we were going in the wrong direction."

"Nay, I told ye we had to go this way," said Ella, and then she smiled and waved her fingers at Brett. "Greetings, Sir Brett. Have ye come to lead us home?"

"Nay, lass, but there are a few Banuilt men here that will do so," he said, and nodded at the three young men who moved to flank the women. "We need to go and find your mother."

"Then ye must go back the way we came. I can show ye, if ye like."

"Nay, lass, it would be best if ye stay with Joan. We may have to do a wee bit of fighting when we get to where your mother is."

"Are ye going to cut up the mon who hit me and feed him to the ravens?" She touched a bruise on her check.

"Mayhap I will. So, ye be a good wee lass and we will bring your mother home soon."

"Just go back the way we came," she said. "Follow my wee rocks."

Brett joined Joan in staring at the child. "Your wee rocks?"

"Aye. When they took me I had my pockets full of them, so I dropped them as we rode away from my mother. She taught me that. She said it would help me find my way home if I got lost. She showed me how to see things right and clear, like trees and cairns, so I could see the path home, and told me to mark it if I wanted. So I marked it. With my wee stones. I didnae want the hairy men to get me lost."

"Ye saw Sir John Grant? Met with him somewhere?"

"Aye. The hairy men took me to him and he was under the big crooked tree with the eagle's nest. He hit me because I told him my mother would cut him into pieces and feed him to the ravens." She glanced up at Joan. "That is what Angus says ye do to bad men." She looked back at Brett. "Then he made the hairy men take me away and I thought we were going back home, but then they stopped and we waited and then my mother came, but she gave me to Joan and rode away with the bad men. I hope they didnae ride on my stones." She frowned. "I liked my stones, but now I lost them."

Brett watched Callum ride up next to Joan, lean down, and, turning Ella's face up to his, kiss her bruised cheek and smile at her. "Ye will have more stones soon, lass. Ye are a verra clever wee lass and should have all the wee stones ye want."

"Wheesht, the mon can charm e'en the wee ones," Brian said as Ella looked up at Callum through her lashes and blushed.

If he had not been so concerned for Triona's safety, Brett knew he would have laughed. Instead he studied the little girl who so blithely told them she had left them a trail that would lead them straight to Sir John. She was not his child, and yet his heart swelled with pride.

"Thank ye for your help, Ella," he said. "Ye have made it much easier for us to find your mother and bring her home."

"I did?" She sat up straight and looked from Callum to Brett and back again. "I helped?"

"Aye, lass, ye helped a lot. Now, go with Joan and we will bring your mother home soon. I promise ye that."

"If I have been so helpful, can I have a kitten?"

It surprised him but he actually had to swallow a laugh. "Best ye wait and ask your mother." He pretended not to see her slump and push her bottom lip out in a pout.

A moment later the women were riding off with the three young men from Banuilt. Ella peered around Joan and waved at him. Brett waved back and then turned his attention to Callum, who was slowly riding back the way the women had come, his gaze fixed upon the ground.

"Wee stones?" Brett asked as he rode up beside Callum.

"Aye, and spaced just right." He briefly grinned at Brett before returning his gaze to the ground. "She was verra careful in dropping them as they rode, just to be sure she could find the path home. Verra clever wee lass."

"I am nay sure I wish to ken why her mother felt a need to teach her such a trick."

"Nay, although it was a verra wise thing to do, even if nothing bad prompted the lesson. That child has a natural instinct for it, for following a trail and marking one. She will ne'er get lost. And did ye nay hear how she marked where Sir John is?"

Brett slowly smiled. "Aye, I did. A big crooked tree with an eagle's nest atop it. A keen eye on the lass. To see something like that she truly had to be studying everything around her as they rode. And Sir John's men wouldnae have kenned it, would ne'er have thought it necessary to cover a child's eyes to hide where they were going."

"Their ignorance becomes our good luck."

For the first time since he discovered that Triona had gone to meet with Sir John, Brett felt the soothing touch of hope. Not only did they now have the means to find her but also a very good chance of finding her before she was wed to the man. Even if they could not stop the wedding, he was confident they could stop it from being consummated.

"We will find Lady Triona, Brett, and we will kill that bastard Grant," said Callum. "For all wee Ella's smiles and cleverness, I could see that he put a touch of fear in that child's eyes. When she spoke of the slap, it flickered there for a moment. With but a moment or two of his time, he bruised her wonderful happiness and sense of being loved and safe. For that alone I want him dead."

"I, too, want him dead. I saw what ye saw, even though I was rather stunned at the moment by how easily she spoke, giving us just what we needed to find her mother. Aye, and I want him dead for how he has treated the people of Banuilt, what he did to all those Banuilt men he tossed into that peel tower and forgot about, and even for how he has crushed the hearts of the people on his own lands and left them so uncertain of their future. And for what?" he asked as he and Callum continued to follow the trail. "A piece of land his forefathers lost through utter stupidity."

Just thinking on all of Sir John's crimes stirred

Brett's fury to life. The man had become a poison to what had been a peaceful area in a country that too often knew little peace. While it was true that the people of Banuilt and Gormfeurach were not clans as his family kenned clans, they were close enough. They were certainly bonded to each other as those in a clan would be, save by blood. The knights who had founded each place had chosen well, and the lairds that had come before Sir John and Sir Boyd had been open to accepting anyone who wished to join, to help build and help protect the place. They had also chosen a place that was remote enough that it had known more years of peace than war.

And he loved it all almost as much as he loved Triona McKee. Brett nearly smiled as he felt the acceptance of that truth flow through him. He would end the threat of Sir John, get Triona safely home, and then he would find some way to return to her and Banuilt. He now knew that it was the only way he could ever be truly happy.

Chapter Sixteen

"Forgive him, Father. He is a grave sinner and kens nay better."

Triona clenched her teeth against a cry of pain when Sir John slapped her for what she had said. He did so with such a cold calm it was terrifying. She wondered if that was how he had slapped her child, and feared it would leave as big a bruise on Ella's soft, innocent heart as it had on her face. The priest the man had dragged her to after binding her hands together at the wrists looked at her with icy contempt, making it clear that he felt she had just gotten exactly what she deserved. She smothered the urge to stick her tongue out at him, even though it was a mild reaction compared to what she wanted to do to Sir John.

"Are ye certain ye wish to wed with such an impudent woman?" the priest asked.

"She has the land that I want, Father Mure," replied Sir John. "This is the only way left to me to get it. Struth, this is the only way to end the trouble she has caused me."

Triona nearly gaped at the man, unable to believe he could blame her for the mess he was now in. Yet, studying his face she could see that he had convinced himself that it was indeed all her fault. She doubted she would ever understand how he could have come to that conclusion. In her mind, it was just more proof that the man was probably mad.

Father Mure looked her over in a way that made Triona feel unclean. "She may be too old to give ye a son."

It was undoubtedly a sin, but Triona desperately wanted to punch the priest right in the mouth. She could barely believe it, but she may have finally found a priest more contemptuous of women than the one that had served at Banuilt before the fever had taken him. She made a sudden, fierce promise to herself and to all the other women at Banuilt. When she got free—and she refused to believe she would do otherwise—and returned as laird of Banuilt, she would make very certain that any priest who replaced theirs did not see all women as weak, sinful, and worthy of nothing but contempt. There had to be one out there somewhere.

"I am but five and twenty," she snapped.

"Married for six years and yet ye gave your husband but one child. A girl."

The way Father Mure said *a girl*, he might as well have said *a demon from hell*. His tone of voice made Ella, the greatest gift Triona had ever received, sound like the worst of failures. Triona was not surprised at how angry that made her, but she was a little shocked to hear herself growl and start to rise to her feet, her hands clenched into tight fists. She cursed when Sir John grabbed her by the shoulder so tightly she could not completely smother a gasp of pain, and then pushed her back down onto her knees.

"I dinnae suppose it would occur to ye big, strong, monly men that the bearing of children is as much the mon's responsibility as the woman's," Triona said. "'Tis his seed used in the planting, aye? Mayhap it was Boyd's fault that I had only the one child and ne'er gave him a son. Mayhap he nay had more than my wee Ella in him."

Father Mure and Sir John stared at her in shock. Triona was not sure if they were shocked by her angry words or by her suggestion that a man could be at fault for such a thing. She could almost see that shock slowly turn into outrage, however, and braced herself for some retribution. Men like them did not like to be contradicted. She had learned that lesson well from her own father.

"Aye, and mayhap making Ella was one of the greatest things Boyd e'er did," she added, and smiled, not caring how they made her suffer for speaking what they probably saw as near sacrilege.

"The laird of Banuilt obviously didnae teach ye how a proper, godly wife should act," said Father Mure.

Triona still found it nearly impossible to believe, but Father Mure was even worse than Banuilt's old priest had been in his contemptuous beliefs about women. There was no more doubt in her mind. Although she could not recall the priest her family had dealt with when she was growing up and had no clear memory of him spouting such hard words, she knew he had never done anything to stop the sometimes brutal way her father treated her and her mother, which made her think the man had been of the same ilk as these two. Both of the men glaring at her right now apparently chose to ignore the fact that Banuilt had been run mostly by women for almost two years and would have done very well if not for Sir John's many attempts to destroy it. Every single thing that had brought her close to failing had been Sir John's doing.

"Are ye absolutely certain there is no other way for ye to gain hold of Banuilt?" asked the priest. "I cannae believe our liege laird wishes it to be held by a woman. It goes against all the laws of God and mon. Mayhap I should go and speak to him for ye."

"It willnae work. The mon honors Sir Boyd's choice."

"I used to serve our liege laird . . ."

"Before he sent ye to me. I ken it. It still doesnae matter. The laird honors Sir Boyd's last will. So the only way for me to get Banuilt is to marry this bitch." Sir John glared at Triona. "Dinnae worry, though. After the way she has sullied herself with that bastard Murray, I dinnae mean to keep her for long."

"Are ye certain ye should be telling the mon that?" Triona asked, even as she wondered how he knew what she had been doing with Brett. "He is a priest and all that. Nay sure ye should be talking to him about your plans to murder me. I may be one of those poor female creatures he appears to think near useless, but murder is murder nay matter who is the victim."

"Did I say I planned to kill ye? I dinnae recall saying anything about murder."

"And I didnae hear him say that, either," said Father Mure. "I did hear, howbeit, that ye, a widow of nay e'en two years, has nay kept herself chaste as is right and proper. It may be past time that ye enter confession and do a penance."

"And I begin to think that ye are as mad as Sir John," Triona said.

It did not really surprise her when Sir John hit her again. It did anger her, however. Triona did not think she had ever been so angry before, and yet within moments after falling into the hands of these two men, she had tasted that fierce anger twice already. She had always considered Sir John Grant vain and spoiled, but she now realized he was far worse. He was a cold brute, one who could deal out pain and cruelty without a twitch of true emotion. She suspected he did not simply see women as something beneath him or view them with disdain. He hated them.

"There is no respect in her for the superiority of men," muttered Father Mure. "She doesnae ken her proper place at all. I am certain our laird, Sir Mollison, would quickly change his mind about all of this if he but kenned what a disrespectful little whore she is."

"Too late," said Triona. "The laird has already given this disrespectful little whore, who just happens to be the laird of Banuilt, the full right to seek whate'er justice she deems needed against Sir John Grant for the kidnapping and imprisonment of my entire garrison. It seems our laird doesnae like it when one of his supplicants nearly destroys a large force of fighting men—good fighting men, allies who have weel proven their worth. There are other crimes too numerous to list, which I now hope the laird will listen to, but what Sir John did to my garrison is what made the laird cast him aside and take away all protection." She saw the priest frown. "Did ye nay ken what Sir John did to my men?"

"Nay, but it doesnae matter," replied Father Mure. "They were, and are, just common men. I am but surprised that our liege laird would discard a weel-born knight like Sir John for such a reason. Men who can swing a sword can be found or bought anywhere, but a true knight of good blood is worthy of more care. I am certain I can change Sir Mollison's mind about heeding all your charges and putting his knight in a state of disgrace. I refuse to believe the mon would hold firm to his mad decision to give a mere woman the right to mete out justice."

Triona barely stopped herself from gaping at the man. Then she decided it was undoubtedly such thinking that got the priest sent away from the laird's lands to languish in the much poorer church at Gormfeurach. Sir Mollison might hold much the same disregard for her as too many other men did, refusing to accept her word over that of a man, but she was very certain that he valued good fighting men like the ones in Banuilt's garrison, common born or not. It was what Sir John had done to those men that had finally caused Sir Mollison to heed her charges against Sir John. Any fool should be able to see that the laird would not be made to change his mind.

"Let us get this done," snapped Sir John. "I wish to have this marriage blessed and consummated before nightfall. Where shall we do this?" He grabbed Triona by the arm and tried to pull her to her feet, only to find himself hanging on to a woman who was as limp as soaking-wet linen.

Something Triona had learned from her father as a way to avoid another blow from his heavy fists was to go completely limp. Not only did he then have some difficulty getting her into a position to strike another blow, but he had had no interest in brutalizing someone who did not appear to be conscious enough to suffer from it. Her mother, long cowed by her father and believing the man could do no wrong, had lectured her on the habit, telling her to stop, but Triona had not heeded her. Now, years of playing that game gave her the skill to remain limp even when Sir John shook her.

"She has swooned," said Father Mure. "Overcome by maidenly fear, I should think."

Overcome by revulsion, Triona thought, and prayed that someone would come and find her soon. The game of going limp had worked with her father because he had given up fairly quickly, but Sir John was in no position to do that. She was not sure how long she could hold off the forced marriage with such a trick. *Any delay is a good one,* she told herself, *for it gives time for someone to come and get me free of this nightmare.*

Brett paused when Harcourt did and then looked around. They were riding for a place not far from where Sir John had imprisoned the garrison. This part of Gormfeurach land was obviously remote and unpeopled enough for the man to do as he pleased without worrying about being seen or caught. He began to wonder if there were even more crimes Sir John was guilty of, ones he had committed in this lonely place with the surety that they would never be uncovered.

"More wee rocks. The child must have been fair weighted down with them," said Callum. "Ye would have thought whoever grabbed her would have noticed that she was a bit heavier than she ought to be."

"And there sits the eagle nest in the crooked tree," said Brian, looking upward.

Following the man's gaze, Brett had to shake his head. It would not have been easy for a small child to have seen such a thing unless she was working hard to notice everything around her. Little Ella had learned her lesson about seeing things right to find a path home very well indeed.

Uven hurried up to them on foot. He had taken the chore of slipping ahead of them, into the trees, to see if he could better judge what was in advance of them. With Triona's life at stake, Brett could not afford any surprises.

"They are just inside those trees," he said, pointing into the thickest section of the woods just beyond the crooked tree with the eagle's nest. "There are about ten men as weel as Sir John, and a tall, thin mon I suspect is a priest. Triona was looking just fine, but a moment before I turned to come back here, she went limp."

"Ye think she is hurt?" asked Brett, holding back his fear for her with difficulty.

"I saw neither mon touch her. Sir John grabbed her and was trying to get her to move toward a place to the left, and she just went limp. He cannae move her, and the mon I think is a priest suggested that she may have swooned."

"Triona doesnae swoon."

"But she has learned that 'tis far more difficult to be forced to do something when she is naught but a wet rag in his hands," said Brian, who shrugged when the others looked at him. "Had a brother who did that whene'er the rest of us looked to be eager to thrash him. He had a limp, ye see, and couldnae run fast." He grinned. "He stopped doing it after the time we simply picked him up and threw him in the pig's wallow."

"Ye would beat on a person with a limp?"

"It was just a wee one, and he was one of those brothers that just seems to beg ye to thrash him every time he opens his mouth." He unsheathed his sword. "Shall we go and save your lady?"

Brett shook his head, unsheathed his own sword, and nodded. "Sir John is mine."

* * *

Triona winced as Sir John began to drag her along the ground. She was about to give up being limp when a bellow cut through the quiet surrounding them. It was a battle cry, and she was sure it was from men coming to save her.

She abruptly ceased to be limp, leaping up on her feet and kicking Sir John in the shins. Triona savored his loud curse of pain, and when his grip on her loosened, she yanked free. Before she could run away, however, the priest grabbed hold of her and she hesitated to hit him. He might be a very bad priest in her opinion, but he was ordained. It was hard to shake the well-taught rules of respect for such a man that her mother had drummed into her head.

"Ye are going nowhere," the man snapped, and dragged her over to a tree.

Ignoring him, Triona looked around just as Brett and the others broke through the surrounding trees into the small clearing. The way the men dismounted, two men quickly grabbing the reins of the horses and moving them out of the way, impressed her. Here was the training she had wanted for her own men. The sight of Brett stole her breath away as well. Tall, strong, his sword held expertly in his hand, he was the brave knight every small girl dreamed of. Triona almost smiled at her own romantic thoughts. After one hard look her way, which she returned with a smile, he turned all of his attention on Sir John.

The other men who had come to rescue her were

busy cutting down Sir John's men and chasing after the ones who had bolted, running for their lives into the forest. A couple of sharp screams of pain told her that they had not managed to get very far. Then she looked at Brian and Callum, who, all the while keeping a watch on Brett, came over to stand in front of her. It was only then that she realized the priest had set her in front of him like a shield.

"Wheesht, what a coward ye are to hide behind the skirts of such a wee lass," she muttered, and could tell by the way the priest clenched his free hand into a fist that her comment had caused his anger to rise.

"I but try to be certain these men dinnae mistakenly kill a mon of the Church, mistaking him for one of the enemy," Father Mure said.

"Nay a mistake," drawled Brian, and grinned at the man. "Ye are a priest willingly helping a mon, declared an outlaw by his own laird, to marry a lass against her will." He poked his sword a little closer and laughed when the priest quickly pulled her more firmly in front of him.

"I am unarmed," Father Mure said.

"But shielded. Ye want me to move the fool, lass?"

"Nay, he is fine where he is." She held out her hands. "I would like these gone, if I might." She stood calmly as he neatly cut through the ropes with his sword. "I dinnae suppose Brett means to capture Sir John alive."

"Nay." Brian did not lower his sword, but he looked where Brett faced Sir John. "He may make him sweat a wee bit first, but he will kill him."

Triona nodded and watched her lover face her enemy. For a moment she feared for Brett, not wishing to see him wounded, or worse. It only took a moment of seeing how he easily and gracefully fended off every swing of Sir John's sword to know that Brian was right. Brett was going to make Sir John sweat a little and then kill him. She knew that should probably trouble her a little, but it did not. She only had to think of her garrison imprisoned for nearly two years for no reason other than this man's greed, and how they must have struggled to survive, losing hope with each passing day that they would ever see the outside again. That was the sort of inhumanity that earned Sir John whatever punishment Brett meant to mete out. She only wished she were a man, just long enough to do it herself.

"Your death should be as slow and painful as the one ye condemned her garrison to," Brett told Sir John, "but I fear I have nay wish to see ye breathe the same air as the rest of us for that long."

"I didnae kill her garrison and ne'er intended to." Sir John grunted when Brett's sword sliced open the front of his jupon, cutting through to split open the skin beneath it. "'Tis nay my fault the guards didnae do what they had been told to. That plan cost me a lot of money."

Brett almost paused to just stare at the man. Sir John was one of those who never accepted blame for anything. He could see it now. He suspected the man even blamed Triona for saying she did not want to marry him for the way he had tried to destroy Banuilt.

They would probably never understand why the man had done all he had, for he did not think clearly or with any sense of the truth.

"I think the people of Gormfeurach will be much better off without ye sitting in the laird's chair," he said, and cut the man's arm.

"So this is why ye mean to murder me, to take what is mine for yourself, just as ye took Lady Triona. She was supposed to be mine. That fool Boyd should ne'er have left her that land, and his error should have been my gain. Instead ye came here and have ruined all my plans."

For a brief moment Sir John fought fiercely, and Brett actually saw the hint of skill in the man's use of his sword. Then he saw how badly the man was sweating, his chest heaving with the effort of continuing the fight. There would be some touch of sweet justice in it if he let the fool fight until he stumbled to his knees and had to stay there trembling, unable to save himself as Brett killed him, but Brett decided he really did not have the stomach for it. If Sir John were a worthy opponent there could have been a sense of victory in it all, but the man was no true warrior, and that would make it a cold slaughter of a weak man.

Despite Brett's decision to be quick about it, Sir John had time to see that he had lost. As Brett drove his sword into the man's chest, Sir John's eyes widened with something that looked much like surprise followed rapidly by sheer terror. Brett pulled his sword free and watched Sir John's body fall to the ground, wondering idly if the man had, in that last breath, caught a glimpse of where his soul was headed. It would certainly not be heaven he saw.

He then looked for Triona and found her standing in front of a tall, thin man who had to be the priest. The man was staring at Sir John in surprise, as if he had believed the man would win. A quick look around told Brett that all of Sir John's hirelings had been killed or captured, so he walked over to stand in front of Triona.

"Why is that mon hiding behind your skirts?" he asked, and very gently touched the bruises forming on her face.

"He is a cowardly priest," she said, "who felt Sir John was doing as he should and that I was just some disrespectful little whore who didnae understand what good fortune had befallen her." She grinned at the look of anger that tightened Brett's expression.

"Were ye hurt in some way?" Brett asked, fighting the urge to beat the man, despite the fact that he was a priest. "Uven said ye had gone limp."

"Aye, just a trick to make it verra hard for someone to get ye to do something they wish ye to do." She saw Sir Brian nod but decided now was not the time to ask why he knew exactly what she was talking about.

"I told ye nay to give him what he wanted," Brett said.

"I ken it, and I was glad ye ne'er asked me to promise ye that I wouldnae go to him. I would have hated to have to lie to you. Do ye ken if Ella and the women made it home safely?"

"Aye, they did. We met them on the way here." Brett told her of how Ella had helped them and smiled at her look of pride. "She thinks she ought to get a kitten for that."

Triona laughed. "Weel, mayhap I will have a look at the kittens in the stables and see if there is one I can abide being treated as if it is a member of the family. Now, I would verra much like to leave this place, but I am nay sure what we should do about this priest."

"I shall need someone to take me back to Gormfeurach," Father Mure said.

"I thought ye might be theirs. Poor people of Gormfeurach. A bad laird and a worse priest. They have been twice cursed."

Father Mure stepped around her to confront her, his face hard with anger. "Ye dinnae understand your place, woman."

"Och, nay, the fool just called her *woman*," muttered Brian.

"Since he has already called me worse, I suppose I shouldnae be surprised. May I?" she asked as she looked at Brett.

Brett noticed how her small hand was curled in a tight fist. "If ye wish."

Triona punched the priest in the mouth so hard he staggered back with a cry. He stared at his hand when he took it away from his mouth and paled at the sight of his own blood. To her astonishment his eyes rolled back and he collapsed on the ground.

"I didnae hit him hard enough for that," she muttered.

"Nay." Brett nudged the priest's body with his foot. "He swooned when he saw his blood on his hand.

Swooned like a wee lass." He started laughing with the other men and slung his arm around Triona's shoulders. "Ye really need to stop hitting priests, love."

"I will do a penance." She turned into his hold and wrapped her arms around his waist, deeply moved when he hugged her back with obvious affection, even though she wished it was more than that. "May we go home now?"

"Aye." He kissed the top of her head before setting her aside. "Just let us clear away the mess and get Sir John's body on his horse."

She nodded and went to her pony. It would not be easy for the little animal to keep up with the men's horses, but there was no need of any great speed. Triona wanted to see with her own eyes that her daughter was safely back at Banuilt, but that was the only pressing need she had. It was going to take her a while to accept that her troubles were now over, at least until a new laird came to Gormfeurach, but she would deal with any problems when they arose.

It took her a moment to wonder why she was not happier. Although she did not wish anyone to die, Sir John would never have given up, and his death did not trouble her at all. Then she realized why there was a growing sadness in her: her troubles were indeed over, and that meant that Brett had no more reason to stay at Banuilt.

Turning away so the men clearing up the bodies in the meadow could not see her face, she fought the sudden urge to weep. He had given her no words of love, just affection and passion. He had made no promises except the one to help rid Banuilt of its troubles, a promise he had fulfilled admirably. Brett, as well as Brian, Arianna, and all the others, had no more reason to stay, and they all would undoubtedly leave soon—and it hurt.

She had tried not to nurse any hope in her heart, but it was evident that her heart had not listened to her and had simply gone its own way. Triona struggled to hide how badly it was breaking. At best she had one more night with her lover. She was not going to spoil it by letting him see her sorrow. There would be plenty of days after he was gone to indulge in that.

When he stepped up, brushed a kiss over her mouth, and then set her in the saddle, she gave him her warmest smile. What little time they had together would not be marred by regrets or unfulfilled wishes. Brett, she decided, was going to be blinded by passion if she had anything to say about it. That way he might miss the hurt she knew she would not be able to hide completely when he said farewell.

Chapter Seventeen

"We will leave in the morning."

Brett looked at Brian and then quickly looked back over the walls of Banuilt. The keen way Brian was watching him was not comfortable. He knew the time to make a firm decision had come, and yet he was still not sure what he wanted, or even needed, to do.

"We will ride with you and Arianna," he said finally and was not surprised to hear Brian curse softly.

Nothing had been said concerning the fact that he had fulfilled his promise to end Triona's troubles and that he would now leave. Not on the whole journey back from where she had nearly been forced to marry Sir John, or after he had come back from taking the priest and Sir John's body to Gormfeurach. If Triona wanted him to stay, she was showing no sign of it, neither trying to nudge him into making any promise nor even just asking him to stay.

And waiting for her to make the first move was the coward's way, he thought, and inwardly grimaced. It

would have helped him with his own unusual inde-
cisiveness, but it would not have been fair to her. He
certainly would not wish to risk being told no to his
face. When he had first taken her to bed, he had more
or less set the boundaries. They were lovers, he would
clear away her problems with Sir John, and then he
would leave. He had given her no hint that that had
ever changed. Why should he expect her to be the
one to do so?

"Are ye still wearing that hair shirt of penance for
the death of that lass?"

"Brenda. Her name was Brenda," said Brett, "and
she wasnae just a lass. She was carrying my bairn, and
I intended to make her my wife. I should ne'er have
played the secret-lover game with her, a game that
soon became verra serious for me. But I should have
been mon enough to go to her father, marched right
up to those gates, and . . ."

"Got kicked right out on your arrogant arse." Brian
held up a hand to silence him when Brett began to
speak. "Ye told me ye had naught to offer her father
for her hand, neither land nor a heavy purse. She was
a weel-dowered lass, aye?"

"Weel, aye, but . . ."

"Bonnie, young, and fulsome, and ready for her
father to choose a mon for her. Nay, ye would have
been verra fortunate if all he had done was beat ye
senseless and toss ye into the mud. Struth, I suspicion
he already had a mon chosen for the lass, one who
could give him something he wanted or needed, and
that is why she insisted on keeping ye such a secret."

"Aye, he did have someone in mind, but naught had been signed and no pledges had been given."

"Doesnae matter. They were undoubtedly still bartering. She kenned it and probably kenned there would be no changing her father's mind, nay for a lad who had a lot of allies, a lot of kin, and nay much else save for a bonnie face. I think she also kenned that she was putting your life at risk when she succumbed to your allure."

Brett opened his mouth to defend what he thought was a somewhat harsh criticism of Brenda, but thought over what Brian had just said. "Succumbed to my allure?" he asked, and frowned at a grinning Brian.

"'Sounds fine, doesnae it?' Arianna bellowed that at me whilst we were still arguing. Something about how badly she wished she had kenned what a heartless bastard I was before she had succumbed to my allure. I liked the sound of that, of her succumbing to my allure."

The man was grinning like a mischievous little boy, and Brett laughed. "She also called ye a heartless bastard."

"I chose to ignore that because she was speaking in anger."

"Of course ye did. And, aye, Brenda kenned I was at risk and probably kenned all else ye think she did. All that doesnae matter. She was but a lass of eighteen who had been weel guarded all of her life. I was nay so innocent. She was coming to meet me that night and we were going to run off together, to marry and raise the bairn she had just discovered she was carrying.

While I waited for her, feeling sorry for myself because she was late and I began to fear she had changed her mind, she was caught by her clan's enemies. Five men beat her, raped her, and left her there in the wood, left her for dead. She crawled the rest of the way to where I sat pouting, then died in my arms."

Brian sighed. "A sad ending, and now I ken where your guilt o'er it all is bred from. Ye, as so many of we men like to do, somehow think ye should have saved her. Should have kenned she was in danger, kenned she was hurt, kenned where it was all happening, and also been able to ride swiftly to her rescue with sword held high. Aye, we men all have moments like that. It shames us when we discover we are nay omnipotent when it comes to the safety of those we love. We all chew o'er the *what if* I had done this or that, or *what if* this had happened instead, when there is a tragedy. Ye were nay there to stop it. Ye were waiting for her as promised. I suspicion ye had nay knowledge that her enemies were close at hand. There is nay wrong there, Brett, only sad mischance."

"I see her," Brett whispered.

"See her? Do ye mean ye see her ghost? Now?"

Brett smiled fleetingly at the way Brian looked all around. "Nay, nay now. I see her when I try to bed down with a lass and seek a wee bit of pleasure. Suddenly there is her ghost, looking sad as she watches me with the woman."

"Jesu, that must be, weel . . ."

"Wilting? Aye, verra much so. If it didnae end all attempts to gain my ease, it certainly stole away the pleasure I may have gained from the act. Even drink didnae banish her, although it occasionally allowed me to gain a little ease ere I was sober enough to see her again."

"Do ye see her when ye are with Triona?"

"Nay, and I confess that is why I stand here struggling to decide if I should go or if I should stay. I still have no lands to call my own, no heavy purse to offer her. She has had two men seek her only for her holdings, nay for herself. Her husband sought the heavy purse that was her dower and Sir John sought this land. I dinnae wish to appear to be a third who but seeks gain through wedding her."

"I dinnae believe anyone here, including Triona, would e'er think that was why ye married her, but I understand. I sought such things when I wed Mavis, although I did want her and I did like her, could e'en see the chance that I would come to love her. When she died so suddenly and I was left with naught, I decided to ne'er do that again. 'Tis why, e'en though I had coin, I hesitated to wed Arianna despite how much I loved the lass. And ye do love Triona, aye?"

"Aye, I do. I wonder if that is why I am nay seeing Brenda when I am with Triona."

Brian nodded. "Could be. 'Tis nay just an enjoyable rutting ye are indulging in. So ye need to find something to make ye feel more equal in standing with Triona, something to make ye feel that ye have brought something of worth to the marriage and nay just gained. Seems to me there is a keep and land near at hand that no longer has a laird. No heirs to cry foul if someone gets hold of it, nay more than a few distant cousins and mayhap a bastard or two aside from the six lassies."

Brett stared at Brian for a moment, unable to speak as his mind was flooded with ideas. "And I have many powerful friends, and kin, who owe me a boon or two."

"Plus enough coin in your purse to pay a bribe or two as weel, if it is needed."

"I think ye mean a wee gift, a show of gratitude."

"Aye. Exactly."

"And it will help if I have a mon or two already holding Gormfeurach."

"The men there do have need of someone strong to hold the place until they get a new laird."

Brett exchanged a grin with Brian. "'Tis good to have a plan."

"And part of that plan is to claim Triona, is it?"

"It is, but I will do naught about that until I ken I can come to her with something of my own to offer. In the end, her husband did right by her, by naming her his heir. He recognized her work here and her worth. I ken I could have her without going to all the trouble I am about to, because the lass cannae hide how she feels even when she tries to. It sounds cursed arrogant to say that, but 'tis there to see in her eyes. Howbeit, for once I want her to be the one who gains something in a marriage. I want her to be the one offered something of worth for the privilege of her hand in marriage."

"Good mon." Brian slapped Brett on the back and

then suddenly sniffed the air. "'Twill be time to ea.
soon. Good cooks they have here, who ken how to
make hearty, tasteful fare with little. Arianna has
gathered a few recipes from them. We do weel, but
there are always the lean times to face—or when ye
just dinnae wish some guests to eat all that game
ye struggled to catch, in but one sitting. Arianna told
me that the lassies in the kitchen said it was your
woman who is most responsible for those meals."

Your woman, Brett thought as he followed Brian
down off the walls. The words stroked him, giving him
pleasure. Even if he could not gain hold of Gormfeurach, he would find something else to offer
Triona, because he knew he had to claim her. Brenda
had been the love of his youth, but he was a different
man now. This man wanted Triona; she was his future.

Triona suspected her blushes would be enough to
heat the bathwater she was in if it had not been well
heated already. All during the evening meal she had
done her best to let Brett know that she wanted him
in her bed tonight, with every smile and light touch
of her hand. Her plan was to greet him in something
more alluring than a plain linen night shift. Bathwater, scented and faintly cloudy with soap, seemed
like a wonderful idea. The way she was tensing at
every small sound outside her door made her think
she had vastly overestimated her ability to be sultry
and inviting.

"Just how cursed long do ye have to be with a mon

to start being comfortable being naked around him?" she muttered as she scrubbed at her foot.

"Most men would like that to be about two minutes," drawled Brett as he quickly stepped inside the room and shut the door, not wanting anyone to see the delightful vision of Triona in her bath.

The sight of her, her pretty face flushed from the heat of the water and the fire the tub was set in front of, stirred the ache of raw need inside him. He liked the way her thick hair was messily pinned up on top of her head, damp tendrils slipping free to curl around her long, elegant neck. Brett realized that the more he saw her, the more he realized she had beauty. It was not the kind that grabbed a man's gaze immediately like some women's did, but it was beauty nonetheless.

Triona squeaked in surprise and nearly sank down beneath the water. Catching herself before she did so, she frowned at Brett. A moment later she recalled she was trying to be sultry, to be a woman he would never forget. *Or a woman he had to return to,* a little voice whispered in her head, and she ruthlessly silenced it. She would not allow herself any false hope.

Brett nearly grinned. She had looked irritated about being startled but suddenly had changed to looking coy and inviting. It appeared that Triona was trying to seduce him. He should probably tell her she did that by simply standing within sight of him and breathing, but he was enjoying her efforts far too much to put an end to them. He walked over to the tub, crouched down beside it, and picked up the little dish of soap.

"What are ye doing?" she asked as she watched him dip the edge of the linen washing cloth into the soap.

"I am about to help my lady in her bath," he said, and reached over to grab one of her surprisingly long and strong legs, all too easily recalling how good they felt wrapped around him as he buried himself deep inside her heat. "Ye just relax and allow me to do all the work."

Her blush revealed her unease with such intimacy, but he calmly ignored it. Brett knew that such reticence disappeared quickly once her desire began to rise. He washed her carefully, enjoying the way her eyes grew heavy lidded and turned a richer blue, as well as the feel of her soft, wet skin beneath his hands. The soft little gasps she made when he spent a long time washing between her legs, stirring her desire with his fingers, delighted him.

Deciding that the game had to end or he would be trying to climb into the tub with her, leaving a mess that would be embarrassing to explain to the maids, he tugged Triona to her feet and helped her step from the tub. He took the same care in drying her lithe yet nicely rounded body as he had in washing it. Except for the few faint birthing scars, her body revealed few other clues that she had borne a child. Her breasts were not quite as firm as a childless woman's but far more so than other women's he had had the privilege of exploring. Triona did not just direct her people in what work needed doing, she lent a hand herself, and it showed in the lightly muscled fitness of her body. He was not a man who cared if childbirth left its mark on a woman, but he also liked the strength and vigor displayed in Triona's form.

Eager to have that fit body wrapped around his, he tossed aside the drying cloth and took her to the bed. The way she watched him as he shed his clothes was so flattering, he knew she could easily make him a bit vain with those looks alone. It had certainly made him prefer to stand before her and remove his clothes rather than just toss them aside as quickly as possible. Instead of just lying down beside her, he crawled onto the bed near her feet and began to slowly kiss his way up her body. When he touched a kiss to the very red curls at the juncture of her thighs, he grinned when her whole body tensed. He then grasped her by the thighs, held her in place, and began to make love to her with his mouth.

Triona was so shocked when he kissed her there, she could not move. By the time she thought she ought to pull away from such an intimacy, he had a hold on her that prevented that. In another moment she did not care, opening to his kiss as the heat of desire flared through her body from each touch of his tongue.

She heard herself make a sound of complaint when he began to kiss his way up her body, for she had wanted *that* kiss to continue. That tautness she now knew led to a delicious burst of pleasure that had begun, and she did not wish it to ease, fading a little as he stopped kissing her so intimately. When he paused to lavish attention on her breasts, she wrapped her body around his, rubbing against the hard length of him with increasing need. By the time he reached her mouth, she was desperate to feel him inside of her.

"Now, lass?" he whispered against her lips.

"Aye, right now if ye wish to live to see another dawn," she said.

Brett laughed even as he kissed her and thrust home inside of her. Triona had the fleeting thought that the touch of laughter, even in the middle of a passionate moment, was very nice indeed. Then her body's need for release blocked all other thought from her mind. Triona was vaguely aware of her nails scratching over his back as her release tore through her, making her cry out his name. Her whole body was still shaking from the strength of it when he found his own pleasure, plunging deep inside and growling out her name against her neck.

It was a little while before Brett regained enough breath and strength to shift most of his body off of Triona's. He looked at her still-flushed face and her lovely mouth faintly swollen from kisses, and the hint of desire stirred in him again. It was going to be a long night of greed, he mused. They had not spoken of it, but they both knew this was their last night together. Only he knew that he would be back.

The decision not to tell her he planned to return had been a hard one. He knew he would hurt her when he left. Yet he did not know how long it would be before he could come back, and he hated to think of her waiting. While he certainly did not wish her to find someone else while he was gone, there was simply too much uncertainty in his future at the moment to leave her with even the most tenuous of promises.

"I think that didnae go quite like I planned," she murmured, turning her head to look at him. "Ye seduced me."

"Aye." He got out of bed, fetched the linen wash-cloth from the tub, and used it to wash them both clean before tossing it back into the tub. "I think I did," he agreed as he returned to her side and idly nuzzled her neck. "That was nay your plan?"

"Nay. I had planned to be the one doing the seducing."

"Ah. So ye did. Ye were naked in your bath."

"That was nay all of it."

"All I needed." He laughed when she slapped him lightly on the back. "Nay, truly. It would probably be all any mon needed. Aha, says the mon as he steps into the room, naked woman in the bath. I must get my clothes off ere she changes her mind." He smiled when she laughed. "I caught the hint of the seduction in the great hall, lass. Ye made my blood heat with all those soft smiles and wee strokes of your bonnie hand."

Triona felt a hint of pride and tried not to show it. She had feared she had no skill in the art of seduction, only what she had seen when others had played the game where she could see them. It was pleasing to think she had seduced Brett. The fact that he appeared to be easily seduced was something she could ignore. Such a thought could stir doubts in her own ability to entice him, and could invite thoughts of how any woman might seduce him with little effort.

She was disappointed that she had not been a little more daring, and then almost smiled as she felt his manhood twitch slightly against her hip. There were more chances to be daring before the night was done, she mused, and slid her hand down until she could curl it around his manhood. The way he tensed and inhaled swiftly was very promising, she decided, and began to stroke him.

Brett closed his eyes to enjoy her touch to the fullest. She had a natural skill, he thought, and almost grinned. It was probably not the wisest compliment to give a well-born lady. Then she turned a little and slid her other small, warm hand between his legs to lightly stroke him there as well, and he decided he really did not want to do any thinking for a while.

The light of the rising sun warmed his face and Brett slowly opened his eyes. It was morning and he did not think he had ever faced one with such reluctance before. He eased away from Triona's light hold and quickly put his clothes on. A large part of him wanted to wake her, make love again, but he knew he had to get his things together. When Brian said morning, he meant morning, and making love to Triona again would take far more than the few minutes he now had to spare. It was easier to flee than to talk, and he was embarrassed that that thought prodded him to leave her side so swiftly.

He also felt a bit like a complete coward as he hurried to his bedchambers, which he shared with Harcourt and had not used since first making love to Triona. His brother was already up, dressed, and packed. Brett quickly washed up, changed his clothes for ones better suited to riding, and shoved his belongings into his saddlebags.

"Ye slipped away like a thief in the night, didnae ye," said Harcourt as he waited for Brett to join him in going down to the great hall to have a quick bite of food before leaving.

"Aye, I did," Brett snapped. "Was I to wake her at dawn just so she can wave good-bye?"

"So, ye havenae told her that ye are going to come back, either."

"If I kenned when that would be, I might have done so. I can say I will be back, but I truly dinnae ken when. I thought it kinder to leave matters as they stand. No promises. I willnae break one to her, and if I dinnae get what I am after, I could need a long time to gather what I need to come and ask for her hand."

Harcourt sighed. "Mayhap all she needs is ye. E'er think of that?"

"A lot, but I will nay be the third mon in her life to come to her with little or nothing, to marry her for my own gain. When I come back it will be with enough that when I ask for her hand she will ken that

that is all I want, just her hand, nay her coin and nay her land."

"I pray I ne'er fall in love. It makes life too troublesome. Do ye still want me to join those two MacFingal lads at Gormfeurach?"

"Aye, unless ye have changed your mind."

"Nay. There is work to be done there, and I have a strange urge to do some of it. So, best ye get your hands on the place or I will be sore angry that all my hard work benefits someone who isnae my kin."

Laughing softly, Brett followed him down to the great hall. He knew it was dangerous to hope for too much, but he let that hope for a future with Triona rest in his heart. It made the parting easier, for he could see the path back into her arms.

Still chewing on an oatcake, he stepped out into the bailey to see their horses readied and Brian already waiting a little impatiently for his wife. The well-padded cart was for her, and she paused in talking to Triona every once in a while to glare at it, but he knew she would be riding in it all the way back to Scarglas—and not just to please Brian. Arianna still held a fear of losing the child.

Triona surreptitiously glanced to where Brett stood. She had woken up in time to see him leave, the warmth of his kiss on her forehead still lingering. For a moment she had been angry that, after the night of lovemaking they had just enjoyed, he would slip away like some thief or a man trying to make certain he was not caught in a wife's bed by her returning husband.

Then she had decided it was the best way for them to part, if only to help her keep her dignity. If he had lingered, made love to her again, she might have been reduced to begging him to stay.

"Ye didnae ask him to stay, did ye?" said Arianna.

"Nay. He gave me no promises and I will nay hold him with tears and pity. He wants to leave, and I will wave fare-thee-weel from the gates." She sighed when Arianna kissed her cheek. "It was good to see ye, Cousin. Take the journey home easily."

"It appears my husband feels the same. Do ye see what he intends me to ride in? As if I am some aging matriarch or have some disease? A cart. He means to make me go back to Scarglas in a cart." She glared at Brian, who just grinned back at her. "I think he means to punish me for leaving in the first place."

"Nay, he but understands your fears and tries, in his awkward monly way, to ease them." Triona smiled when Arianna laughed. "And here comes my Ella to wave fareweel, too."

Triona watched as Ella kissed Arianna and then went to kiss each of the men, tensing when her daughter stopped before Brett. She actually started to move toward them to hear what was being said and stopped herself. It would be wrong. Ella had the right to say what she wanted, and considering some of the things the child might say or ask, it might also save her some embarrassment if she did not venture near enough to overhear. She just hoped Brett did nothing to add to the sadness she knew her child would feel when he was gone.

"Why can ye nay stay here?" Ella asked. "I thought ye liked us."

Crouching in front of the little girl, Brett said, "I do, my wee angel, but I have to go and do something right now. It is important that I get something before I come back." He kissed her cheek. "But dinnae tell your mother I said that. I am nay sure when I can come back, and I dinnae wish her being sad as she waits."

"I will be sad as I wait."

"Nay, ye will be playing with your friends and the kittens and helping your mother. Ye will be too busy to be sad. Just be a verra good lass for your mother."

"If I am a verra good girl may I have a kitten?"

He laughed. "I told ye to ask your mother about that."

"She will say nay."

"Then ask again later, for ye can ne'er ken when she might change her mind."

He talked with the little girl for another moment as Brian settled his complaining wife in the cart, and then he walked over to Triona. There were so many things he could say, from formal, polite words of thanks to asking her to wait for him, but he could not think of which words or what to say. Instead, he pulled her into his arms, gave her a passionate kiss, and then went and got on his horse, joining his hooting friends and relatives as they all rode out.

"Did he say he is coming back?" asked Joan. "That looked like an *I will come back* kiss to me."

It had rather felt like one, but Triona beat down the surge of hope that tried to fill her heart. She needed more than a passionate kiss before he rode away to let that hope live. For now, she intended to go to her bedchamber and spend a few hours sunk in morose self-pity, and then she would pick up the pieces of her shattered heart and get to work.

"It was just a kiss, Joan," she said as she turned to reenter the manor. "Just a kiss from a mon who obviously didnae have anything he wished to say to me."

"Some men cannae easily speak what is in their hearts."

"And some men dinnae have anything in their hearts to speak about. Now I am going to slip away and be alone for a few hours and wallow in feeling sorry for myself because I was foolish enough to let a tiny ray of hope enter my heart. Once I have it completely throttled to death, I mean to get to work. For once we can work without having to stop to fix damage done by Grant."

She paused in the doorway and looked out through the gates at her retreating visitors. "And for that we can thank all those people." She looked at Joan. "I can also thank Sir Brett Murray for showing me that what can be between a mon and a woman can be verra fine indeed. It might have hurt a little in the end, but that is something I am indeed verra, verra grateful for."

And she was. She just wished that she had been able to make him love her with his heart as well as he had loved her with his body.

Chapter Eighteen

"Weel? Are ye now a laird or nay?"

Brett sat down at his brother Payton's table, smiled at the man's wife, and helped himself to some food. "Aye, I am now the laird of Gormfeurach."

"Congratulations," said Payton. "That went more easily than ye thought it would, aye?"

"If ye consider *easily* a few bribes to be allowed in to see people; stepping up the highest ladder I have e'er climbed as I went from laird to laird to laird, starting with Mollison, until I reached the one who had the power of a final aye or nay; and e'en fighting to nay take the name of Grant just to sit in the laird's chair of a place few of the Grants e'en realized existed. It cost me most of what coin I had, too, but I am happy the few Grants that briefly thought they might want to fight for the place preferred money o'er land. I e'en enlisted the aid of all my friends and kinsmen, and kinswomen, to speak for me when it was needed." He sighed as he took a chunk of bread and dipped it into a small dish of herbed butter. "I am nay sure I have a favor left to ask of anyone I ken."

"Then ye shall need to gather up a new crop."

"Or the lass ye are trying so hard to win can do so," said Kirstie and she reached for the last piece of bread, only to get into a silent tug-of-war with Payton over it.

Brett watched his older brother and his wife playfully fight over the last piece of bread. They had been married for almost fourteen years, had seven of their own children with another on the way, and always had a small horde of orphans or cast-off children around. Chaos often surrounded them and many thought them odd in the way they cared for the lost or forgotten children, but he knew without a shadow of doubt that Payton was happy, would not have his life any other way. That was what Brett wanted.

"Triona may have a favor or two owed her e'en now, if only out of a need for some to apologize for nay heeding what she told them about Sir John Grant," Brett said. "I believe Mollison's guilt o'er how he did naught to help her, didnae listen to her, is why he welcomed me as a possible new laird and ally. The connection of his keep with those of both the McKees and the Grants appears to be important to the Mollisons, mostly for food. Cattle, sheep, crops.

"The three clans have long had a tradition of sharing when there is a lean year, and they work together on many another thing. Mollison's lands are poor producers, Banuilt has good lands, and Gormfeurach has modest ones. Banuilt has some of the best weavers, who often spin and weave wool from Gormfeurach and Cromcraobh, Mollison's lands. Gormfeurach has excellent tanners. Cromcraobh has excellent thatchers. And there is more. Much more."

"So, they all need to continue to be allied if they are to prosper," said Payton, cutting the last piece of bread in half and tossing one half to Kirstie, who neatly caught it. "For one to hurt another is to lessen all three. I can see both good and bad in that, but it has obviously worked for them for a verra long time."

"Since the first three knights settled there and chose their pieces of land. It has suffered of late because the lairds of Banuilt and Gormfeurach werenae interested in much more than being lairds. Their predecessors were better but nay by much. Mollison ruefully admitted that he hadnae liked seeing a wee lass do a better job as laird than Sir John and Sir Boyd and their predecessors. He was ashamed and embarrassed by how he left her in danger simply because he believed the word of a mon—a friend though nay a particularly close one—over hers."

"And ye took full advantage of that."

"I did indeed. Then he sent me, papers in hand, to another laird. And so it began."

"Are ye certain Sir John Grant's kin will cause ye no trouble?"

"Nay interested in fighting for the place. As I said, few of them e'en kenned it existed, the bloodlines having grown so thin. Sir John left a will but left it all to his legitimate heir, as yet unnamed. No legitimate heir exists. Coin interested his kin more than a place they have ne'er seen. They also sought to please some of the ones who spoke in my favor, making it clear that they wanted me to have the land. So it all would have languished, for e'en Mollison couldnae simply hand it o'er to a friend or kinsmon without taking the same journey I just did, and he had no interest in doing so. Thus, disinterest in working to gain Gormfeurach is one reason I am now its laird."

Payton raised his tankard in a salute and took a drink. "Ye should have married the wench first, and then ye could have had pleasant company as ye sought the right to call yourself a laird."

"Nay, love, your brother acted correctly," said Kirstie. "Triona needs him to seek her out, e'en though he has nay need of a dower from her. Mayhap if her first husband had been a good one, been kind and at least a wee bit caring, it wouldnae have mattered, but she has had two men who made their disinterest in her as a woman all too clear— the one she married and the one who demanded she marry him. Each needed something of hers and would have wed anyone who had it." Kirstie smiled at Brett. "Ye will go to her needing nothing she has, and have also already shown how hard ye will work to help her hold on to Banuilt."

"That is how I pray she will see it." Brett grimaced. "I but hope she hasnae found another, for I have been gone far longer than I had planned to be."

"How long?"

"Three months. And it will take me at least a sennight to return, mayhap longer, for I must go to

Gormfeurach first. The people there need to be told who their new laird is."

"Weel, eat. Fill your belly and be gone in the morning."

"Kirstie," Payton said, laughter tinting his voice and weakening what had been intended as a gentle scold.

"I mean it," she said. "If the woman truly loves ye, Brett, three months is too short a time for her to rid her heart of that love and turn to another. Three months can, however, make her nay verra willing to see ye ride up to her gates, for she will have spent much of that time trying verra hard to get ye out of her heart."

That was exactly what Brett feared. With each passing day away from her side, he had become more determined to return to her. Yet, because he had left her with no promise to return, no words of love, she would be spending each of her days away from him trying to tear him from her heart and mind. Brett had never thought it would take so long to lay claim to Gormfeurach, envisioning either a quick, clear no or a not-so-quick but still clear aye. Nothing had prepared him for the twisted route he had had to take to have his bid for the keep accepted. Otherwise he might have left Triona with at least enough of a promise to return that she would watch for him and wait for him, if only for just a little while.

"Ye *are* certain she loves you, aye?" asked Payton, watching Brett closely.

For a moment his heart clenched with uncertainty, but then Brett remembered how Triona would look at him as he shed his clothing, and the warm, rich blue of her eyes after he kissed her. She trusted him, had proven it time and time again, and he knew how important that was. She also trusted him with her little Ella, and when he had helped her bathe the mud off the little girl, he had caught a glimpse of the wish for more children, his children, on her face before she had swiftly hidden it. He knew he had not been mistaken in what those looks were telling him about what was in her heart.

"Aye, she loves me, or is so close to doing so 'twill need but a wee nudge to capture the prize," he replied.

"Then best we plan what ye need to take with ye for your journey and homecoming. 'Tis past time ye went to your Triona and did a little nudging."

Brett fought the urge to turn around and race for Banuilt as he rode through the gates of Gormfeurach a week after leaving Payton's home. Now that he was close to Triona, he wanted to do nothing more than hold her, but the people of Gormfeurach needed to know what their fate was. He dismounted and nodded to the youth who took the reins, and then grinned at his brother Harcourt as the man walked up to him.

"Ye did it, didnae ye, ye bastard," said Harcourt.

"Aye, I did, and best nay let our father hear ye talk so about our mother." He laughed when a grinning Harcourt slapped him on the back.

"Best ye tell all these people then, as they have

been growing more and more uneasy with nary a word about who would come and sit his arse in the laird's chair," said Harcourt.

Brett went and stood on the steps leading to the doors into the keep while Harcourt gathered as many of the people as he could. The looks on their faces told him how they had suffered as they waited to hear who would soon lead them. Brett knew many feared for their places at Gormfeurach, as a new laird often meant the better positions within a keep went to the ones the new laird favored. There would also be those who feared that, although their last laird was not a very good one, the next one could be far, far worse. Brett would undoubtedly have some of his kin come to Gormfeurach, but he would be certain he did not displace anyone. They would have to wait and see what kind of laird he would be, for he knew swearing to be a good one would convince no one. They did not know him well enough to know that when he gave his word, it was a vow one could trust in.

The announcement that he was to be their new laird was met with silent shock, and for a moment Brett feared he would have a rebellion. Then the men began to smile, and soon everyone was congratulating him. Even the news that he would remain a Murray did not dim their welcome. He suspected the loyalty of the people at Gormfeurach had long been to the land more than the laird. Whatever else they might think about him, the people of Gormfeurach were obviously more than willing to give him a chance. He suspected Harcourt's work here had helped that happen. All the men of the garrison quickly pledged themselves to him, and then the people began to disperse, many heading out to tell others the news.

"That went far better than I thought it would," he said to Harcourt as they sat down at the large work-table in the ledger room. "I have a feeling I might owe some of that welcome to ye and whate'er work ye have done here. Where is Gunn?" he asked when he realized how at home Harcourt was in the room.

"He assists, as does his son," Harcourt replied, and poured them each a tankard of ale. "They are gone for the day now and have a verra fine wee cottage in the village. I made sure of it, for Sir John had them living in little better than a hovel, despite all the work the mon did for him, work that kept this place from falling into complete ruin. I but like to go over the work. There is promise here, Brett, of a fine keep. And it appears that Gormfeurach is actually the first line of defense for all three keeps."

"Ah, that would make sense." And that would please a man like Harcourt. "Who leads the men?"

"'Tis Duncan now, as the ones who did lead are all dead. They were close with Sir John and kenned everything but said nothing. They died with him the day we last rescued Triona, but even if they had lived and returned, it is doubtful any of these men would wish to follow them."

"Probably for the best, as they would have been trouble for anyone who came here as the new laird. For me, they would have been a great deal of trouble, as I am the one who killed Sir John." He frowned. "Do the people here ken that?"

"Aye. Felt it was nay good to hide the truth. They simply didnae care. All they worried o'er was who would take his place. Gunn told me that neither Sir John nor his father would listen to his gentle hints that they should breed more legitimate heirs, or find cousins to favor, nay matter how distant they might be. Neither wished to hunt down cousins with few true blood ties to the clan whose name they held. Gunn began to think that neither of the men truly cared for more than what this place could gain them while they lived, that plans for the future, after they were gone, didnae interest them at all."

"A shame, as this is a good place, and I think there are a lot of good people here."

"There are."

Brett studied his brother. "So ye would stay on and hold my place if I can get Triona to marry me?"

"Aye, I believe I would. I wouldnae have thought so when I first came here to hold it until a laird would be found, but I have discovered that I like the work. I find myself making plans, imagining how to improve this or that. I am nay sure I like to admit it, but it is as if I have settled."

"Good. Then unless ye find land of your own and need to leave, ye hold my place. I mean to stay with my wife." He frowned. "She hasnae got anyone wooing her, does she?"

"Nay." Harcourt smiled faintly. "And I think ye had best hone your skills at wooing ere ye go to her. I have seen her now and then, and she isnae thinking fondly of ye at the moment."

"I feared that might be so. Weel, after a hearty meal, a few talks with some of the people here, and a good night's rest, I best go and begin my wooing. Have Callum and the others returned home?" he asked, recalling that the three had said they would join Harcourt when Mollison had been unable to settle the matter of who should be laird of Gorm-feurach.

"Aye, they have, and nay long after ye left Mollison. Callum got word from his kin and needed to go home, so Uven and Tamhas went with him. The two MacFingal lads stayed. I am thinking they may ne'er leave, as they have settled in verra firmly."

"Ah, weel, I suspect there is room for them to make a good life for themselves here, and they are wise enough to see that."

"They are, and I have found them most useful in the training of the men." He held up his tankard. "And now, I raise my drink to the new laird and wish him all good luck in wooing his lady."

Brett touched his tankard to Harcourt's and smiled a little ruefully. "I fear I will need it."

"Och, aye, ye most certainly will," said Harcourt, and laughed.

Brett controlled the urge to throw his tankard at Harcourt's head. He had earned the laughter. He had made a grievous mistake in keeping silent, in thinking it best to wait to speak his heart to Triona until he had all he thought he needed. Brett could only hope she would be understanding.

Triona crossed her arms over her chest and studied the small thatched building that would serve as a bathing house for the garrison. It was well built and attractive, tucked up against the high wall, so she no longer worried about how it would fit into the area within the bailey. Brett had been right. Her garrison had developed a strong need to stay clean. The bailey had often been muddy from the water used to wash away the sweat and dirt from training. This should solve that problem, for inside was a well, a hearth, buckets, and tubs. The clever man who put the well in the cottage so that water could be drawn right there had also put in a drain that allowed the dirty water to be poured away, beyond the walls. Now if she could just find some way to make a shelter for the men who would slip outside of the tower in the dead of night to sleep in the open, she mused, feeling a pang of pity for the scars their long imprisonment had left them with.

There was little she could do to help them, and she knew it. Triona doubted the men would accept much help, anyway. The few attempts she had made to talk about what troubled them had been politely but firmly brushed aside. She knew they would shy away from sympathy because they would see the need of it as unmanly. They had each other, each one having shared that horror, and she had to hope that would aid in their healing.

Just looking at the bathing cottage again, as she thought to see that it did not need any more done to make it right, began to make her think of Brett and she almost cursed aloud. The man would not stay out of her head. She could go for hours, and then there he was, in her mind, causing her heart to pinch with pain. Her dreams at night were a constant torment, filled with all the memories of the passion they had shared. The mornings were spent struggling to still the aching need those dreams left her with. Being cured of Sir Brett Murray was taking far longer than she thought it ought to.

"Ye dinnae like it?" asked Joan from where she stood beside Triona, also studying the little house. "I thought it actually looked quite good."

"It does," Triona replied. "And I think it will work out verra weel and nay just for the garrison. This could work for when we have visitors. It will be much easier to send the men here to seek a wash than to carry the water to the rooms. I fear I just recalled who told me the men may need to be clean, more than they ever had before, and that roused my temper."

"Ah, Sir Brett."

"Aye, Sir Brett of the smile and the wave who barely left a trail of dust behind him as he rode away. I was but annoyed at how often the mon still comes to mind."

Joan put her arm around Triona's shoulders. "A mon like that is difficult to forget."

"Weel, he shouldnae be, as I am fair sure he has forgotten about me."

"Ye cannae be certain of that. I still feel there was more to that kiss than fareweel."

"If there was, there should have been some word from him. I could, mayhap, believe he couldnae think of what to say when everyone waited for him to leave with them, but he has sent me nay one word since then. It shouldnae take a mon three months to compose a letter or e'en a wee tiny message."

"He sent that wee carved cat to Ella."

"Aye, to Ella. And nary a word to me when it was sent."

Joan grimaced. "Aye, I thought that was badly done. I dinnae ken what to say. Despite his silence, I just cannae believe he means to ne'er return. He appeared to be so much more to ye, with ye, than a lover."

Triona sighed. "I thought so, too, and mayhap we are both just fools. Ye havenae had all that much more experience with men than I have."

"Nay, I havenae. I was waiting for my Aiden. Loved that mon since he was a lad with feet he kept tripping o'er. If it hadnae been for that, I may have had me a mon or two. But I kenned what I wanted and I wasnae going to settle for less."

"I settled for Boyd. Not that I had much choice. My father wanted me to wed the mon. But do ye nay see? I was wrong about Boyd. I saw charm and kindness and thought he and I could have a verra good marriage. Instead, he turned out to be a mon as cold as a December night who but wanted a fat purse and a son. Sad to say, that was better than remaining under my father's roof.

"Yet here I stand, wondering if I was mistaken in a mon again. I thought Brett was, weel, I thought he cared for me. I thought what we shared was more than just a lusting, e'en on his part. A mon who has a caring for a lass doesnae love her into exhaustion in the night and then ride off with naught but a smile and a wave, ne'er to be seen or heard from again."

She cursed and kicked at a small stone on the ground. "I must nay let my mind prey on the matter. He gave me no words of love and no promises. If I am unhappy that he is gone, thcn 'tis my own cursed fault. I hoped. I tried not to, but I did. He didnae ask me to, didnae encourage me, so it isnae his fault."

"Nay, although I do wish I could curse him for telling ye lies or the like."

Triona smiled. "It would be easier to root him out of my heart if that was the way of it, but it wasnae. My heart didnae care that there were no words of love or promises. It just kept filling itself up with need for him."

Hooking her arm through Triona's, Joan started toward the manor. "The heart does as the heart pleases."

"Weel, my heart needs to be taken into a corner and slapped about until it regains its senses." She smiled faintly when Joan laughed.

Triona spent the next few hours keeping herself as busy as possible, but for reasons she could not understand, Brett lingered in her thoughts. She finally went back inside the manor to the great hall to do some mending. Ella was so hard on her clothes that there was never a shortage of that somewhat tedious work to do.

She had barely finished mending one little shift and was reaching for another when she knew it was not going to work. Brett was not going to be dismissed from her thoughts so easily. The days when she could not shake him out of her thoughts had grown fewer, and she had begun to hope she would soon be left with only the night and her dreams to worry about.

Staring into the fire, she sighed. It was time to accept the sad fact that she might never be able to forget the man. He had burrowed his way so deeply into her heart and mind, there was no shaking free of him. She had the strong feeling that he had burrowed at least a part of him somewhere else as well.

Placing a hand over her belly, she suffered a feeling that was an uncomfortable mixture of excitement and terror. She had not bled since he rode away. It had taken her a while to realize that, for she had worked herself so hard that exhaustion drove her to her bed and those dreams she could not stop. She wanted the child she was now sure she carried, but she did not want to shame all the people of Banuilt by bearing a child when she had no husband.

What she needed was another man, she decided, and then cursed. There were no suitable men around Banuilt she could look to. If there had been, she might have found an attractive one and been with him before Brett had ever ridden inside her gates.

Triona doubted there was a man at Gormfeurach who would suit, either. She was stuck with the one that lived in her mind and heart but obviously did not care to live with her in person. She would not try to trick a man into marrying in order to give a name to her child, either, and she sincerely doubted a man would willingly wed her to give his name to another man's bairn. The mere thought of trying to find Brett to tell him about the child made her blood run cold, for she knew it would kill her to have him turn away from her—or worse, marry her out of a sense of duty.

It was difficult not to wonder what was wrong with her. Triona hated the doubts about herself that would creep into her mind at such times, yet there was no ridding herself of them permanently. She suspected every woman in her place would suffer from the same doubts, but thought she might have more right to them than most. Her father had cared nothing for her. Her husband had seen her as no more than a female to breed with. And Sir John had wanted nothing more from her than the land she held, had not even liked her and done nothing to hide that fact.

"Brett liked me," she whispered, and then glanced around to make sure no one was near enough to have heard what even she thought sounded childish.

There was some truth in it, and she knew it. Liking and respect had been there. Triona was certain of it. It just had not been enough.

"M'lady! The new laird of Gormfeurach is at the gates!"

Pushing aside her mending, Triona looked at

Angus, who was standing in the doorway to the great hall. The youth looked so excited she was surprised he was not shaking from the strength of it. She was not sure why the choice of a new laird for Gormfeurach should be of such import for him, however.

"Who is it, Angus? Anyone we ken?" she asked as she stood up and started toward the door.

"Ye must come and meet him."

He was definitely excited, she thought as she reached him. "That is what I am about to do. Do ye mean to escort me out to the bailey?"

"Aye, ye shouldnae be going out to greet someone alone."

At least he had finally learned that much, Triona mused as she watched him hurry off without waiting for her. Angus was trying to learn how to be a proper man-at-arms. Aiden had decided that until Angus was older, the youth should serve as her personal guard within the manor and village. Whatever was happening in the bailey, however, had apparently pushed most of the lessons Angus had so painstakingly learned right out of his head.

She stepped outside and looked at the men who had just ridden inside her gates, and shock made her tense, pushing all clear thought from her mind. The men were not the ones she had expected to see, not the Gormfeurach garrison. As they dismounted, she told herself she was seeing things, that her mind was still lost in memories. That could not be the tall, black-haired man that had haunted her dreams for over three months.

Chapter Nineteen

"Brett?"

Triona stared at the man striding toward her. Despite the hurt he had left her with when he had ridden away, longing still filled her abused heart whenever he came to mind. Which was far too often, she thought crossly as she looked him over, finding no signs of any horrible wounds that would explain why he had been gone for so long. That longing rushed through Triona now, so strongly she had to fight the urge to fling herself into his arms, and she firmly reminded herself that he had sent no word that he would return, given her no hope that he ever would. Even if he had changed his mind, had decided he wanted to stay with her, it should not have taken him so long.

"I was told that I was to meet the new laird of Gormfeurach," she said, tensing against the rush of heat in her veins when he kissed her hand.

"And so ye have," he said.

She frowned in confusion. Then she looked around

him but saw only a grinning Harcourt. There was no stranger around, not even one of the men she might recognize from the rare times Sir Mollison had sent someone to Banuilt. And then the look of mischief on Brett's face, one blended with a very large dose of pride, began to push aside her confusion.

"*Ye* are the new laird of Gormfeurach?" she asked, not surprised at how small her voice was as the realization sunk in—that the man she loved, the man who had left her with no more than a smile, a wave, and not even the tiniest hint of a promise, was now going to be living close at hand. It would be impossible to hide her secret from him.

"Aye," he replied. "Once they were left with no laird, and none amongst them could clearly be named an heir and thus step up to be named laird, I thought I might have a chance to make a claim. It took far longer than I thought it would, for it appears the ones who built Gormfeurach were too arrogant to think they could be left with no heir at all. The Grants couldnae e'en make a true claim, for their close blood ties to the men of Gormfeurach were lost a long time ago. 'Tis a verra long tale, Triona."

"I am certain it is, Sir Brett Murray," she said, and nearly nodded in approval when she heard the courteous chill in her voice.

Brett nearly winced. He had had warmer greetings from complete strangers. It was foolish of him, but he had rarely considered the possibility that Triona would be furious with him, either for leaving as he had or for never sending her word of his plans. It was only recently, during talks with his family, that he had begun to think he would have to do a lot of soothing and explaining. He began to soothe his own unease with memories of their time together and the knowledge that Triona was not a fickle woman, nor one who gave her affection lightly, and would not swiftly and easily cast aside what she had felt for him.

"I would verra much like to tell ye all about it," he said, smiling at her and ignoring the way she narrowed her eyes at him instead of smiling back.

Triona wanted him to go away. There was an urge within her to grab him, hurl him to the ground, and take what she wanted, that hot passion that had haunted her dreams every night since he had ridden away. At the moment it was an urge easily controlled by the anger she felt over how he had acted, but she did not trust herself to hold that anger up as a shield for too long, especially if he decided to be charming. She sternly reminded herself that she needed him but swore that she would not allow him back into her bed and her life unless she was absolutely sure that he wanted to be there.

Questions clamored in her mind so loudly that she had to bite the inside of her cheek to keep herself from giving voice to them. Why had he left without a word if he had always planned to return? Had he returned just for Gormfeurach, or for her? She had to clench her hand into a fist, hiding it in the folds of her skirt, to stop from rubbing her forehead in the vain hope of quieting her mind.

"Then mayhap ye can tell it all as we dine," she said,

refusing to be a bad host just because she wanted to throttle him. "The evening meal will begin soon." She nodded toward Angus, who looked as if he was going to do a little dance of joy over Brett's return, and that thoroughly irritated her. "Angus, please show our guests to a place where they can wash away the dust of their journey. I will see to the setting of extra places at the table." And more food, she thought as she turned and walked back inside the manor, refusing to see it as a retreat.

"Weel, at least she didnae have a weapon," said Harcourt, "or I think I would be trying to get your blood off my boots right now."

Brett glared at the MacFingals, standing behind Harcourt, but it did nothing to silence their laughter. "At least she didnae have me tossed outside the walls and the gates closed to me." He sighed. "I was a fool nay to think that anger would be awaiting my return, especially considering the women in our family."

"Aye, ye were. Ye have time now to think of how ye may soften it."

It was not going to be easy to do, Brett thought as they followed Angus inside. There was a good chance that Triona would do her best to make certain they were never alone, and all his best ideas for soothing her anger required some privacy. Then he saw Ella coming toward him, her smile of welcome easing a little of the chill her mother had left behind. She was slow to come to him when he held his arms out to her, and he suddenly noticed that she was moving with an odd, shuffling gait. Brett walked up to her and crouched down in front of Ella, giving her a kiss on the cheek, idly wondering if that soft growling noise he heard was her stomach rumbling with hunger.

"Have ye hurt yourself, Ella?" he asked, leaning back a little to look at her feet.

"Nay, I have a kitten," she said, and lifted her skirts up to her knees.

Between her plump little legs sat one of the kittens they had played with in the stables, although it was nearly full-grown now. Its markings were a swirl of black, brown, and copper with an occasional splash of white. It was also staring at him with eyes uncomfortably similar to Harcourt's, its black tail with its white tip twitching back and forth. Then, still staring at him, it reached up with one paw that had far too many claw-tipped toes, caught the edge of Ella's skirts, and tugged downward, causing the child to drop her skirts back down over the cat. Brett felt as if he had just been given the feline equivalent of a door slammed in his face, and the poorly smothered laughter of his companions told him he had not imagined it.

"He likes it under there," said Ella as she leaned forward, put her arms around his neck, and gave him an awkward hug.

Brett was sure he had just heard a soft snarl from beneath her skirts. "What did ye name him?"

"Clyde," she replied. "I like the sound. Clyde. 'Tis a fine name."

"Aye, that it is."

"Are ye going to stay with us now?"

"That is my plan."

"Mother is a wee bit angry at you, I think. I will get ye some flowers to give her."

"Thank ye, Ella. That would be verra helpful." He watched her start to shuffle away. "Mayhap ye should try to teach Clyde to nay walk with you like that. Ye could fall." This time he had no doubt that Clyde had just snarled at him.

"Nay, I am used to it, and he doesnae do it all the time. Sometimes he rides up on my shoulder."

Brett stood up and watched her leave, catching the occasional glimpse of that white-tipped tail flicking out from beneath her skirts. He looked at Angus. "Are ye certain that Clyde is actually a cat?"

Angus sighed. "We are nay too sure some days. Come along, m'laird. It isnae much longer ere the food will be set out."

Brett found the meal a torture. Triona was all that was courteous, the food was good, and everyone listened with gratifying interest to his tale of how he had become laird. When it came to Triona, however, he felt as if she had never been in his arms, had never cried out his name in the throes of passion. It had been difficult to even sit next to her, as she had obviously done her best to see that he did not. He supposed he ought to be pleased that she had underestimated his stubbornness.

It was not until the fruit and tarts were set out that he decided he had had enough. They needed to talk, and yet he did not want to lay out his heart in front of everyone. He knew they were all aware of why he was there, or had guessed—everyone except Triona—but that did not mean he wished to let them sit and hear everything he had to say to her.

"I would like to have a private word with ye, Triona," he said, and nearly winced at the look she cast him, her anger not hidden well.

"I am nay sure what ye think we have to speak about, Sir Brett Murray," she said.

If she called him that one more time he was going to say or do something that could embarrass them both, he decided, and leaned closer to her so that he could whisper in her ear. "Ye will come somewhere private with me now, lass, or I will pick ye up, toss ye o'er my shoulder, and carry ye to a place of my own choosing."

Triona turned her head slightly to look him in the eye. It had not been easy to sit next to him and maintain her air of calm and distance. Even the scent of the man had her stomach tied up in knots of desire too long unfed. Yet she did not know if she wished to speak alone with him. Without the shield of all the others, keeping her wanton urges at bay was going to be dangerously difficult. The look in his eyes, however, told her he would do exactly what he had threatened to.

"As ye wish, Sir Brett Murray," she said, and could see in the way he narrowed his eyes how that angered him. "If ye would follow me, we will go to my ledger room."

She stood up without waiting for him and started to walk away. Brett slowly stood up to follow. He could understand her anger and tried to battle his own.

However, although he had not expected to be greeted with open arms, this coldness she was showing him was hard to bear. It made him afraid, which fed his growing anger.

"Shall we prepare some bandages?" asked Harcourt.

Brett grabbed a hunk of bread and tossed it at his brother's head before following Triona out of the great hall. His mind busy struggling with what he would say, he looked around as he strode after her. The signs of improvement at Banuilt were obvious. The place had always been orderly and well cared for, but now it nearly shone, it was scrubbed so clean. He had to wonder why Triona had worked so hard when it had not really been necessary.

Once inside her small ledger room, she sat behind the worktable and stared at him. Brett wanted to grab her and make love to her right there. He clenched his hands at his sides and sat in the chair to face her across the table. Soothing her anger this way would require a skill with words he was not sure he possessed. He had hoped to use seduction to his advantage, but it was difficult to seduce an angry woman when one could not even touch her.

He leaned forward, rested his forearms on the table, and was pleased to see her tense. If his getting even that close made her look so defensive, he felt he had a chance. She was not feeling as cold as she pretended to be.

"Is there something ye wish to change about the customary arrangements between Banuilt and Gorm-feurach?" she asked.

There was a slight tremor in her voice, and Triona silently cursed when she heard it. It was easier to hold that chill between them during a meal with other people around. Now there was nothing to divert her attention from the look in his eyes. She could not guess what he had to say, but he was obviously intent on talking about something, and she had the feeling it was not about his being an ally.

She bit her tongue against the urge to scream questions at him, to demand to know what game he was playing with her now. Triona prayed he was not about to suggest they be lovers again. She did not want that, now that he was back and would be staying at Gormfeurach. To be used like that would destroy her.

The problem was that she carried his child. It was not something she could hide, and yet she had no idea what to do. She did not want him at her side because he felt only some sense of responsibility for his child. She needed so much more from him.

"I am nay here to talk about the alliance between our lands," he said. "I am here to discuss ye and me."

"There is nay ye and me," she said, and knew her ability to hide her anger and hurt was disappearing rapidly. "Ye left."

"Aye, that I did, and I had good reason to do so."

"Without a word that would imply ye might return."

"Because I didnae ken when I would return. It may have been wrong, but I would offer no promise of returning when I didnae ken if I could get what I sought, or how long it would take. I needed something ere I came back, and if I didnae get what I first sought, I would have had to seek out something else. What was I to say? 'I will be back when I can,' which might be months, mayhap e'en longer?"

"Aye, unless ye didnae wish anyone to wait for ye."

Brett sighed and dragged his hands through his hair. "I did wonder if I was mistaken in my plan. I just didnae wish ye to wonder why I was nay yet back as the weeks went by and I didnae return. It seemed better to just say nothing. I always meant to come back, Triona," he said quietly, and reached out to clasp her hand in his, ignoring her attempt to pull it away. "Always. I but needed to get something before I did."

"What? What could ye need to get if what ye wanted was here?"

"In a way, I sought a dower to bring ye."

She stared at him and slowly blinked. That made no sense. A man did not need a dower. He sought one from the woman he chose. That was always the way. At best a man had to show he was a good match in blood and breeding, mayhap show he could defend his wife or provide her with a roof over her head, but all men expected the woman to bring a nice, fat dower to the marriage. For once she had been perfectly happy to have something a man might want—Banuilt being her very nice dower—and yet he went to find something else?

"I dinnae understand," she said, and idly noted that he now held both her hands in his and she had no urge to yank them free.

"Ye told me that Boyd wed ye for your purse, and we both ken why Sir John was trying to marry ye. I

decided it was time that a mon asked for your hand
without expecting anything from ye. So, with Gormfeurach without a laird, I saw my chance to gain my
own land and thus come to ye with nay need of yours."

She found the strength to yank her hands free of his
and stood up to pace the room. Her heart was pounding so hard she was astonished he did not hear it and
remark upon it. Triona tried to make sense of his
words but was afraid to believe in them. He sounded
as if he was after her hand in marriage, and everything
inside her wanted to yell out aye, but the thought that
she might have heard him wrong made her hesitate. It
would be so humiliating if she was wrong.

Brett did not hesitate to take advantage of the fact
that a table no longer separated them. He leapt up
and caught her in his arms as she walked by him, too
lost in her thoughts to evade him. For a moment she
stood like a pillar of stone in his arms, but slowly she
softened, her body resting against his.

"I kenned that when your troubles were solved and
it was time for me to leave, I did not wish to leave ye,"
he said as he rested his chin on the top of her head
and savored how it felt to have her back in his arms.

"But ye did."

"I realized I had a chance, though it may have been
a small one, to claim Gormfeurach. Then I could
come to ye with something of value. Ye should have
that, should have a mon who comes to ye and wants
nothing but ye. Nay your purse or your land. I can do
that now."

She leaned back a little and looked at him. "Ye want me?"

"Och, aye," he whispered, and lightly brushed the backs of his fingers over her cheek. "I did for a long time ere I left. I was just a wee bit slow in seeing exactly how much I wanted ye."

"Weel, ye got what ye wanted," she muttered, and blushed.

"Aye, or so I thought, but then I wanted more. Yet I was wary. I loved a lass once, and I lost her. For years I have blamed myself for her death, was so certain I should have been able to save her. We were planning to run away and get married when she was murdered. I think the fact that she carried my child at the time only added to my guilt o'er not being able to save her. She was attacked so near to me as I sat awaiting her, unaware of how she needed me."

"How verra sad. Why did ye feel guilty, though? Was it your enemies who murdered her?"

"Nay, they were enemies of her clan. And Brian made me see that I have been, as he put it, wearing a hair shirt o'er something I could nay change. I wasnae there. 'Tis that simple. I would have done all I could if I had been, but I wasnae. I didnae heed him much at first, but that realization has settled in now."

"And ye still love her?" she asked quietly, bracing herself for him to confess that he did.

"She will always have a small place in my heart, if only because she was going to be the mother of my child, but ye dinnae need to fear that she still holds my heart as she once did. For a long time, though, I was so troubled by what had happened, and my guilt, that I had difficulty being with a woman."

Triona thought of how often and vigorously they had made love, and frowned. "I didnae sense that ye had any trouble."

"I didnae with ye. This is going to make ye think I am mad, but I would see her ghost whene'er I tried to be with a woman."

Triona stared at him and could tell that, even though it made him uncomfortable to tell her, he was speaking the truth. "A ghostie like Ella sees?"

"Something like that. She would appear and that would end my desire to be with the woman I was with. Nothing stopped the vision of the ghost save for a great deal of drink, but that only made it go away whilst I was blind drunk. So, when I didnae see her when I was with ye, I began to think it was because of ye, because it was ye I was about to bed down with. Nay, it was because I wasnae bedding down with ye but *making love* to ye."

He watched her closely as she thought that over. The fact that she had not immediately told him he was mad or telling her a lie allowed him to relax. It had been right to tell her. He doubted he would see Brenda's spirit again, but he did not wish to hide such a thing from Triona if he did.

"I see. So ye wish to stay with me because ye dinnae see the ghost?"

"Nay, I want to stay with ye because I cannae abide being away from ye." He kissed her, his kiss quickly revealing how hungry for her he was when she did

not push him away. "I want to marry ye, Triona," he
whispered when he ended the kiss and brushed his
lips over her cheek. "I have my dower and I have shed
that cursed hair shirt I have worn for seven years and
I wish to make ye my wife."

"Why?" she asked.

"Ah, lass, because I cannae be without ye at my side.
Ye are what I need to be happy. I kenned that before
I left, and the knowledge just grew stronger every day
we were apart. I ne'er realized how alone I had
become until I rode away from here that day, and I
dinnae want to be alone anymore."

Triona gave herself over to his kiss, craving the
taste of him. It was not until he started to push her up
against her worktable that she regained enough of
her scattered senses to push him away, although only
far enough to put a small distance between their
bodies. She knew what he wanted right now, did not
have to feel the hardness of him against her to know
it. It was there in his kiss and his eyes. Triona also
knew that she would somehow find the strength to
say no.

For a moment she thought on all he had said.
There had been one glaring omission. He had not
said he loved her. He had said he wanted her, needed
her, felt alone without her by his side, but had made
no declaration of love. That stung, but she told herself not to be an idiot. The man had gone to a lot of
trouble just to come to her and ask for her hand in
marriage, in a way that could never make her think he

did it for Banuilt. For now, that and all he had offered
would be enough, at least for her to say aye.

"So, are ye formally asking me to be your wife?"
she asked.

"Aye, Triona, marry me. Be my wife. Have my bairns
or nay, as ye please." He grinned. "Although I would
verra much like to have a bairn or two with ye."

He would get that far sooner than he planned, she
mused, and almost told him. But then she bit her lip
against the words. There would be time for that after
they were married. For just a little while she wanted to
be only a bride. She also intended to be a bride before
she became his lover again, and pushed him away far
enough to slip free of his hold.

"Triona?" he asked, his whole body aching for her.

"This time we willnae be slipping into a bed"—she
blushed and looked at the worktable he had been
pushing her up against—"or hopping on a table until
we are properly married."

"But we have already been lovers, and everyone
here kens it," he protested, even as he struggled to
cool his need because he could tell that she was very
serious about this.

"I ken it, but nay this time. The next time we are
in a bed together, I want to call ye my husband."

"Then ye had best start preparing for a wedding, as
I will be off to fetch a priest as soon as the sun rises."

She grimaced. "I fear that will have to be Father
Mure. He is still at Gormfeurach."

"Nay the best choice. We could go . . ."

"Nay, it can be him. I willnae wait any longer than

it takes to fetch him." She reached out to caress his cheek. "I have missed ye as weel, Sir Brett Murray. I dinnae wish to wait weeks to find another priest willing to journey here to marry us."

"Then ye had best find your friend Joan and talk to Nessa, for I was nay jesting when I said I will be off to fetch the fool in the morning."

After giving her a kiss that left her slumped against her worktable struggling to catch her breath, Brett left. Triona was torn between wanting to dance about the room and wanting to fret over the fact that he had still not given her any words of love. It was going to take work not to think about that too much and be happy for what she had. The man her heart had been aching for was back and intended to marry her, even spoke of how much he wanted and needed her, even missed her. She would get the rest of what she needed after they were married. Triona refused to believe she would fail to win his heart, for the thought of being trapped in another loveless marriage was enough to make her want to run away. Brett desired her, liked her, and respected her. The seeds of love were there. All she had to do was make them grow strong enough to last a lifetime.

Chapter Twenty

"The priest wasnae happy about being dragged out of bed."

Brett looked at Harcourt even as he finished donning his plaid. "I dinnae care what Father Mure is happy about or nay happy about. This is the least he can do, and with a smile on his face, after what he was willing to do for Sir John."

"Verra true. I was a wee bit surprised when ye returned so soon to the great hall to tell us all that ye would be married." Harcourt grinned. "Rather thought we wouldnae be seeing either of you until the morning."

"Nay, although that was my plan yesterday, but she wishes to be married first. She willnae let me come to her bed unless I do so as her husband."

"Do ye think she doesnae trust that ye will go through with it?"

"Nay, she trusts me. Triona is a verra moral wee lass, for all that she let me be her lover for a wee while. She thought I wouldnae be staying once her troubles here were ended, didnae she?" He shrugged. "I am nay leaving this time, and mayhap to please her people or simply because she slid off the righteous path for a time and doesnae wish to do so again, she means to do this properly."

Harcourt nodded. "That makes sense. She is verra conscious of her place as laird here."

"I told her about Brenda," Brett said abruptly and, after taking a deep breath, confessed everything about his old love, her ghost, and the trouble he had had with women because of it. He felt as if a burden had been lifted from his shoulders when he was done.

"Jesu," Harcourt whispered, and then he shook his head. "I am nay sure I would have told her if I had been in your place, but I suppose that once ye told her that ye loved her now, Triona wasnae too troubled by the tale."

Brett paused in pinning on his brooch and stared at his brother. He carefully thought over all he had said to Triona before she had joined him in the great hall so that they could announce their forthcoming marriage. Search his words though he did, he could not find those three very important words in anything he had said to Triona.

He almost rushed from the room to go and tell her now. A part of him was suddenly terrified that she would realize his omission and leave him standing at the altar. Brett stood where he was, his brooch clutched so tightly in his hand he knew it would leave a mark.

"I didnae tell her," he said, stunned by his own stupidity.

"What?"

"I didnae tell Triona that I loved her."

"And yet she still said she would marry ye?"

"Aye." Brett slowly began to relax, his sudden fear easing away. "Aye, she did. What I said was enough for her to ken that I am nay marrying her just because I dinnae see Brenda when I am with her or because I covet her land."

He could not believe he had babbled on and on and never once truly told her what she meant to him. Wanting, needing, missing. *Look at me, I am now a laird and I do not see a ghost when we make love.* Brett had to wonder why Triona had not just punched him in the mouth.

"Might I suggest that ye make verra sure ye say it to her on your wedding night?" Harcourt frowned. "Ye *do* love her, aye?"

"Och, aye. I am fair certain she loves me, too, although I begin to wonder why she would."

"I but pray she hasnae thought too long on what ye didnae say that she changes her mind about this."

So did Brett, because he suddenly knew he had not given her very much to cling to as she took her vows. Triona had so many skills and so much strength, he forgot all too often about that vulnerability he had seen in her too many times. There had not really been any man in her life who had shown any true feelings for her. In an odd way, that could be what saved him from the consequences of his own idiocy. Triona

might believe she was getting so much more than she
had before, she needed to say aye. He was going to
enjoy letting her know the truth about his feelings for
her, letting her know just what a treasure she was in
his eyes.

"He didnae tell me that he loves me, Joan," Triona
said as her friend and Nessa helped her dress for her
wedding. "Mayhap I shouldnae do this until he does
tell me."

"Dinnae e'en think about nay doing this," said
Joan. "Of course he loves ye. He was just being an
idiot of a mon. They do often think they dinnae need
to say the words, that a lass ought to ken how he feels
from his actions or his loving. As if men dinnae show
far too many lasses their skills at loving before they
pick one to wed. Ye just make certain that your mon
says it tonight."

"And just how am I to do that?"

"Ye could always say it first," said Nessa, and
shrugged when Triona glared at her. "Just a wee passing thought. He might be needing the wee nudge,
too, to unstick the words from his gullet."

"If he didnae say it, then why did ye say aye when he
asked ye to be his wife?" asked Joan.

"People of our ilk dinnae marry for love, so I
didnae think on it," Triona replied.

"Love be why ye are wedding the fool now, and
dinnae try to tell me otherwise."

"Aye, it is why I am about to marry him despite the

lack of those words. He spoke of needing me, wanting me, and missing me sorely whilst he was away from me. I felt that was far more than I have e'er been offered before. And he went out and gained hold of Gormfeurach for me, so that he could actually present me with a dower."

"Why does his having Gormfeurach matter?"

"He told me he wanted to be the one to offer me a dower when he asked for my hand, that I had had two men who showed they cared only for what I could give them, and he did not want to be a third." She frowned when Nessa and Joan just stared at her. "Ye find that a poor reason to wed with the mon?"

"Nay, I but think he is a wonderful mon and would almost take back the talk of his idiocy. He kenned what ye needed, lass," Joan said, and Nessa nodded in agreement. "Ye might nay have seen it, but he did. This time, and especially with this mon, ye needed to ken for certain that he actually gains nothing at all when he marries ye. I think that says quite a lot about how he feels about ye. So let us hurry and get ye ready so that ye can go and make that mon all yours."

It was what she wanted, Triona told herself. All that she had dreamed of since he had ridden away was Brett returning to Banuilt and making her his wife. She told herself there was nothing to worry about. Even if she never heard him speak of love, he would give her so much more of a true marriage than Boyd ever had.

* * *

Brett watched the women lead his wife to the small shaded knoll where he waited with Harcourt and the priest. It was the area where they had once thought to put a church, but had yet to find a new priest. The old church in the village was in too much disrepair to consider using it, and he had wanted the ceremony to be somewhere other than the great hall. The marriage was being done hastily, but he had seen no reason why something could not be done to make it a little festive.

Triona deserved it, he told himself. The people of Banuilt deserved a celebration as well. He could tell from the fields and the condition of the cottages that a lot of work had been done and a good harvest would soon be brought in. This was a good reward for all of that hard work.

Glancing around, he had to admire the efficiency of the women at Banuilt. They had arranged a spot for the priest to stand beneath a large rowan tree, spread a white cloth upon the ground for him and Triona to kneel on, and draped other bolts of cloth on the trees all around the knoll, adding a bit of a festive air. Flower petals were strewn along the path that led to where he waited for Triona, and a lot of little girls, clean and dressed in their finest, stood along the path holding flowers in their little hands. Everyone from Banuilt appeared to have gathered around, and even the sun graced them with a warm day. Brett was not sure he could have asked for anything better.

He wished his family could be there but hastily pushed the wish aside. Harcourt was with him, and that was enough for now. Later he would try to think of some way to get his family to come to Banuilt, perhaps put on a celebration later for the family alone. His mother would be disappointed, especially since she had been pressing him to get married, but he knew she would love Triona and forgive him his hurry.

When Triona reached his side, he took her by the hand and sent the priest a warning look. The man had been very unhappy about being dragged to Banuilt to perform this ceremony. He had said but one unkind thing about Triona before Brett had made it clear that he would be very wise to say nothing more save for the marriage rites. Why the man was still at Gormfeurach, he did not know, but he would make sure he was not there for much longer.

The ceremony went on without any problem, although the priest was far from pleasant. With a surprising grace, Angus appeared beside them with the old church ledger for them to sign. Once done, Brett turned to the people gathered, grinned, and kissed his new wife. The cheers of the people of Banuilt rang through the clearing, and he did not think he had ever felt so at home since he had ceased living with his parents more years ago than he cared to count.

Everyone went down into the village, where a feast awaited them, tables were set all along the road through the village so that everyone at Banuilt could join in the celebration. There were people there from Gormfeurach as well. Toasts came from anyone who was inclined to raise his tankard. Brett caught a glimpse of Ella with her cat draped over her shoulders, telling the MacFingals—Ned and Nathan—some tale that had them both laughing.

"Ye are smiling so widely, Brett," said Triona. "Have I missed something?"

"Nay." He leaned over to brush a kiss over her mouth. "I was just thinking that it is a glorious day."

"Aye, it is. It is indeed. Even Father Mure could-nae spoil it."

He laughed and put his arm around her shoulders. It was going to be difficult to wait until the evening when he could finally be alone with her. Not only did his body ache for her, but Brett now knew that he would be able to tell her with ease how much she meant to him, and had every intention of doing so. Before the night was done, Triona would know just how deeply rooted in his heart she was, and he would be sure to have her say what was in her heart as well. They would start the first night of their marriage with no more doubts between them.

Triona smiled at him, leaned into his side, and the lingering worry she had nursed faded away. He had not said the words, but if he did not exactly love her now, she began to be more certain that he would soon. It was there to see in how pleased he was with their marriage, even how he teased her as they ate and drank. There may not be love there yet,

but her heart told her the seeds had already begun
to take root.

Triona tried not to be nervous as she waited in the
bed for the arrival of her new husband. She was
wearing a delicate, lace-trimmed shift that she hoped
would look alluring. Her hair was brushed out and
neatly draped over her shoulders. She was clean
and nicely scented, all prepared and ready for her
husband to come and claim her. Triona wondered
why that was making her far more nervous than she
had ever been when she and Brett had been lovers.

She pondered what Nessa had said, that she should
be the first to speak of love. It was probably what
would be needed to try to get Brett to be more fulsome about his own feelings, but she wondered why
men had to be so difficult. He was the one who had
proposed, the one who had worked so long and hard
to get what he thought was needed to offer her his
hand in marriage. It was a bit odd that he would then
lack the stamina to tell her what was in his heart. She
could not completely still the little voice that whispered that he might not actually hold her in his heart.

The door opened and he stumbled in, pushed by
his laughing brother, the MacFingals, and Aiden.
Triona stared, for he was wrapped only in his plaid. If
there were not so many people wandering around the
manor at the moment, she suspected they would have
tossed him into her bedchamber naked.

She had not forgotten how fine he looked, but

seeing him in the flesh again was a lot different from seeing him in her dreams. Triona clenched her hands into tight fists as she fought the urge to leap up, run over to him, and stroke all that smooth skin stretched taut over muscle, the few battle scars he carried only adding to the manly beauty of him.

Before she had a chance to weaken and give in to that need, Brett was there beside her bed. He wasted no time in shedding his plaid and climbing into bed with her. A heartbeat later he was tugging off her night shift. Triona gasped with pleasure when their skin touched for the first time in far too long.

"I was going to love ye slowly, dearling," Brett said as he crouched over her and looked his fill at her body, "but I dinnae have the strength for any patience just yet."

The way her body ached, Triona decided that she did not have any patience, either. She was starved for the pleasure he could give her, for the feel of his strong body joined with hers. Not surprised to see her hand tremble, she reached out and touched him, slowly running her hand down his back.

"I am nay feeling all that patient, either."

Brett kissed her and knew the first time was going to be fast and a little rough. He had to keep a tight grip on his control just to try to ready her for his possession. Kissing her, smelling the sweet scent of her passion-heated body, and hearing her soft sighs of pleasure made clinging to that control an arduous task. The way she was stroking his skin everywhere she could reach him only made it harder. Slipping his hand between her slender thighs, he found her already weeping with welcome and nearly shouted out his relief. Taking her mouth in a hungry kiss, he joined their bodies with one greedy thrust.

Triona wrapped herself around him and reveled in his greed for her. It was a glorious feeling to know she could drive the man to such heights of need. Then her own passion swept her under its waves and she let herself go with it, savoring the sound of him crying out her name as he spilled his seed deep inside of her.

Once he got his breath back, Brett cleaned them both off and then rejoined her in their bed. *Their bed,* he thought, and smiled as he pulled her into his arms. There would be no need to slip back into his own bedchamber anymore. A little matter but an important change.

"I willnae be staying at Gormfeurach," he said, and silently cursed himself as a coward.

Now would be the perfect time to tell her what was in his heart. They were momentarily sated, at peace, and newly wed. Instead, he opened his mouth and out came talk of his new lands. Brett wondered if he could get Harcourt to slap him a few times until his wits returned.

"But ye are their laird now," she said as she raised herself up to look down at him. "Shouldnae ye be there?" She knew she should have considered that they were both lairds with responsibilities to two different lands, and living together all the time could be very difficult to do.

"Harcourt is going to do it. I will go there now and

then to see what is being done and what needs doing, but my brother has been taking care of the place since Sir John died, and he likes it. I intended to find someone anyway, as I have nay intention of sleeping away from my wife, but this is perfect. My brother now has a place of his own in most ways, and I get to stay here with ye."

She moved so that she straddled his body, her hair covering her in a way that gave her an odd sense of modesty. "I think it the perfect solution. And the people of Gormfeurach are already accustomed to him acting as laird, so ye are nay even asking them to suffer yet another change."

Brett slid his hands up beneath her hair to stroke her breasts, and enjoyed the light flush of desire that colored her cheeks. "I wanted the place mostly for ye, Triona. I couldnae bear the thought that ye would be facing yet another mon who sought to gain from marrying ye. I needed ye to ken that I had all I needed and didnae depend on any of your coin nor require any of your land."

Triona brushed her lips over his. "It was nay something I was concerned about, but I thank ye for doing it. Once done, I realized I may have nurtured a concern or two, and that sort of thing can be a slow poison in a marriage. Now we are equals."

"It will be Murray land now, too."

"It was ne'er really Grant land anyway. Just as this isnae really McKee land. The name was here, but nay more than that."

She slid down until she covered his body with hers

and began to kiss his strong throat. His murmur of appreciation encouraged her sudden boldness. Triona had imagined doing things to him in her dreams that they had not done when they were lovers. She now wished to try a few of them. Perhaps, if she could get him caught up in passion's grip, she would find the courage to tell him she loved him. If she was very lucky, he would give her the words she craved.

It was the possibility that she would say them and he would not return them that made her hesitate to speak. Triona knew that would hurt, and she feared it could create a distance between them that would be hard to overcome. She would not wish to nurse her hurt but suspected she would, her mind constantly preying on the matter.

As she kissed his broad chest, he combed his fingers through her hair. Triona knew he was silently encouraging her to continue her seductive play. It gave her an odd sense of power to take the reins in their lovemaking. She just prayed he would not be unpleasantly shocked, because she was going to do something to him that Joan had told her Aiden loved.

Brett closed his eyes and savored the feel of her warm mouth on his body. The silken glide of her hair over his skin only added to his pleasure. They still needed to talk, but he was not about to interrupt her attempt to seduce him. When her small hand stroked his erection, he was not sure how long he could enjoy the game, however. His hunger for her was still too hot and greedy to allow for too much play.

The touch of her lips on his manhood had him

opening his eyes so fast they stung. He bit back a cry,
terrified she would think it was disapproval. Brett
struggled for control as he lightly clenched his hands
in her hair and tried to subtly hold her right where
she was. Then she took him into her mouth and he
could no longer be a silent, appreciative lover. He
watched her love him with her mouth and whispered
the occasional hint about what he would like her to
do. To his astonishment, she did it. Teeth gritted as he
fought for the control to enjoy her loving, he finally
had to stop her.

"Now, love," he said as he grabbed her under the
arms and pulled her up his body. "Ride me. Ride
your mon."

As he gave her some gentle assistance in mount-
ing him, he was thrilled to find her wet with welcome.
The sight of Triona astride him, her breasts bouncing
as she rode him, was, he decided, the most beautiful
sight he had seen. The moment he judged her close
to finding her release, he pulled her into his arms and
sat up. Then he kissed her as she quickly adjusted to
the slight change in position and took them both over
the edge. Brett was not surprised to hear himself yell
out those three words he had been having so much
difficulty saying aloud.

Triona lay sprawled over Brett's chest after they collapsed back onto the bed as one. She fought to regain
her composure, easing their bodies apart as she did
so. His words of love were still ringing in her ears, but
she was not sure she ought to make any mention of
what he had said. It had been wondrous to hear him

say he loved her, so wondrous it had sent her tumbling into her release, but she feared talking about it would lead him to say something that would spoil it all for her.

"Triona, do ye think ye might return my feelings?" Brett asked as he combed his fingers through her hair.

She lifted her head slightly to peer at him through her hair. "So, we can talk about what ye bellowed then, can we?"

He brushed a kiss over her mouth. "We dinnae have to discuss it like one would the possibility of a new bull or ram, but I was rather hoping that ye would have a response."

Triona lightly rubbed her nose against his and smiled, suddenly so full of joy she did not know why she was able to lie there quietly in his arms. "Aye, Sir Brett Murray, I love ye." She laughed when he hugged her almost too tightly and then kissed her. "I have for a verra long time, even though I kept reminding myself that ye would be leaving as soon as my troubles were o'er."

"Ah, Triona, I believe I have loved ye for nearly as long. I was but a wee bit cowardly and also a bit loathe to change my life. I truly thought I had had my chance and it had passed. And then Arianna decided to run away to her cousin."

"By marriage, many times removed," Triona said, and they both laughed.

"So now we build Banuilt and we build Gormfeurach into prosperous keeps, and we build our family.

I am five and thirty and a bit old to be starting a family . . ."

"But nay too old, as I can attest," she said as she watched him closely and then laughed over the openmouthed look he gave her as her words suddenly sank into his mind.

"Ye are with child?" Brett asked, his voice barely above a whisper because her words had stunned him and he wanted them to be true so badly he dared not believe.

"I am. I had but fully accepted the fact when ye rode up to announce that ye were the new laird of Gormfeurach." She placed her hand over his when he put it on her belly. "I was concerned about what to do or how to tell ye before ye arrived, though. I didnae want ye to come back just to marry me for the sake of the child."

"I ne'er would have done that, love. E'en if ye had kenned it earlier and sent me word, I would have still come back just for ye." He pulled her into his arms and held her tight. "Ye are my heart, Triona. Ye are what I need to see that I have a future and that I can be happy in it. We will build strong homes for our children."

"Already planning more than one?" she teased.

"With this bairn I already have more than one, for your child is mine as weel. E'en if Ella wasnae such a wee angel. I wed ye and ye have a child, so I wed the child as weel. 'Tis how I see it. Soon Ella will have a brother or sister to teach things to."

"That could be a curse we dinnae wish to unleash

on the world," Triona drawled, and laughed along with him.

She felt him suddenly tense and her heart skipped a beat in alarm. Brett was staring toward the end of the bed, but she could see nothing there. His ghost had returned, and it terrified her. It also angered her that another woman would enter her bedchamber on her wedding night.

Brett blinked, unable to believe his eyes. He had seen nothing of Brenda for quite a while. It did not please him to be seeing her spirit now. He knew he loved Triona, knew it without a single doubt in his heart and mind, but he did not know what he would do if Brenda began to haunt him again. His guilt over her death was just a tiny thing now, and he had fallen in love with another woman. Brenda should not be here and should definitely not be looking at Triona.

Then Brenda's spirit looked at him, smoothed a hand over her belly, and smiled.

Ye were nay to blame, lover.

His heart pounded in his chest as he heard her voice in his mind.

Enjoy your life, for ye were nay to blame for the end of mine. I didnae tell ye about our enemies because I didnae want ye to tell me to stay home. Love your lady and that bairn I can see within her. I have been needing ye to let me go.

Before he could ask what she meant by that, the vision was gone.

"Was Brenda just here?" asked Triona.

"Aye, and I do believe she just gave us her full approval."

"She said that?"

"Nay, she said I was nay to blame, that she had kept things from me that led to her death. Then she said she has been needing for me to let her go. I am nay sure what that meant, but 'tis the oddest thing—I can feel that she truly is gone now."

"Mayhap your guilt held her here."

He kissed her and rolled so that she was beneath him. "She just wiped the last of it away. 'Tis what I have needed for a long time, but 'tis nay easy to be rid of something like that. Now I can just put all my mind, heart, and soul into ye and our child."

Triona wrapped her arms around his neck and kissed him. "Good. No more ghosts. No more guilt. Use my love to soothe the last remnants of both, for I do love you, Brett Murray. I will love ye until I watch my last sunset."

"I truly hope I will be watching it with ye, so that we both may take our last journey together. Ah, love, I am a lucky mon. I have all I need now, all I shall e'er need."

"Weel, I would say I am verra close to having all I need, but there is one tiny thing more, something Banuilt needs that will finally make everything right."

"And what would that be?"

"A new priest," she drawled, and grinned when he laughed.

Epilogue

One year later

"Come, Brett, we must be in the bailey to greet him."

Brett looked up from the ledger he had been working on and smiled at his wife. She was flushed with excitement, her arms full of their son, Geordan. As if catching her excitement, Geordan was bouncing up and down on her hip, his plump hands clasped around her braid, drool running down his chin.

"Greet who, love?" he asked as he stood up and walked over to kiss her and Geordan on their cheeks.

"Our new priest. Since ye sent Mure on his way, neither Gormfeurach nor Banuilt has had a priest near at hand to deal with all those things priests do. I told ye that we were to finally get one, and one I was promised wouldnae be like all the others I had to deal with."

As he walked her out into the bailey, Brett struggled to recall what she had told him about the priest. It was not something he had much interest in, but he knew she had been anxious about it. He felt all was right in his world now, but Triona was determined to believe that Banuilt would not be completely right, their lives would not be completely right, until they had a priest that she could like and trust. The man would be settled in a small stone church, built between Gormfeurach and Banuilt so that he could serve both clans. The only rigid requirement Triona had had was that the man could not be one of those priests who disdained women. She had had enough of such men. Considering the few candidates Sir Mollison had sent to her, it had proven to be a very difficult requirement to meet.

A crowd had gathered in the bailey. Brett grinned at all the women standing with babes in their arms. The return of Banuilt's garrison had proved to be very fruitful. The village was full of life again, even though it was not as busy with people as it had been before the fever had taken so many. The joy was back, though, and that made life much better at Banuilt.

Then he saw Ella standing next to Joan, who held her son Gillis. Sitting on Ella's shoulder, its strange paws on top of her head and its tail curled around her neck, was Clyde. When he stopped next to them, Clyde snarled. Brett snarled back, as had become his habit, and Ella giggled.

"Have ye met this mon?" he asked Triona. "I dinnae recall a priest coming to talk to ye lately, but I have spent a lot of time o'er at Gormfeurach o'erseeing all the work that is being done."

"He didnae come here, but I was assured that he is

just what I wanted." Triona looked at all the women standing around with their babies in their arms, trying to hide how badly they wanted the children blessed. "He will be verra busy christening bairns for a while, and marrying some of the parents of those bairns. I could have gone along weel enough without a priest, but I could see how, with each bairn born, with each lying-in, the women were becoming more and more fretful about the lack."

"They are worried for the souls of their bairns."

"I ken it, and 'tis nay my place to spout words about priests and churches, most of which are born of my own experiences with priests that needed to be punched in the mouth. Their fear is real, Brett, and I had to see something done to ease it. I truly hope this priest is the one we need."

Brett started to ask again just who had sent them a priest but then saw the two men, flanking another dressed in a monk's robes, ride through the gates. "MacFingals? Ye got a priest from the MacFingals?" If anyone had ever asked which clan would be the least likely to produce a man of the Church, the first name that would have come to mind would have been MacFingal.

He thought of all he knew of the MacFingals, their father, and the scores of bastards the man had bred. Some of the sons were not all that much better than the father. Brett was not even sure the clan as a whole had much use for the Church. One could not forget that old Fingal and several of his clan members liked to dance naked under the full moon, their aging bodies painted blue. He doubted the Church would approve of that behavior.

"Aye. Sir Brian assured me that the mon will be perfect for us," Triona replied, her gaze fixed upon the MacFingals. "Said he was at a monastery but truly wanted his own flock, wanted the village life in some ways. The monastery life he lived was too separate from the people and he wanted to be in the midst of them, christening bairns, marrying people, teaching those who wished to learn, and all of that. Sir Mollison agreed to allow him to come here."

Sir Mollison had developed a true affection for the laird of Banuilt, Brett thought, and would have had a hard time denying the woman anything. Shortly after Brett had returned to the keep, Sir Mollison had arrived for a visit. By the time the man had left, his balding head full of ideas of how to use many of Triona's own techniques at his own keep, the man had been completely won over. If the man had not had two score and ten years on him, a wife he unabashedly adored, and six children, Brett might have been jealous.

Brett greeted Nathan and Ned MacFingal as the two younger men dismounted and then turned to the monk, who was already getting himself introduced to Brett's son and Joan's. When the man did not even blink an eye over Ella and her cat, Brett relaxed. Clyde had not hissed at the man, had even allowed the priest to scratch his ears. Nothing could have better eased Brett's concerns than that open acceptance of the ill-tempered cat. He greeted the monk with a smile when the man turned to him.

"Ye are a priest, aye?" he asked, glancing over the man's monkish attire.

"I am. I am but too accustomed to this garb to change. I am Father Lundie MacFingal, cousin to these lads who are so woefully in need of confession."

The way the man smiled when Ned and Nathan each gave an ill-tempered grunt in response to that teasing told Brett a lot about the man he now knew, almost without a doubt, would be their next priest. Father Lundie liked people, all people, even those whom other priests would condemn as sinners. He had the look of a MacFingal, with the black hair, blue eyes, handsome features, and tall, lean body. The man's handshake hinted at strength as well. When he introduced Triona as the laird of Banuilt and the man greeted her with all the respect and courtesy due her, Brett began to compose a letter in his mind to Brian thanking him for this man.

"And look at all this," Father Lundie said as he stood beside Triona and surveyed all the women with their babies. "I believe I shall be verra busy for a while, giving blessings to so many new souls."

"Aye," Triona said, watching the man closely. "Our garrison was wrongly imprisoned for two years but freed and brought home a year ago."

It was an outrageous thing to say to a priest, even though it was the truth, but she needed to see how he would respond to such earthy humor. When the man laughed with delight, every doubt Triona still held concerning Brian's assurances that this man would be perfect began to fade. His laugh made her almost certain he would not condemn the women who still needed to be married to the fathers of their children.

"Ah, m'lady, I was told of your trouble and the sickness that took so many from their loved ones. A sad time for ye and your people." He held his arms out and looked around again. "But let us now look at how God has blessed ye. So much new life here, so much." He looked at the older children watching him. "And mayhap one or two with a wish to learn."

"I wish to learn," said Ella as she stepped up next to the priest. "I am clever. Everyone says so."

Triona nearly grabbed Ella and shooed her away from the priest. The man appeared to be good-humored and not condemning of the way some of the villagers may have ignored the first step to building a family: getting married. Yet a girl asking to learn was something few men would tolerate, and she did not wish Ella to be hurt when he turned her down. Then again, she mused, it might be time for Ella to understand that other places were not as free or accepting of differences as Banuilt.

"Weel then, ye shall learn whate'er ye wish to." Father Lundie looked at her cat. "I think ye may have a clever cat as weel."

"Aye, Clyde is verra clever. He snarls at Papa. Papa always snarls back."

"And so he should. Mayhap it is just cat talk for hello and your papa understands that."

Triona moved to stand next to Brett as others cautiously approached the priest, who stood listening patiently as Ella told him all about Clyde. "He is perfect."

Brett wrapped his arm around her shoulders. "I do believe he is," he agreed. "So now do ye have all ye want?"

She leaned her head against his shoulder and looked around at the people in the bailey. The women who had feared for their children, the ones who had been waiting so long to be married, and the few remaining elderly who knew they might not live to see another spring were content now. She had a good man for a husband, who loved her and kept her warm at night with his desire. The harvest was promising to be a good one, the weaving was bringing in much needed coin. Her daughter was alive and healthy, as was her son.

Triona stood on her tiptoes and kissed Brett on the cheek. "Aye, I have everything I could ever want, and it is all verra fine indeed."